Pride Publishing books by L.M. Brown

Mermen & Magic
Forbidden Waters
Tempestuous Tides
Dangerous Waves
Shifting Currents
Hidden Depths

Heavenly Sins
Between Heaven & Hell
Between Good & Evil
Between Life & Death

Mermen & Magic

HIDDEN DEPTHS

L.M. BROWN

Hidden Depths
ISBN # 978-1-78686-379-9
©Copyright L.M. Brown 2018
Cover Art by Erin Dameron-Hill ©Copyright October 2018
Interior text design by Claire Siemaszkiewicz
Pride Publishing

Published in 2018 by Pride Publishing, United Kingdom.

Pride Publishing is an imprint of Totally Entwined Group Limited.

HIDDEN
DEPTHS

Prologue

The Isle of the Gods

Caspian drummed his fingers on the table as he waited for Andaman to begin the meeting.

Andaman didn't appear to be in any hurry to do so and kept glancing at the newly awoken Tempest, Goddess of the Storm.

"What?" Tempest asked. "Is there something on my nose?"

Andaman coughed and lowered his gaze. "I thought you might like to chair the meeting, being that you're the most powerful immortal among us."

Caspian cringed as Medina, Goddess of Love, glared down the table at Andaman. When she had awoken from her slumber, Andaman had not offered her the same courtesy.

Tempest waved her hand in a dismissive gesture. "Let's get on with things. I've far too much to do to be wasting time here."

Andaman coughed again and shuffled the scrolls in front of him.

Caspian's sister, Cari, nudged him in the arm. She grinned wickedly and nodded between the fumbling God of the Forge and the irritable Tempest. He forced a smile to his lips. Yes, he had noticed the obvious infatuation Andaman had for Tempest. It seemed his affections had only grown stronger in the centuries while Tempest had slept, along with so many other Atlantean immortals.

The table they sat around was quite crowded compared to a few years before.

"Caspian, Cari, pay attention!"

Caspian startled at the reprimand from his mother. Odessa was another newly awoken goddess—and didn't he know it. He certainly hadn't missed her scolding over the centuries. For the first time, he wished his father, the God of War, would hurry up and wake from his stasis. At least then his mother's attention would be focused elsewhere.

"Well, Caspian?"

While his mind had been wandering, it seemed the meeting had begun and Caspian had no idea what they were talking about.

"Really, Caspian." Odessa sighed loudly. "Aren't you listening at all?"

"Apparently not," Caspian snapped. "What was the question again?"

Andaman growled in annoyance. "I asked which of our brethren you believe will wake next. Which stirred when you visited their temples during the recent battle?"

Caspian straightened in his seat. At least he knew the answer to the question. "My father was the nearest to rising, though several others also appeared briefly. I think we can expect the God of War to be with us in the next few months and the Goddess of the Sea may follow within the year. Despite the quakes caused by the stirring of the gods, the God of the Earth is very much in stasis."

Andaman scribbled notes as Caspian spoke. "Then you believe Cynbel is the only one likely to wake soon enough to assist us when Mariana returns?"

"Yes."

Tempest frowned as she looked up and down the table. "Do you fools intend to wage all-out war on the Goddess of Sea Creatures?"

"She has declared war on *us*," Cari said. "I see her returning to Atlantis within the year. We need to be ready for her. We only defeated her last time thanks to the element of surprise."

"*Who* defeated her?" Tempest asked. "When I arrived, I rather got the impression you were losing until my intervention."

Cari sank low in her seat.

"You're quite right," Andaman hurried to assure her. "We are most grateful for your timely assistance in ridding Atlantis of the goddess who would do such harm to the city and its inhabitants."

Tempest glared down the table. "The mer mean nothing to me. Make no mistake about that."

"What have the mer ever done to you?" Medina asked. "They are a peaceful, loving race, who have opened their hearts to us."

"They're animals," Tempest replied. "Humans keep pets, which show them equal affection. It doesn't mean I want them in my home."

"The mer are half human," Cari pointed out.

"And half fish," Tempest retorted.

Caspian placed his hand on his sister's arm, silently urging her not to lose her temper. There were more important issues to be discussed than the physiology of the merpeople.

"I think perhaps we should move on to the main problem we have right now," Caspian said.

"I thought Mariana *was* the problem," Andaman replied. "Hence, why she was not invited to this meeting."

"She's *a* problem but not the only one," Caspian said. "Unfortunately, the departure of the goddess, along with her sea dragons, has resulted in the city of Atlantis becoming visible to all those who happen to be in the area. Shark attacks on the mer have increased tenfold since the sea dragons were freed, and there are humans navigating the nearby waters who could stumble across the city and the mer within weeks."

"Or even days," Cari added. "My visions tell me those who are most persistent in searching for Atlantis are descendants of the banished Atlanteans. They won't give up their search, because the city beckons them. It's merely a matter of time before the location of Atlantis is revealed to the world — and with it, the mer."

Medina smiled brightly. "But isn't that a good thing? If humans discover Atlantis, people will believe in us again and our powers will be increased."

"Good for us isn't necessarily good for the mer," Caspian said. "Humans today are not as understanding of other beings as they once were."

"Jake seems to accept the mer well enough."

"He does," Caspian agreed. "As do the few others who have been privileged enough to know them, but there are far more who would see them captured and studied in scientific laboratories — or worse, killed. I don't believe the risk is justified. The mer *must* remain hidden, and right now that means we need to find a way to hide Atlantis."

"None of us has the power to make the entire city invisible," Andaman reminded them. "Our own individual temples, perhaps, but nothing more. Even Mariana didn't have that power, only her sea dragons did. I think we have to resign ourselves to the fact that the mer may have to relocate if they wish to remain hidden from the world."

"And where do you suggest they go?" Caspian snapped. "There's nowhere left in the oceans where such a large community can not only hide but also survive."

No one around the table offered any suggestions.

"Atlantis will be discovered," Cari said. "I've seen it for myself."

"How long do we have?" Andaman asked.

"I don't know, but certainly within the lifetimes of my current Oracles."

Caspian had no idea what to suggest. His vow to protect the mer had become a full-time occupation. He hoped he was up to the job.

Chapter One

Jake clicked the link on his tablet's browser and frowned as he read the story about a group of deep sea explorers searching for the mythical city of Atlantis. He glanced at his two lovers, kissing languidly beside him. *Or not so mythical.* He returned to the article.

The general feeling of the reporter was that the group of divers were wasting a lot of money that could be spent far more wisely. The writer clearly didn't believe Atlantis had ever existed.

What worried Jake was the location the explorers were searching in. They were far too close to the true location of the sunken city for his liking. Not that he cared if the city itself was discovered... His concern was for the merpeople who resided within its boundaries – and especially Kyle's family.

Kyle, the merman he had found washed up on the beach nearly three years earlier, suddenly grabbed the tablet from his hand and tossed it to the far end of the bed.

"Hey!"

"I can't believe you're sitting reading some boring news report with two naked men in your bed," Kyle teased.

"You have something else in mind for a Sunday morning?" Jake asked. He could tell them about Atlantis later. There was no sense in worrying them before he had to, and it wasn't like there was anything they could do about the human divers right now.

Kyle climbed over him, leaving room for Finn, the youngest of the trio, to move closer to Jake as well.

Finn ran his fingers along Jake's thigh, toying with the hem of his boxers. "I can't believe we *still* haven't cured you of this ridiculous habit of wearing clothes to bed."

Jake laughed. "Many humans wear even more than I do," he pointed out.

Finn slid his hand into the underwear, and Jake gasped as Finn grabbed his cock and squeezed it lightly. "They're fools, and if all humans shared their beds with the mer, they'd soon be happy to spend their days naked, too."

Jake opened his mouth to make a smart remark but his words were halted by Kyle, who chose that moment to kiss him, swallowing his retort in the process.

He could feel Finn battling with his boxers and he raised his hips a little so his lover could remove them. Finn didn't waste any time once they were off. He dove on Jake's cock, swallowing it to the root with ease.

Jake groaned into Kyle's kiss as Finn sucked him eagerly. He reached down blindly, finding Kyle's stiff rod and taking it in hand. He stroked the thick length in time with Finn's sucking on his own.

Kyle deepened their kiss, thrusting his tongue into Jake's mouth. Jake let him take control.

Farther down the bed, Finn continued to use his mouth to bring Jake exquisite pleasure.

"Fuck, how long is it until the solstice? I need that spanking so badly."

Jake pulled out of the kiss so quickly that Kyle accidentally bit his lip.

"What is it?" Kyle asked as he tested his lip for blood.

"I'm not sure," Jake said.

Finn pulled back, leaving Jake aching with need. "Is something wrong?"

Jake wondered if he had imagined Finn's voice in his head, but he had to ask to know for sure. "I thought the mer couldn't communicate telepathically in human form."

"We can't," Kyle confirmed. "It's one of those things I wish we *could* do."

Finn nodded. "Kyle's right. Why do you ask?"

"I thought I heard your voice in my head," Jake said. "I guess it must have been my imagination. Don't worry about it."

"What was I saying?" Finn asked. "Anything interesting?"

Jake shrugged. "You wanted to know when the next solstice was."

Finn paled visibly.

"What is it?" Kyle asked.

"I *was* thinking about the solstice," Finn whispered. "I…"

"Why?" Kyle questioned. "You're a horny devil every day of the year. Does it make any difference whether it's the solstice?"

Finn wouldn't meet Kyle's eyes and Jake knew that — somehow — he *had* heard Finn's thoughts a few minutes before.

"Finn" — Jake held out his hand and beckoned his young lover closer — "come here."

Kyle sat back so Finn could settle between them.

"Did you hear what else I was thinking?" Finn asked. "About—"

"Yes," Jake said.

Finn hung his head, his cheeks flushed with embarrassment.

"What did he say?" Kyle asked.

"*Think*," Finn corrected. "I didn't *say* anything."

"But you should have," Jake said. "How can we give you what you need if you don't tell us?"

"It's not the solstice," Finn said. "I don't *need* anything except then."

Jake wrapped his arm around Finn and tugged him into his side. "Finn, you *have* to talk to us."

"Can one of you tell me what you're talking about?" Kyle interrupted. "You're not making much sense right now."

"Finn," Jake prompted, "for whatever reason, I heard your private thoughts. I'm not going to tell Kyle what you were thinking, but I would like for *you* to."

Finn sighed and wouldn't meet Kyle's eyes. "I was thinking I needed a spanking."

Jake hugged Finn closely, proud of him for giving voice to his desire.

"You mean you want that outside of the solstice?" Kyle asked.

Finn nodded. "I don't know why, but I've wanted it for a while now."

Jake tipped Finn's chin so he could kiss him on the lips. "You only had to ask, baby."

Kyle bounded off the bed and headed for the chest where they kept their toys. When Finn had finally admitted he needed to be spanked to break his mating fever, he had also persuaded Jake to let him purchase a couple of paddles, pointing out it would make it easier on Jake's hands, too.

Finn pointed to the one in Kyle's left hand. "That one."

Kyle put the other away and returned to the bed. "Me or Jake?" he asked.

Jake was the one who usually gave Finn the spanking he needed on the solstice, but there had been a couple of occasions when Kyle had had the honors.

"Jake, please," Finn said as he eased himself out of Jake's arms and settled himself over his lap, his arse in the air. Jake could already feel Finn's stiff cock poking him in the leg.

Kyle passed Jake the paddle and Finn moaned in anticipation.

"Ready?" Jake asked.

"I've been ready for months," Finn muttered.

"Then you should have said something *months* ago," Jake replied as he brought the paddle down on Finn's backside.

"More," Finn whimpered. "Harder, Jake, harder."

"Whatever you want, baby," Jake said as he struck him a second time.

Kyle ran his hand over Finn's arse in between smacks and Finn moaned with pure need.

"Such rosy cheeks," Kyle whispered as Finn raised his arse to meet the paddle when it swung down for the third time. "Are you close?"

Finn groaned. "Yes, so close. Jake, please, spank me. Please make me come."

Jake put the paddle aside and brought his bare hand down on Finn's arse with one hard smack that tipped Finn over the edge. His lover howled as he spilled over Jake's thigh and the bedsheets.

Kyle gathered Finn into his arms as Jake scrambled into the bedside cabinet for the lotion to soothe the burn of Finn's tender arse.

"Feeling better now?" Kyle asked as Finn recovered. Finn nodded.

"Good, because if you don't tell us what you need, when you need it, you'll be getting another spanking, but I'll make you wear a cock ring while you're having it."

Jake knew Kyle's threat was an idle one. While they had quite a stash of toys in the chest, none of them owned a cock ring or anything of that sort.

Finn scooted over to Jake's side and gave him a mock pitiful glance.

"Don't look at me for sympathy," Jake scolded. "Kyle is right. I thought we were long past a time when we couldn't discuss our needs."

Finn hung his head. "I'm sorry."

"Why did you feel you couldn't talk to us?" Kyle asked.

"I guess I was embarrassed."

"I thought we already went through this the first solstice we spent together," Jake said.

"No one can control what their mating trigger is," Finn said. "On the solstice, I can only break my fever when someone spanks me. I *had* to say something or else continue to go through the pain of going without release. The rest of the time, I can still find release, so I kept quiet, rather than feel like less of a man than I already do."

"Less of a...?" Jake shook his head and pulled Finn into his arms. "Neither me nor Kyle would ever think that of you. I thought you knew us better than that."

Kyle nodded his agreement until he realized Finn wasn't looking at him. "Jake's right. I love you, Finn, but sometimes you can be a bit of an idiot."

Finn clung to Jake, who gave him another squeeze of assurance.

"Next time you want something from us, tell us," Jake said. "Now, I think we should probably get out of bed since, in case you've both forgotten, we have guests."

"What about the other issue?" Finn asked.

"What other issue?" Kyle questioned.

Finn gestured to Jake. "How did Jake hear my private thoughts?"

Jake shivered. *How did I forget such a crucial point?* He wasn't hearing either of his lovers' thoughts right now, but he had a feeling this wasn't a one-off occasion.

* * * *

Despite Jake's insistence that they couldn't leave their guests to fend for themselves, it was still some time before the three of them made their way downstairs.

Finn had pointed out to the others that he was the only one who had come, which had led to him sucking his lovers off one by one in the shower.

Finally, they arrived in the kitchen, eagerly tracking down breakfast.

Finn stared at the door, wondering how long it would be before Delwyn joined them. He hadn't seen his oldest friend in more than two years and was eager to catch up on his news. Delwyn had arrived the previous evening and had met Jake on his arrival. Unfortunately for Finn, Jake had insisted on letting Delwyn and his lover, Fabian, have all the time alone they needed.

"Stop staring at the door," Jake teased. "I'm not letting you disturb them."

Kyle chuckled. "I'm going to go check on Marin. I'll see if he wants anything to eat."

"Take him something," Jake said. "He's barely eaten a thing since he arrived."

Finn didn't blame the merman for his lack of appetite. Marin had been brought to them from Atlantis by Caspian, the Atlantean God of Justice. He had barely spoken a word since his arrival. The kind, friendly merman had lost his lover during the battle raging in the sunken city, and the only thing driving him now was the need to return and avenge Calder.

Calder had been the leader of the city guards and he had died saving Marin and other unarmed mermen from the attack of the sea dragons.

Marin, the worst recruit the guards had ever seen, had been training every waking minute since, perfecting his technique with both spears and tridents.

He had blasted to smithereens at least half of the junk room contents and was the only merman in the house who seemed able to conjure sea-fire at will and with accuracy.

"I'll come with you," Finn said as he crammed the last of his bacon into his mouth.

They found Marin in the makeshift training room. Finn wondered what time he had gotten up or whether he had slept at all. From the dark shadows under his eyes, he suspected not.

"Breakfast?" Kyle said. "We've brought you what Jake calls a *proper* English breakfast."

"I'm not hungry," Marin replied. He blasted a burn into the back of a broken chair before swiftly turning around to aim a thrust at a damaged table.

"If you plan on returning to the sunken city, I'd suggest eating something first," Kyle said. "You'll need your strength for the swim."

"I don't intend to swim back," Marin said. "Caspian brought me here, and he can damn well take me back again."

Finn picked up a spare trident and the tip glowed blue. He quickly put it aside.

"I don't think Caspian will agree to take you back," Kyle said. "He was pretty adamant that we keep you here on land."

"I don't care," Marin snapped. "I'm going back, and if he won't help me, I'll find someone else who will."

"Medina might help," Finn said.

"Would she?" Kyle asked.

"Maybe. Marin has lost his love and wants to avenge him. She would understand his loss. Maybe we should ask her next time she comes to visit Jake. In the meantime, we can help Marin practice and build up his strength."

Finn pointed to the plate of food Kyle still held.

Marin put aside the trident and took the plate. He picked at a fried tomato. "Human food is strange."

"You get used to it," Finn said. "Some of it is great, though I don't get why Jake cooks tomatoes either. Try the bacon instead."

Marin ate a bite and nearly managed a smile of pleasure.

"What's it like living on land?" Marin asked in between bites.

"I love it," Finn said. "But anything is better than being held prisoner in the sunken city."

"I sometimes miss the ocean," Kyle admitted. "And I miss my family. I don't like to think of my sister and niece being in danger so far away, when I'm not there to protect them."

Finn rubbed Kyle's arm. "I'm sure Lynna is fine."

"I hope so. I want Delwyn and Fabian to emerge from their room so I can ask Delwyn if he can check on her."

Delwyn was an Oracle of the Past, bound to Cari, the Goddess of Prophecy. He had the ability to see anything that had already happened and was the only one in the house who could assure Kyle his family was safe.

"Delwyn and Fabian are already awake," Marin said. "I saw them heading into the pool room earlier. They're probably still there."

Kyle and Finn exchanged a quick glance. Finn didn't want to leave Marin alone, but they were both eager to see Delwyn.

Marin seemed to sense their hesitation. "I don't need a bodyguard," he said.

"We'll be back to check on you later," Finn assured him.

Grabbing Kyle's hand, Finn pulled him from the room and back down the stairs toward the indoor pool.

Delwyn was in his mer form in the middle of the pool. Finn watched as he splashed water at Fabian, his human lover. Something was wrong with that picture, and he tried to put his finger on what.

"I thought the Oracles were blind when they were in their mer form?" Kyle whispered into Finn's ear.

"They are," Finn confirmed. Kyle had pinpointed what was bothering Finn with perfect accuracy.

"Finn!" Delwyn waved from the water and swam swiftly to the edge of the pool. Fabian followed behind him at a much slower pace. No human could ever hope to keep up with one of the mer when it came to moving through the water.

Finn ran to the poolside and knelt so he could wrap his arms around Delwyn's back. "I've missed you so much. How are you? How is it you can see?"

Delwyn laughed. "I renounced the Goddess of Prophecy, which means I'm a plain old boring merman now."

"Never boring," Fabian said as he finally caught up with his lover.

Delwyn flashed Fabian a grin while at the same time yanking Finn into the pool.

Finn was glad he didn't bother with clothes around the house, unless they had human guests, because whatever he'd have been wearing would have been ripped to pieces the moment he transformed into his half-fish form.

"You always were too slow," Delwyn teased.

"Not that slow," Finn replied as he ducked Delwyn under the water.

Delwyn wrestled himself free and they chased each other around the pool. Finn couldn't recall ever being happier. Now that Delwyn was here in England, he felt as though his family was finally complete. He knew Delwyn must have left his parents back in Atlantis, but Finn hoped they might join him here soon.

He glanced at Kyle, who sat on the edge of the pool. Of course, there were some who insisted on staying in the sanctuary, even if it meant splitting families in two. Lynna, Kyle's younger sister, had chosen to stay in the sunken city.

"Delwyn," Finn began, "I know you're not an Oracle anymore, but do you know anything about Kyle's family?"

Delwyn swam over to Kyle. "As far as I know, there were minimal losses during the battle between Mariana and her sea dragons and the mer. I'm sorry. I don't know about Lynna personally. I never met her, but I believe all the casualties were among the guards."

Kyle nodded. "I had hoped you might be able to check in on her, but I guess that's out of the question."

"I'll ask Medina to find out how your family is," Fabian offered.

"Jake was going to do the same thing," Kyle said. "We're hoping she'll stop by for a visit soon."

"Why doesn't he call her?" Fabian asked.

"I think he doesn't like to bother her. She can be a little temperamental."

Fabian chuckled. "She sure can. I'll give her a call. There are advantages to being the nephew of a goddess."

Finn covered his ears as Fabian yelled — at the top of his lungs — for 'Aunt Medi'.

Loud as his call was, it seemed to be quite effective, too. Medina appeared and took a seat on the sun lounger.

"Was that *really* necessary?" she asked as she sipped from a glass containing a strange purplish drink. "I'm not deaf."

"I thought you might be busy," Fabian said as he climbed out of the pool.

"If I were, it wouldn't matter how loud you yelled. Now, what can I do for you?"

"I hoped you might go check on Kyle's family in Atlantis. He's worried about his sister and niece."

Medina sighed dramatically. "I suppose you want me to bring them back here, too?"

"Would you?" Kyle asked.

"If they wish to come, then yes, but I won't transport them here against their will."

Kyle nodded. "I understand, but if you can try to talk them into coming here, that'd be great."

Medina gave them all a bright smile, placed her glass on the table and vanished.

Kyle, the only one not in the water, walked over to the table and picked up the glass. He sniffed the contents and gave it a dubious look. "I've never seen a drink this color before," he commented.

"Give it a try," Fabian called.

Finn could hear the mischief in Fabian's voice, but he held his tongue until Kyle had taken a sip. "What is it?" he asked.

"I can't say for sure, but it looks like some of my aunt's special brew."

"Which does what?" Finn asked.

Fabian lowered his voice to reply. "For immortals like my aunt, it simply tastes pleasant. For humans, even half-humans like you guys… Let's just say, it's a good thing Kyle has two lovers, because one sip of that and he'll be insatiable for the next few hours. I doubt one man would be able to keep him satisfied."

Finn laughed. "Like that's any different to normal."

Kyle put down the glass and shrugged. "It tastes all right, nothing special."

Finn snickered into his hand.

"What has you so amused?" Kyle asked.

"Nothing." Finn choked on his laughter while Delwyn and Fabian made no effort to hide their own mirth.

Kyle, like Finn, chose to remain naked in the privacy of their home. As such, Finn could see the moment the drink began to take effect. Kyle's cock, previously hanging between his legs following their earlier activities, rose in an instant.

Finn gaped at his lover. He had never seen him get hard quite so quickly.

Kyle glared at them. "You do realize she'll be back any minute? What will she think when she sees me like this?"

"She'll probably offer to give you a hand with it," Fabian suggested. "Though, if you take her up on that, give me a chance to get out of here first. I *really* don't need to see my aunt like that."

"You're not funny," Kyle said. "Finn, stop laughing. Come here and help me get rid of this thing."

Finn guffawed as Kyle frantically tried to get himself off before the goddess returned.

"Why don't you jump in the pool and transform," Finn suggested.

Kyle gave him an annoyed frown. "That won't help. I'll still be aroused, but with no way to fix it."

A few minutes later, when Medina reappeared, Kyle was still trying to get his raging erection under control.

Medina smirked at him and picked up her glass.

Kyle hurriedly tried to cover his groin with his hands — not that he had any hope of managing such a feat.

"Would you like another drink?" Medina asked, holding the glass out to him. "I should warn you that it's quite addictive."

Finn and the others in the pool spluttered as Kyle appeared torn between taking the glass and continuing to hide his cock from the goddess.

"A shy merman?" Medina said. "Such a rarity."

"Aunt Medi, stop teasing him," Fabian called.

Medina laughed. "You could have warned him what it would do. Now, about Kyle's family…"

"You've spoken to Lynna?" Kyle asked.

"Yes, and her mate Xane. They are both quite well, as is your young niece."

Kyle gave up trying to hide his erection and sighed. "I take it they don't want to come here?"

"They're settled in Atlantis and don't wish to leave Xane's family or the safety of the city."

"Is the city still safe?" Fabian asked. "Without the sea dragons hiding it from predators, both human and sea-life, Atlantis is visible to anyone or anything in those waters."

Medina nodded. "You're quite right, and the pantheon is already discussing the implications of this."

"What do they intend to do about it?" Fabian asked.

"None of us has the power to hide the entire city. Only dragons, those of the land and sea, have the power to become invisible and mask their surroundings to such an extent. Land dragons are now extinct and sea dragons are on the verge of the same."

"Are there other sea dragons besides those loyal to Mariana?" Delwyn asked.

"A handful, but they're wild and uncontrollable, except by the Goddess of Sea Creatures herself. I'm sorry, but Atlantis can no longer be hidden. It's just a matter of time before humans discover its location."

"They're already hunting way too close for my liking," Jake said from the doorway. "I've been reading reports on the Internet and the deep-sea exploration vessels are heading directly for Atlantis. Without knowing the exact location, I can't say for sure, but I'd say the city could be discovered within a few years."

"Years is foolishly optimistic, I'm afraid," Medina agreed. "While the immortals don't have modern technology to keep an eye on things, we have other methods. The human science vessels are within five hundred miles of the city."

"Fuck!" Jake swore. "Will they find the city for sure?"

Medina nodded. "Many of those who are drawn to the ocean carry Atlantean blood in their veins. Some are swimmers and surfers. Others are sailors and explorers. The call of Atlantis has always been strong in those who are descended from the original inhabitants of the city. As the rest of the gods wake, the lure of the city grows stronger. It's silent but as seductive as the call of the sirens, and for as long as there are Atlantean descendants walking the earth, there will be those who seek Atlantis."

"Are there many Atlanteans?"

"Yes. Those who were banished were scattered across the world, with no memories of their lives there. They married, had children, grandchildren and thrived in their new lives. They outnumber the mer by at least a thousand to one."

"Why is that?" Fabian asked. "The mer far outnumbered the Atlanteans before the humans were banished."

"Because the mer are a cursed race," Medina explained. "But that's a problem we cannot do anything about today, so let's leave it at that and concentrate on the issues we can try to manage."

"What do you intend to do about those approaching the city?" Jake asked, though he wondered why the mer had been cursed. Kyle and Finn didn't seem to be under any form of magic, not like poor Lucas and Justin had been when the latter had angered the goddess in front of him. Reminded of how they were hexed was enough for Jake to resolve not to bring up the subject of the curse again. The last thing he needed was to anger Medina.

Medina paced the floor. "There's nothing we can do while so many of the mer insist on staying in the city."

Finn swam to the edge of the pool and climbed out. "Are any of them intending to leave for safer waters?"

Medina nodded. "A few have already been scared away by Mariana and the other rising immortals. Unfortunately, far more are staying in the city. You rarely left Atlantis except to come here. You don't realize how much of the ocean has been contaminated by humans or is frequently explored by them. Places where the mer can safely hide are few and far between."

"Medina is right," Kyle said. "My clan traveled extensively before we sought shelter in the sunken city. The oceans of the world may be vast, but for the mer, there are very few places we can still hide as well as thrive. I want my family here in England, where at least I know they'll be safe."

"She refused to come," Medina reminded him.

Kyle sighed. "Then I guess I'm going to be making plans to go there and bring her back myself."

Kyle's words hit Finn in the gut. He didn't want to return to Atlantis, but he knew he'd never let Kyle make the journey alone.

Chapter Two

Medina disappeared in a flurry of perfumed robes, wishing everyone a happy love day.

"What's a love day?" Jake asked.

"It's Medina's personal equivalent of Valentine's Day," Fabian explained. "Her powers are increased today, and her priests used to get extra horny. If we were still in the era where she was at the height of her glory, she'd never have answered our call to come here. She'd have been far too busy having her harem of men attend to her."

"Her powers increase?" Jake questioned. *Could that be why I heard Finn's thoughts this morning?*

"Yes, though whether they still do now is another matter. They used to increase because of Atlanteans celebrating her day. Now that there are none to remember her, it may be that her powers don't grow either."

Kyle pressed up against Jake, rubbing his hard cock against Jake's thigh.

"Kyle, we've got company," Jake said, trying to put a little distance between them.

Finn snickered.

"Is Kyle's behavior something to do with Medina, too?" Jake asked.

"No, that's because he took a drink of her aphrodisiac potion," Fabian explained. "Depending on how much he drank, he'll be extra horny for an hour or two."

Jake disentangled himself from Kyle, who did nothing to assist, merely continued to hump his leg.

"Or maybe longer," Fabian amended. "It may be the effect on the mer is even stronger than on humans."

"If alcohol is any indication, I suspect you could be right." Jake tried again to put some distance between himself and Kyle. "Kyle, for fuck's sake, get yourself under control."

Finn laughed. "Maybe we should take him to bed and let him wear himself out before dinner tonight."

"Good idea," Jake muttered. "If he's still acting like this when it's time for us to go to dinner with your parents, I swear I'm leaving him at home."

* * * *

After several hours in bed, as well as on the floor, in the shower and over the kitchen table, Kyle seemed to be more his usual self, and Jake and Finn decided perhaps it might be safe to take him to Finn's parents' anniversary dinner.

They arrived at the best restaurant in town, where Finn's family was already gathered. Every person at the table gave them knowing looks as they took their seats. They were quite used to the three men arriving late, and no one had any doubts as to why.

"And how can I help *you?*" the waiter purred at Jake, while completely ignoring the rest of the table.

Jake picked up the menu. "If you could give us a bit more time to choose, please."

"Of course." The waiter leaned in a little too close for Jake's comfort. "I'm Tim, so ask for me *personally* and I'll be at your service for *anything* you want."

Finn glared at the waiter's back as he retreated. "What a wanker."

"Finn!" his father, Malcolm, snapped from the other end of the table.

Malcolm's sister, who everyone called Aunt May, shook her head with disappointment, too.

"Really, Finn," his mother added. "Your language was never this bad back in Atlantis. The young man was just doing his job."

"He was hitting on Jake," Finn replied, sulking.

"Just ignore him," Jake said. "I don't want another man in my life. You and Kyle are all I need."

Across the table, Finn's twin brother Alex snorted. "Are you sure about that? Kyle's looking kind of tired. Maybe you're wearing him out."

Alex's wife Summer smacked her husband on the arm. "Shut up. You're embarrassing them."

"Let's order," Malcolm said. He passed the menu to his wife. "What would you like, Coral?"

"You can order for me," Coral replied with a smile. "You know what I like." "*Hmm, whipped cream, now that brings back some memories. You, licking it off me.*"

Jake choked on the sip of water at Coral's words. No one else seemed to have noticed anything out of the ordinary. *Maybe I imagined it?*

He glanced at Finn, recalling hearing his lover's thoughts earlier that day. Hearing Finn's secret desires had been a shock, but it hadn't bothered Jake too much. Finn should have been talking to them about his needs and now that things were out in the open, Jake hoped he would in the future.

Hearing Finn's mother's private thoughts was a whole different matter. Malcolm had been like a father to Jake, and even though Jake and Finn weren't married, he and Coral were very much the in-laws. Jake did not want to hear private thoughts about their sex life, now or ever.

Jake hoped it had been his imagination and went back to studying the menu.

Kyle's hand on his thigh took him by surprise. His mermen lovers were very sexual beings, but they tended to avoid public displays of affection, particularly in front of Finn's parents. Jake stilled as Kyle moved his hand higher on his leg, dangerously close to Jake's groin.

At his other side, Finn moved his chair closer and leaned on Jake's shoulder. To the others at the table, it might appear as though Finn were reading the menu. Jake could tell he was doing nothing of the sort. A few more inches and Finn would be crawling onto his lap.

Then, even more disturbing than having his two lovers getting *very* up close and personal in public, Jake felt a foot rubbing his ankle.

The angle was wrong for it to be either of his lovers, which meant it must be someone else at the table. Directly opposite Jake, Alex smiled at him and winked.

Jake jerked his foot, delivering a sharp kick to Alex's leg.

"Fuck!" Alex swore and reached under the table to rub his ankle.

"Alex!" Malcolm snapped.

"Jake kicked me," Alex muttered.

"It was an accident," Jake replied easily.

Alex glared at him for a moment before his face transformed and he offered the table a bright smile. "I'm sure it must have been. Jake would never want to hurt *me*, would you, babe?"

Babe? What the hell has gotten into Alex tonight?

Finn growled beside him and shot his brother a venomous look. "Did you call my boyfriend *babe*?"

"A slip of the tongue," Alex said.

"Alex, are you drunk?" Summer asked.

"I've not touched a drop." Alex smiled at his new wife.

"Then stop winding up Jake and your brother."

"What about me?" Kyle asked. "You think it isn't annoying *me* when your husband calls my boyfriend 'babe'?"

"Sorry, Kyle," Summer offered. "You didn't seem as angry about it as Finn did."

"Well, I *am*," Kyle snapped. "Jake's my boyfriend, too, even if you all seem to forget it half the fucking time."

No one bothered to scold Kyle about his language.

"Okay, let's calm down everyone," Malcolm said. "We're disturbing the other patrons, so let's order our food and try to enjoy the evening."

Jake nodded and searched for the waiter. Tim hovered right behind him, pad and pen in hand.

"What would you like to eat?"

Since Tim seemed to expect it, Jake chose what he wanted first. Finally, everyone had placed their orders and Tim, somewhat reluctantly, went to put them in.

"Would you like anything else, *darling*?" Finn mumbled under his breath.

Jake wrapped his arm around Finn's shoulder and gave him a quick hug. "There's no need for jealousy, so stop worrying."

Finn kissed him in response and Jake had to restrain himself from deepening the connection. He reminded himself they were in public and not everyone was comfortable with seeing two men kissing each other.

"I guess I'm not going to be getting a kiss while we're here."

Jake knew, without looking, that Kyle had not spoken aloud the words he had heard.

"Finn's the public boyfriend and I'm...the other one, I guess."

Jake frowned as Kyle's words sank in. *Is that how Kyle sees himself?* He thought back on the times he had been out in public with Kyle and Finn and he accepted that Kyle might have a point.

He wasn't sure how or when it had happened, but somewhere along the way, Finn had become the more traditional boyfriend. When the three of them were out together, Finn's hand was the one he held as they walked down the street. When he introduced his lovers to someone, he referred to Finn as his boyfriend but occasionally had stumbled a little with what to call Kyle. People simply didn't expect there to be more than two people in a relationship.

Jake realized he had been so busy trying to reassure Finn that he wanted him and that he wasn't simply a substitute for Alex, he had been neglecting Kyle.

They pulled out of the kiss and Jake resolved in that moment to change the way he acted when he was out with his two men. Kyle's place in Jake's heart was as secure as Finn's, and it was about time Jake made that clear.

Jake turned to Kyle and drew him into a kiss of his own, just as deep and long as the one he had shared with Finn.

When they parted, Kyle gaped at Jake for several long seconds.

"No jealousy," Jake murmured, "of *anyone*."

Kyle raised his fingers to his lips. "You *heard* me?" he whispered back.

Jake nodded. "You're my boyfriend, just as much as Finn is, and I'm sorry if anything I've done has made you feel as if you weren't."

"You have *two* boyfriends?" Tim appeared at the other side of Kyle. "Got room for a third?"

"No!" Jake snapped. "Is our food ready yet?"

Tim pouted. "Not yet. Would you like the wine menu?"

"That'd be great," Aunt May interrupted. "I hope you have some non-alcoholic options on it. We've quite a few people here with low tolerance."

Jake knew she referred to the mer, who all got drunk faster than anyone else. One drink and they were pretty much wasted.

"And one of us who can't drink right now," Summer added with a shy smile and pat to her flat tummy.

Coral squealed. "Really?"

Summer nodded. "We've been waiting for the right time to tell you."

"Congratulations," Jake said. "When are you due?"

Summer glanced at the waiter. "I'm not sure of the exact date yet."

Jake guessed it might be difficult to estimate in her unique circumstances. From what he had learned from his lovers, mermaid pregnancies lasted five months. Summer was human, but her husband was a merman.

Of course, this was something they couldn't discuss in public.

Malcolm clapped his hands. "We'll have to drink a toast to my future grandchild."

Everyone offered their congratulations, and by the time the food arrived, everyone seemed to be happy and content—everyone except Jake, who felt penned in by his two possessive lovers, as well as annoyed by the return of Alex's foot nudging his own.

By the time they had finished the main course, Jake needed to escape for a few minutes.

"I'm going to pop to the gents," Jake announced while they waited for their desserts to be served.

He practically ran from the table and into the loos. He sought sanctuary in the farthest stall from the doorway.

What the hell is wrong with Alex tonight? His best friend since childhood had always been straight, something that had broken Jake's heart as he'd watched Alex and Summer slowly fall for each other.

Alex trying to play footsie with him all evening was totally out of character, even without Alex's wife, his parents and Jake's boyfriends, one of whom was Alex's twin, sitting right there at the table.

"Are you all right in here?"

Jake jumped at the sound of the vaguely familiar voice. He had a horrible feeling the waiter had come to track him down. "I'm fine, thank you."

The footsteps drew nearer instead of moving away. "Are you sure?"

"Very sure."

"Okay."

Jake listened for Tim leaving, and when he heard the click of the outer door, he emerged from the stall.

"You don't look okay," Tim said, from where he stood leaning against the door, trapping Jake inside the men's room.

"I thought you'd gone," Jake said as he washed his hands.

"I know you did." Tim smirked at him. "But it's my job to make sure all our customers are *completely* satisfied."

Jake dried his hands and stalked toward the door. "I'm fine. Now, if you'll excuse me, I'd like to return to the table."

Tim trailed a finger down Jake's chest. "Are you sure you don't want to stay here a while?"

Jake smacked Tim's hand out of the way. "Don't you have work to do?"

"I *am* working," Tim purred. "Now, how can I ensure you have *everything* you need?" Tim grabbed Jake's cock and squeezed.

"Get your fucking hands off me, right now," Jake stated.

"But you're so hard for me."

Jake pushed Tim's wandering hand away. "I'm hard because I've had my boyfriends sitting up close to me all night. It has *nothing* to do with you. Now let me pass or I'll report you to the manager."

Tim pouted but didn't move.

The door to the bathroom opened, forcing Tim to step aside. "Jake, are you still in here?"

Jake had never been so glad to see Alex in all his life.

"What's going on here?" Alex asked. "Jake, you're not seriously cheating on my brother with this sleazy waiter, are you?"

Jake pushed Tim away. "Of course not."

Alex stepped closer. "I would hope not. If you're going to fuck anyone besides your two boys, it's going to be *me*."

Jake had heard enough. "Alex, have you lost your fucking mind?"

Tim, who couldn't seem to take a hint, even when his job was in peril, plastered himself to Jake's side. "Jake and I were getting to know each other. But I *might* be willing to share him with you, if you ask me nicely."

"I don't share," Alex replied.

Alex swung his fist at Tim's head, but the waiter ducked just in time, and Alex's punch caught Jake squarely on the jaw.

Pain burst through his face and Jake stumbled toward the nearest sink.

What the fuck is wrong with everyone tonight?

Behind him, Alex and Tim were fighting, each cursing and swearing that Jake was theirs.

The door to the bathroom opened again, this time to admit Kyle and Finn.

"Alex, what are you doing?" Finn asked.

Kyle ran to Jake's side. "What happened to your face?"

"Alex punched me," Jake mumbled. It hurt to talk and one of his teeth felt loose.

"You punched my boyfriend?" Finn shouted.

Jake stared in horror as Finn and Kyle dove into the fray. He didn't know what Tim was usually like, but this was definitely not normal behavior for the other three men.

When the door opened once more and Malcolm entered with a woman wearing a badge reading 'Manager', Jake breathed a sigh of relief.

"What the hell is going on here?" Malcolm roared.

"They've all lost their damn minds," Jake muttered.

The arrival of the manager seemed to bring Tim to his senses and he raised his hands in surrender.

Kyle stepped back as well, but Finn landed one more punch on Alex before he, too, stopped.

Malcolm glared at each of them. "I think we're going to call it a night. Alex, your wife would like you to take her home. Jake, I suggest you get Kyle and Finn out of here until they've calmed down. If the manager here agrees, I'd like to stay for dessert with my wife and sister, and we'll continue our anniversary dinner alone."

The manager nodded. "You're most welcome. I must insist, however, that the rest of you leave and don't come back here again."

"What about me?" Tim asked.

The manager shook her head. "I'm sorry, Tim. You're one of the best waiters we've ever had, but I can't condone this sort of behavior. I'll have to ask you to leave, too."

"I'm fired?"

The manager sighed. "I'll have Kathy cover your tables for the rest of the evening."

Jake almost felt sorry for Tim, especially when he considered the way everyone else had been acting all night. Maybe Tim was also affected by whatever had the rest of the young men in the room behaving so oddly.

Something else was happening here and Jake had a horrible feeling he knew who might be responsible.

"Medina," he muttered under his breath. Having men throw themselves at him without any real control over their actions was right up her alley. He hoped the damage could be repaired.

* * * *

By the time Jake arrived home, Kyle and Finn were getting on his last nerve.

They had argued about who would sit in the front passenger seat until Jake had told the pair of them to get in the back while he drove.

Then they had been playing with his hair, distracting him from the road and making Jake wonder whether it might be prudent to get his head shaved.

His two boyfriends squabbled for most of the—thankfully, short—journey about which of them loved Jake the most, almost as if it were a contest.

Jake called for Medina as he walked through the front door, but the goddess didn't appear. He shouted louder and Fabian appeared in the doorway.

"She's probably found someone to share her bed tonight," Fabian said. "If she doesn't appear the first couple of times you call, she has no intention of doing so."

Jake tried to discourage Kyle from pulling out his cock in front of their house guest. "I really need her to answer me. Everyone has gone crazy."

"Men throwing themselves at you?" Fabian asked as he gestured to Kyle and Finn.

"Not just these two," Jake replied. "Finn, for god's sake, get a hold of yourself."

Fabian chuckled.

"You can stop laughing, as well. Our waiter hit on me and so did Finn's heterosexual brother, right before they all got in a fight in the bathroom and we got thrown out of the restaurant."

"Don't worry too much about it. It'll only last for today."

"What will?" Jake asked. "Did you know this was going to happen?"

Fabian shook his head. "No, but sometimes, when you have gifts from the gods or you're related to one, you have to expect a few oddities."

"Well, I definitely didn't expect tonight," Jake complained as he tried to extricate himself from his lovers. "Are you sure this is going to end after today?"

"Pretty sure," Fabian replied. "On my aunt's love day, anyone she finds attractive fawns all over her, and when darkness falls, it tends to become an orgy. I try to stay out of her way, but everyone in the pantheon knows how it works. With the awakening of the other immortals, everyone's powers are growing, including those like yours. It sounds like every man you've been attracted to this evening has made a move on you."

Jake frowned. He'd had a crush on Alex long before he had met Kyle or Finn, but he hadn't been attracted to their waiter, had he?

Fabian sighed. "You can't help who you're attracted to, and it doesn't mean you'd ever act on the impulse, but there must have been something there for men to be throwing themselves at you."

Jake headed into the living room and sank onto the sofa. "The powers from your aunt are a bloody menace."

Finn and Kyle both tried to straddle Jake's lap at the same time and Fabian laughed. "There are *some* advantages, Jake. You have to learn to take the rough with the smooth."

Jake sighed as he tried to concentrate on the conversation, despite his lovers. "If everyone who threw themselves at me tonight did so because I fancy them, why aren't you doing the same?"

Fabian raised a brow. "Are you saying you're attracted to me?"

Jake shrugged. "You're a handsome man. Most gay men would be happy to share your bed."

Finn smacked him on the chest. "Stop ogling Fabian and pay attention to *me*."

Fabian laughed. "Maybe I'm not affected because I'm related to Medina. Who knows? I'd suggest you take your boys to bed and tomorrow will be a whole new day."

Jake took Fabian's advice, and after he'd finally escaped from under his two lovers, he took them by the hands and led them upstairs to the bedroom.

He sat Kyle and Finn on the end of the bed and knelt at their feet. He wanted to talk to Kyle about what he had been thinking back in the restaurant, but he knew that would have to wait until tomorrow. They all needed a clear head for that discussion.

Finn and Kyle had wasted no time in stripping out of their clothes, which wasn't anything unusual, and Jake gazed at their equally fine bodies with awe that they were his.

"What do you want tonight?" Jake asked quietly.

"You," answered his lovers in unison.

Jake smiled and shook his head. "I think I'd like to see you two come together. How about it?"

Finn and Kyle exchanged a quick glance before nodding eagerly.

"Great." Jake pointed at the bed. "Move to the other end so I can climb on, too."

Without hesitation, the two mermen scooted down the bed, and Jake joined them a moment later, though he sat out of touching distance.

"Kyle, kiss Finn," Jake ordered.

Finn opened his mouth as Kyle pressed their lips together, moaning loudly as he obeyed Jake's command.

For a moment Jake wondered whether they were doing what he told them because of some other power from Medina. He hoped that wasn't the case. He didn't like the idea of forcing his lovers to do things together. Then he remembered who shared his bed, two mermen with rampant sex drives that wore him out on a daily basis. No, regardless of any power Jake might be wielding, Kyle and Finn were never less than eager to kiss, touch and make love, whenever the need arose.

Looking at the two mermen now, Jake could see they were definitely in need. Their hard cocks rose between them, brushing together as they shifted closer.

Jake, who was still dressed in his suit, wished he had taken the time to remove his own clothes. The fabric over his groin stretched tight as the sight of his lovers kissing turned him on.

Finn wrapped his legs round Kyle's back and pulled himself so close Jake could no longer see space between them.

The sound of lips smacking together, combined with moans of desire, filled the room.

Jake slid down the zipper of his trousers and slipped his hand inside the opening. Shielded by his loose shirt, neither Kyle nor Finn would be able to see his cock, but he knew they would have no doubt about what he was doing.

He enjoyed watching his men find pleasure with each other. He had never felt jealousy at such times, only desire and love. Until hearing Kyle's thoughts, Jake hadn't even considered jealousy to be an issue in their relationship.

As he stared at the delectable sight before him, Jake heard his lovers' thoughts once more.

"Need you so badly, Finn."

"Love you, Kyle, so much."

"Jake, get over here and fuck me."

"Need to bury myself in you, Kyle."

Underwater, the two mermen could communicate telepathically, as could Jake, since he'd discovered his Atlantean heritage. Right now, though, neither of them could hear the other, but Jake could.

Jake considered Finn for a few moments. The youngest of the three of them, he often took the most submissive role in the bedroom. He yearned to be held down and taken, to be fucked hard and fast, to be held over a man's knee and spanked until he came.

Rarely did Finn top either of his lovers, yet it was clear from his thoughts right now that he wanted to.

Had Jake not been able to hear him, he'd no doubt have fucked Kyle followed by Finn, or possibly the other way around, and he'd never have known his youngest lover needed something else.

"Finn," Jake said, "fuck Kyle."

The surprise in Finn's silver eyes was clear, as was his eagerness to do as Jake had said.

Kyle frowned a little. "Is that what you want, Finn?"

"Yes." Finn looked at Jake. "How did you know? Did you read my mind again?"

"Yours *and* Kyle's," Jake admitted. "We have to work on our communication skills."

Kyle ducked his head and blushed bright red.

"All of us," Jake said. "Kyle, tomorrow, when we're all a bit less aroused, we're going to talk about our roles in this relationship, okay?"

Kyle nodded and twisted out of Finn's embrace so he could position himself on his hands and knees. He faced Jake but remained out of his reach. Finn crawled behind Kyle and bent his head. Kyle, who couldn't see what Finn was doing, squealed when Finn licked along the line of his crack.

"That's it, Finn," Jake encouraged. "Taste him and fuck him with your tongue."

Kyle moaned loudly and pushed back against Finn's mouth.

Jake gripped the base of his own cock, desperately holding back the orgasm. He couldn't come yet. It was far too soon. Yet it had been a long time since he'd been this turned on, without even touching his lovers. When had they drifted into the monotony of routine sex?

"Oh fuck, oh fuck, oh, Finn, fuck, yes, right there." Kyle encouraged Finn with shouts and cries of pleasure until Jake wondered whether Kyle might come just from Finn rimming him.

Kyle whimpered when Finn pulled away, but Jake knew it was only a temporary withdrawal. He returned a moment later with lube in hand and set about preparing Kyle, stretching him with his fingers and massaging his prostate.

Jake squeezed his own shaft, all the while rethinking his position on cock rings. He could do with one right now if he wanted to keep from coming in a matter of seconds.

When Finn pushed his cock inside, Kyle screamed in pleasure. Jake hoped the rest of the household couldn't hear them. They always placed guests as far away in the mansion as possible, but Jake knew they could all be pretty loud when they lost control.

"Feels so good," Finn gasped as he seated himself fully in Kyle's arse. "Been too long."

"You should have said something," Kyle muttered.

"So should you," Jake reminded him.

"And what about you?" Kyle asked. "Are you keeping any secret desires from us?"

Jake didn't think so, but he was hesitant to say no without giving it some thought. He didn't want another man in his bed, but was he getting everything he needed from his lovers?

"I think maybe there's something else he wants from us," Finn said. "But I think it might have to wait at least a few more minutes, because we're a little busy right now."

Jake laughed. "We'll talk tomorrow. Right now, I want to watch you fuck Kyle into the mattress."

"Yes!" Kyle cried. "Do it, Finn, as hard and fast as you can."

Finn took him at his word and thrust his hips over and over, sending Kyle slipping across the silken sheets.

Jake moaned as he watched Finn take Kyle. His hand flew over his cock, slick with the cum he had already spilled.

Kyle's neglected dick hung heavy between his legs. Finn gripped Kyle's hips and Kyle's own hands were planted firmly on the mattress. Jake suspected it wouldn't matter. Kyle was too close, too aroused. He was ready to come any second.

As Jake watched, Finn changed his angle, and with the next thrust, Kyle howled as he spilled across the sheets below him. The sound of his lover coming went straight to Jake's cock and he followed him a moment later, his seed spraying in an arc across the bed.

Finn screamed and stiffened as he came too, buried to the hilt in Kyle's arse.

The three of them collapsed onto the sheets, panting and struggling to draw breath.

Jake wasn't sure which of his lovers recovered first, but he became dimly aware of the sensation of a tongue licking at his balls. Fingers and hands tugged at his clothes, stripping him bare. Then there were two tongues and two mouths, sucking his soft testicles and licking along the length of his cock.

When he opened his eyes and stared down the bed, both his lovers' heads were buried between his legs. Jake spread his thighs wider, opening himself to his lovers.

Finn reached between Jake's legs with a slick finger. He gazed at Jake questioningly and Jake responded with a quick nod.

With an eagerness Jake hadn't seen in a long while, Finn pressed his index finger against Jake's hole, rubbing around the edge, before slipping the digit inside the tight channel.

Jake whimpered as Finn slowly fingered him. How long had it been since either of his lovers had taken him? Six months? Longer? Jake didn't know, but it had clearly been far too long.

He bore down on Finn's finger and moaned. "More, Finn... Give me more."

Finn did as he'd begged, slipping a second finger in alongside the first. Then Kyle added a third and Jake gasped. He spread his legs wider, urging his lovers on.

In perfect unison, Finn and Kyle pressed their digits inside Jake's arse, fingering him more thoroughly than he could ever recall them doing before.

Jake's cock, so recently spent, twitched with renewed interest. Another gift from Medina, he guessed. Although his mermen had a fast recovery time — something common to their species — Jake didn't. Yet his dick was showing a definite interest in the proceedings, and Jake had no doubt he would soon be as hard as he had ever been in his life.

He could see both Kyle and Finn were thoroughly aroused once more, and he wondered which of them would take him.

"Who do you want in you?" Finn asked quietly.

Jake moaned as one of them brushed their finger over his prostate. "I don't know, don't care. Fuck me, please."

"Blindfold him," Finn said.

Kyle withdrew his fingers and climbed off the bed. When he returned to Jake's side, blindfold in hand, Jake lifted his head so Kyle could secure it behind him.

Between his legs, the two mermen shifted and moved until Jake could no longer tell which of their cocks poked at his entrance.

"Shush," one of his lovers whispered, causing the other to chuckle lightly.

Strong hands lifted Jake's legs, hooking them over the shoulders of one of his lovers. He felt long hair brushing against his calf. *Finn.*

The only feature that enabled people to easily tell apart the Mitchell twins was their hair. Both men were natural blonds, but while Alex wore his hair in a short modern style, Finn had never cut his in his life and his long hair reached down to his waist.

Kyle, like Jake, generally kept his hair short, pointing out that longer hair got in the way underwater. Neither man could understand why Finn didn't get frustrated with his lengthy locks drifting this way and that. Finn had laughed and flatly refused to shorten his hair.

Lucky for Jake, Finn's telltale long hair told him who was about to fuck him. *No*, he corrected himself. His men were making love to him. There had never been a time for Jake when what they did together was nothing more than fucking. His heart had been involved right from the start.

He relaxed his muscles and let Finn inside, welcoming him with his body.

When Jake moaned, he felt something familiar brush against his lips and he opened his mouth. Kyle kissed him and sucked on Jake's tongue as they explored each other's mouth.

"Suck him," Finn said.

Kyle laughed. "Who do you want to suck who?"

"Good question," Jake said. He didn't mind whether Kyle sucked him or fed him his cock — with Finn slowly driving him back to the brink of orgasm, he wouldn't last long even without a hand or mouth on his dick.

Kyle, who had never been a selfish lover, even on the night of the solstice, dove on Jake's cock before Finn could answer.

Jake screamed in pleasure from the dual sensations of being sucked and fucked at the same time.

Finn filled him completely, while Kyle swallowed him down to the root.

His balls drew up and he could tell he was close. Surely there was nothing left in him to shoot? Yet, somehow, there was. Whether by fluke or some magic of Medina, Jake was coming in Kyle's mouth, and Kyle took everything he had to give. Between his legs, Finn stiffened and the heat of his release filled Jake's arse, even as his love for the two mermen filled his heart.

Kyle removed Jake's blindfold and Jake took hold of Kyle's cock, tugging him to completion, until his lover spilled across Jake's chest.

They lay together in a sticky, sweaty heap, no one making any effort to move.

"Do we still have to talk tomorrow?" Kyle asked.

"Yes," Jake replied. "We really do."

Chapter Three

The next morning after breakfast, Jake ordered Finn and Kyle to dress and took them out in the car. Thankfully, whatever magic of Medina's had been around the day before seemed to have dissipated with the dawn.

"Where are we going?" Kyle asked as the scenery passed in a blur. In the back seat, Finn appeared rather green around the gills. Even after two years, he still didn't like traveling in human vehicles. Kyle wasn't particularly fond of them himself, and he hoped the journey wasn't going to be a long one.

The car traveled down the coastline for miles, before finally, when Finn declared he was about to lose his breakfast, Jake pulled off the road and into a dusty car park.

Kyle stepped out of the vehicle and looked down at the deserted beach past the dunes. "Where are we?"

"The Point," Jake replied. "It's quiet here, and we need to talk, somewhere we won't be disturbed or distracted."

"We could talk just as easily at home," Finn pointed out, "without the need for car rides down long, winding roads with lots of bumps."

Jake chuckled. "If we tried talking there, we'd just end up having sex. Besides, you two are beings of the ocean, and I think talking here might help you be more honest."

Kyle nodded and began the walk over the dunes. "This place looks pretty deserted. Are you sure we won't end up having sex here, too?"

"Maybe," Jake admitted. "But not before we've talked."

They found a place on the sand and Kyle waited for Jake to say something.

"Kyle," Jake began, "what you thought in the restaurant last night... It's not true, you know."

"What *did* you think?" Finn asked.

"It's nothing," Kyle mumbled. "It's not important."

"I disagree," said Jake, his voice firm and making it clear that if Kyle didn't tell Finn, *he* would.

Kyle sighed, realizing he didn't have any choice other than to come clean. "When Jake kissed you, I was jealous. Sometimes, especially when we're with your family, I feel as if you two are a couple but that I'm not really a part of that."

"What?" Finn gaped at him. "That's ridiculous! How could you think that?"

Jake placed a calming hand on Finn's arm. "It's not ridiculous at all. Kyle picked up on something that *we* missed. Three men in a relationship together is unusual anywhere, and especially so for a small town like this one. Whether we meant to or not, we made Kyle feel like he's not a part of what we share, when, in fact, he's what holds us together."

Kyle's eyes watered at Jake's declaration.

Jake took Finn's hand with one of his own, and Kyle's with the other. "From now on, no matter where we are or who we're out with, I promise I'm going to make it clear that you're my partner, every bit as much as Finn is."

"You don't have to do that," Kyle said. "I know we're all in this together."

"That's not the point," Jake replied. "I think everyone else needs to know that too."

"But it's like you said, three men together is unusual, and I think we all know it's not socially acceptable, either."

"I don't care," Jake said. "You, me and Finn... That's how it's going to be from now on, and anyone who has a problem with that can deal with it or fuck off."

Finn grinned widely. "Great, so now that's sorted, can we have sex?"

Jake shook his head. "Not until we've got everything out in the open, including whatever it was that was bothering you yesterday in the pool. Care to fill us in?"

"You could tell I was upset about something?"

"Do I really need to answer that?"

Finn sighed. "I guess not. I'm just worried about going back to Atlantis. My father—King Nereus, that is—won't be happy to see me again. You'll remember how we left."

Kyle cringed. "He was pretty furious, but we've heard from others since who've seen him, and he seems to have forgiven you."

"I hope so," Finn said. "If not, I'll be spending the rest of my life in the palace dungeons."

"I'm sure it won't come to that."

"*You* didn't shoot the king with sea-fire," Finn reminded him.

Kyle sighed. "He was angry with all of us, if I recall correctly. He threatened to set the sea dragons on us if we went back."

Finn grimaced. "On the bright side, at least he won't be able to carry out that particular threat. If they reappear, they won't need any encouragement from the king to attack us."

"There is that," Kyle said with a chuckle. "You do know you don't have to come with me? It's *my* family who are being stubborn about leaving. I should be the one to go talk some sense into them."

Finn poked Kyle in the ribs. "Your family is *our* family. If you go back there, we come with you."

Jake paled and Kyle squeezed the hand that still held his. "You're Atlantean. You have the ability to survive underwater at great depths and for however long it takes. You just have to believe you can do it."

Jake snorted. "I know I can do that. It's the swimming for weeks on end that puts me off the whole idea. I might be Atlantean, but I'm still human. I'm not half fish like you two."

"I'm sure Medina would be able to help," Finn suggested. "She really seems to like you."

"Yeah, so I gather. Her little gifts are just one way of showing me how much."

"The mind-reading thing is kind of weird," Finn admitted.

"Not as much as having every man I'm attracted to throwing themselves at me," Jake replied. "That poor waiter got fired because of me. And I don't think your family is too impressed with last night either. I feel I need to apologize to everyone, but I don't know quite what for."

"Did you really fancy that waiter?" Finn asked.

"I guess I must have or else he wouldn't have thrown himself at me. But that doesn't mean I'd have ever done anything with him or even encouraged him. You *have* to know that."

"Of course we do," Kyle said. "We trust you, just as we always have. You know all our secrets. You know who we are, *what* we are and where we came from. You could have sold us out to some science laboratory or the government as soon as you discovered I was a merman."

Jake looked at him aghast. "I'd *never* do that."

"We know," Finn assured him, "and don't worry. I've accepted you'll always fancy my brother."

"I'm sorry," Jake said. "I can't help it, not when he looks just like you."

Finn grinned. "Well, we *are* both devastatingly handsome. I'm just thankful he prefers women. Otherwise I'd have to fight him for you."

"You certainly put in a few good punches last night," Kyle teased. "I never knew you had it in you to scrap like that."

Finn laughed and released his arms so he could flex his muscles.

Jake shook his head and tutted. "You do realize we're now banned from the best restaurant in town because of last night?"

Kyle did know that, and when Finn stopped his preening and hung his head, he could tell the truth had sunk in with him, too.

"Maybe if we go and apologize, they'll change their minds," Finn suggested.

"I don't know," Jake replied. "That manager was awfully pissed off. Let's not worry about it. I think finding somewhere else to eat out is probably the least of our problems right now."

Kyle agreed. "Are there any other issues you think we need to get out into the open?"

"I don't think so," Jake said. "We just have to make sure we communicate properly in the future. *All* of us. Relationships are hard when there are just two of you in them. With three, we've got to take extra care that we're not neglecting one or another of us."

"Agreed," Finn said. "So, Kyle, next time you think you're not being included, let us know."

"It's not always that easy, not in public, but I'll try."

"And you, Finn," Jake said. "If you feel you need something from us, sexually or otherwise, you've got to speak up, right?"

Finn nodded. "And what about you?"

"I'm going to work hard to make sure you're both happy."

"I'm pretty sure that's not what he meant," Kyle said. "We're not stupid, you know. We can tell your powers are growing, and I don't think it's just because yesterday was some special occasion for the Goddess of Love."

Jake ran a hand through his hair. "I'm not sure it was, either," he admitted quietly. "Yesterday, I know for sure I was hearing the thoughts of those around me, but there have been occasions—not many, but a few—where I already thought that might have been happening, at least with you two anyway."

"How long has this been going on?" Finn asked.

"A few weeks."

"What about your other powers?" Kyle asked. "The ones that make people do stuff without them meaning to?"

"I've been really careful about what I say to try to avoid that happening again," Jake admitted.

"Maybe you should test it?" Finn suggested.

"I was considering asking Fabian about it," Jake replied. "As Medina's nephew, he seems to know a lot about her and her powers, and I think he might be more forthcoming with information than she is."

Kyle and Finn both agreed.

"As soon as you get home, track him down," Finn said. "You can fill me in when I get back."

"Why? Where are you going?" Jake asked.

"I've had enough of that smelly contraption for one day. I think I'd like to swim back instead."

Jake frowned. "Just be careful you aren't seen."

"You worry too much," Finn teased. "We've never been spotted before."

"I'll go with him," Kyle said.

Jake snorted. "So instead of worrying about one merman hiding from the locals, I get to worry about two."

Kyle pulled Jake into his arms and hugged him tight. "Merpeople have remained hidden from humans for centuries. We know how to be careful. We'll see you back home later."

Kyle released Jake and stripped off his clothes. Beside him, Finn did likewise and a few minutes later they ran into the surf, leaving Jake to carry their clothes back to the car.

* * * *

"Aaaah," Finn said as he stretched his fins. "It's been so long since I swam in the sea that. I'd forgotten what it feels like."

"Me too," Kyle replied. "You'd better make the most of it. When the weather gets warmer, the tourists will arrive in their droves. Then we won't be able to come out here at all."

"We'd just have to be careful."

"No, we'd have to talk Jake into letting us come," Kyle said. "We both know he's a worrier, and the warmer weather means we'll have to make do with the pool."

Kyle floated on the surface of the sea, his silvery blue tail alongside Finn's pure silver one.

"Can I ask you something?" Finn said suddenly.

"Of course you can. Didn't you hear what Jake said about us communicating properly?"

"Yes, I know. I was wondering... What will you do if Lynna refuses to come here?"

"I don't know," Kyle answered truthfully. "I've not thought that far ahead. I'm hoping she'll see sense, especially since the sunken city is no longer hidden from predators."

"Would you stay in Atlantis if she refused to join us in England?"

Kyle twisted around to tread water, so he could face Finn. "You and Jake are my family, and I don't think either of you would want to live in the sunken city — you because of the bad memories and Jake because he's human. My place, regardless of what Lynna decides, is with you."

"But if she won't leave..."

Kyle took Finn in his arms and kissed him thoroughly, slowly sinking below the waves as he did.

"If Lynna won't come voluntarily, there are two choices. I leave her there or I bring her here by force. Neither option is particularly appealing."

"Or you could stay with her," Finn pointed out.

"That's not an option. My place is with you and Jake, and nothing my sister decides is ever going to change that."

Finn didn't say anything in response, but he deepened their kiss as they ran their hands over each other's body.

Slowly, they sank below the waves until they landed on the seabed. They spent the next few hours teasing each other with touches, knowing they couldn't climax in their mer forms but enjoying themselves just the same. Tonight, when the beaches were deserted and it was safe for them to return to shore, they would be so tormented with lust that Kyle knew it would take only the lightest of touches to send him over the edge.

* * * *

The two mermen swam along the coast, carefully avoiding the humans both on and in the water. Thankfully their keen eyesight along with fast moves gave them plenty of warning if they were about to be discovered.

They slept on the seabed during the afternoon. It wasn't particularly comfortable, but there weren't any other choices.

Then, when the darkness above indicated the sun had set, Kyle and Finn swam back to the surface.

"Damn," Finn muttered as they took in the sight of the beach party.

"Why in the world would anyone want to hang out on a beach at night in February?" Kyle asked.

"They look like they're settling in for a while, too," Finn commented.

"Don't they have homes to go to?"

As they watched, another car pulled up and more revelers emerged.

"I bet my dad's not too happy about them," Finn said.

"You think he might send them off elsewhere?"

Finn shook his head. "No, he'll just moan about the noise and tomorrow complain about the mess they leave behind. But I guess we're going to be sleeping on the seabed tonight."

"We could try swimming to the next cove."

"You know the coast as well as I do. Even if we find one that's clear, it would be a long walk back to Jake, not to mention some clothes. I just hope Jake isn't too worried."

"I'm sure he'll have seen for himself that we're stuck out here," Kyle replied. "He's no doubt at Malcolm's house right now."

"At least he's going to have a comfortable bed to sleep in," Finn complained.

Kyle laughed. "Poor baby. Come here. You can use me as a pillow."

Finn elbowed him in the ribs but not hard enough to hurt. "I don't like you as a pillow. You fidget and you snore."

"I don't snore."

"Yes, you do. I prefer my Jake pillow."

Kyle sighed. "Yeah, me too. But there's no point in complaining about it. Let's just get some sleep and come back up in the morning."

Chapter Four

"I think they're going to be stuck out there for the night," Jake said, as he watched the group of teenagers on the beach.

"No doubt," Malcolm said. "I'm sure we were never so noisy when I was their age."

"Yes, you were," Coral teased. "You have a selective memory. I do hope the boys are being careful and that they won't risk trying to come ashore until the party is over."

"I'm sure they'll stay out of sight," Jake said. "I'm going to head home for the night and be back in the morning."

"Are you sure you don't want to stay here?" Malcolm asked. "Your old room might be taken, but you're welcome to the couch."

"No, but thanks for the offer, and apologies again for what happened last night. I hope it didn't ruin your anniversary too much."

"Oh, don't worry about it," Malcolm said. "Just try to get a hold on those powers you've got before they get you into even more hot water."

Jake grimaced. "I'm trying. Believe me, I'm trying."

* * * *

Back at the mansion Jake shared with his lovers and their various house guests, it didn't take long to track down Fabian.

"If you're looking for your boys, I've not seen them," Fabian said as he glanced up from the job section of the local newspaper.

"They're swimming offshore and likely to be there until morning."

Fabian gave him a look of confusion.

"There's a party on the beach, which means they're stuck out there until it's safe to come in."

"Have they been out there all day?"

"Pretty much."

"I'm surprised you aren't out there with them."

"We drove down the coast this morning. They decided to swim back, but I came in the car."

"And you've been waiting for them all day?"

"Not really. I knew they'd be out there for a while. I've been over at Malcolm's working on the accounts for the business."

Fabian gestured to the newspaper. "Looking at the jobs available, it seems like accounts are something I should know. I'm not qualified for anything in here."

"Don't worry about it. You can stay here for as long as you want. That's why Caspian gave us such a large place—for all the strays from Atlantis to come to until they find their feet, literally and figuratively."

"I guess, but I've never had to rely on others for shelter and food before. I like being able to pay my way."

"I'm sure something will come up soon."

"Easy for you to say," Fabian muttered. "You and your men have jobs."

"Yeah, but I've worked for Malcolm for years, and while Finn has joined us in the shop, he's not exactly happy there. 'Bored out of his skull' is how he usually refers to himself when he's there. As for Kyle, he got lucky with the job at the aquarium. A merman held the position before him, and Kyle took over temporarily as a favor while the guy swam off to Atlantis. When he didn't come back, they hired Kyle permanently. If it weren't for the fact that Lucas stayed with us while he was tracking down Justin, we'd never have known about the job vacancy, since it wasn't advertised in the press."

Fabian sighed. "I hope we aren't imposing on you."

"Of course not. I'm happy to have you, and I know the others are, too."

"Still, I would like us to be able to contribute something while we're here."

Jake understood that feeling very well. He had felt uncomfortable accepting the house when Caspian had told him it was his. The sprawling mansion was well out of his price range and were it not for the funds Caspian had provided to Kyle and Finn, they'd have been wallowing in debt for the rest of their lives.

"There is something you *could* do," Jake said.

"Just name it," Fabian replied.

"You and Delwyn could look after this place while we're gone. I don't want to put Treacle in the kennels and Malcolm won't have time to watch him, not when he's going to be two members of staff down already."

"What do you mean?" Fabian asked. "Where are you going?"

"It looks like Kyle's sister is going to take a bit of persuading to get her to leave Atlantis, so we're going to travel there to see if we can talk her around. From what Kyle and Finn have said, it takes the mer six weeks or longer to swim there from England, and I'm not mer. I have a feeling two to three months is going to be a more realistic estimate. And that's just one way... There's the time we'll spend there and the swim back, too. I think we'll be gone at least six months."

As he spoke, Jake thought of something else Fabian could do to help, too. "We could also have a word with Malcolm about you, and maybe Delwyn, to see if he wants helping out in the sandwich shops. You might not be able to assist with the accounts side of things, but he'd definitely be grateful for the extra sets of hands."

Fabian nodded. "I think I speak for both of us when I say we're happy to help. We'll keep an eye on Marin, too, if you want?"

"I'm not sure Marin will let us leave him behind, however much I think it's a bad idea for him to go charging after Calder's murderer."

"According to Delwyn, Urion has been driven out of the city, along with Mariana and the other sea dragons. Even if he comes with you, there's no one there for him to attack."

"But he could swim off in search of him," Jake pointed out. "I'd rather he stay here, safely out of the way, but I know he won't like that idea."

"I guess we'll have to cross that bridge when we come to it," Fabian said.

"Yes, though I suspect it might be sooner rather than later. Now, I hate to change the subject, but there's something else I wanted to talk to you about, too."

"Yes?"

"You're Medina's nephew, so I'm hoping you know more about her powers than I do."

Fabian chuckled. "My aunt's powers are all about love, lust and all that sort of stuff. My own were connected to the creatures of the sea — and still are, in fact. Even though my power to survive underwater and my demi-god status have been removed, I *do* still have a few powers."

"Such as?"

"I can communicate with Delwyn when we're underwater, even if I can't stay down there for any longer than a regular human being. I can also still hear the thoughts of other sea creatures when they're in the vicinity. Not that there are many around here, but it's kind of nice to know that not everything I was has been stolen from me."

"I'm glad to hear it. Having your life turned upside down isn't a great deal of fun."

"I have no doubt you speak from experience," Fabian said. "So, what powers are giving you the most trouble?"

"All of them," Jake muttered.

"Care to be a little more specific?"

"Well, there's the hearing thoughts of others, having random men throwing themselves at me, accidentally forcing people to be intimate with each other and I daren't even pick up a trident in case I smash something else."

Fabian laughed. "The trident takes practice. That's nothing to do with Medina. You'd have the same problem no matter what, simply because you're Atlantean. I'd suggest giving it a try—but not around anything valuable."

"Okay, and what about the rest?"

"The men throwing themselves at you should be a yearly thing, unless your powers grow so that you have the ability to draw men to you, but you'd have to do it deliberately outside of Medina's love day. I think the best thing you can do regarding that one is to stay home with your boys for the whole day."

"I'd already decided the same thing, and I'm glad to know that'll be just one day a year."

Fabian tapped his fingers on the table, seemingly unsure how to proceed. "Well?"

"Well, what?"

"I'll take that as a no," Fabian said.

"What are you talking about?"

"I was trying to send my thoughts to you, but you obviously didn't hear them. Let me try again, now you know what I'm attempting."

Jake concentrated as hard as he could, but still nothing came through. "I don't think this is working. Maybe it only works once a year, too."

"I don't think so. Let me try one last thing."

"I wonder if Delwyn knows how much I love him."

Jake gave a small sound of joy. "I heard that."

"Are you sure? What did I think?"

"You wondered if Delwyn knows how much you love him, and I'm sure he does."

Fabian grinned. "Let me ask you... What other thoughts have you heard? Were they all love related?"

"Love, lust, sex... That sort of stuff," Jake confirmed.

"Then I guess I'd better watch what I'm thinking around you," Fabian said. "I'll warn Delwyn, too."

"Well, that's a great help around the house but not so much the rest of the time. I *really* don't need to know about my boyfriend's parents' sex life."

Fabian laughed. "I don't imagine you do."

"Do you know how I can switch it off?" Jake asked.

"I'm sorry, but I don't think you can. Medina herself can't switch it off entirely. She learns to 'filter it out', as she puts it."

"Damn."

"I'm sorry, but sometimes the gifts from the gods are a double-edged blade. Now, what was the other thing, causing people to do things?"

"Yeah. It's not happened often, because I try to be careful about what I say, but again, I'd like a way to make it stop."

"I'm afraid I don't know of any, but you could always ask Medina herself."

"I tried talking to her before, but I get the impression she thinks I should be grateful for her gifts and not question them."

"Yeah, that sounds like Aunt Medi. In that case, I'm not sure what to suggest, though, like I told you before, as the rest of the immortals rise from their slumber, the powers of all the gods will increase, and so will those who have been gifted by them."

"Sometimes I wish she'd take her gifts back," Jake muttered.

Fabian patted his hand. "You have to remember that she didn't just gift you with powers. She also brought you the love of two wonderful men."

Jake smiled as thoughts of Kyle and Finn banished his worries about his out-of-control powers. Yes, they were definitely worth a few magical mishaps.

"One more thing," Fabian said as he rose from the table. "Medina has the power to send you and your men back to Atlantis magically. It might be worth asking her if she'll do that, rather than spending months swimming there and back."

Following Fabian's advice, Jake wasted no time in calling for Medina. Thankfully, she showed up a few minutes later, much to Jake's surprise.

"Ah, Jake." Medina greeted him with a kiss on each cheek. "How did you enjoy yesterday?"

Jake snorted. "I can't say I enjoyed hearing my mother-in-law thinking about sex or having men throw themselves at me. Some poor waiter even got fired."

Medina tapped her lip with her painted nail. "Well, that won't do at all. I'm afraid there's nothing I can do about your mother-in-law, but I'm sure Caspian can help the waiter get his job back. Caspian!"

Jake jumped at Medina's yell for the other god. He wasn't sure whether to hope the bad-tempered God of Justice appeared or not. If he did arrive, he wasn't likely to be in a very good mood after being summoned so rudely.

"Medina," Caspian said as he appeared in the kitchen. "Is there any particular reason you shouted to me quite so loudly?"

"I wanted to make sure you heard, of course," Medina replied sweetly. "I need a teeny little favor from you."

"Of course you do," Caspian said. "And what makes you think I'd be willing to do *you* any favors at all?"

"Well, it's not for me, exactly," Medina explained as she gestured to Jake. "I'll let Jake explain."

"What?" Jake glared at his distant ancestor. Trust her to leave him to break the bad news to the glaring god at the other side of the table.

"Well, tell him," Medina prompted. "It's rude to keep a god waiting, you know."

"But you—"

"Oh, just spit it out," Caspian interrupted. "I don't have all day."

"Um, Medina said you might be able to help with this waiter—Tim—who threw himself at me in a restaurant last night."

Caspian raised an eyebrow. "Two mermen aren't enough for you?"

Jake bristled. "Of course they are. Tim was badly affected by it being Medina's special day."

"And what do you want *me* to do about it?" Caspian asked. "Whatever magic caused him to act the way he did, it's over now. Besides, horny men aren't my area of expertise."

"That's a matter of opinion," Medina said.

Jake flinched at the glare Caspian shot at Medina. "He lost his job because of it," he blurted.

Caspian turned his attention back to Jake. "He did?"

Jake nodded. "He got in a fight with Finn, Kyle and Finn's brother, and the manager fired him and barred the rest of us from the place. Can you get him his job back?"

Caspian remained silent for a few moments before he gave a sharp nod. "I'll see it's straightened out."

In the blink of an eye, Caspian vanished.

"There, you see? All sorted." Medina sounded quite pleased with herself.

Jake guessed there was no time like the present to ask for a favor. "Medina, can I ask you something?"

"Of course, what is it?"

"Would you be able to transport me, Kyle and Finn to Atlantis? Kyle wants to talk to Lynna and we don't want him going there alone."

"I'll have you there in two shakes of a lamb's tail. Where are Kyle and Finn?"

"They aren't here at the moment. They're waiting for the party on the beach to finish before they come ashore."

"Oh, there's no need for that," Medina said as she snapped her fingers.

A moment later Finn and Kyle appeared, fast asleep and locked in each other's arms in the middle of the kitchen table.

"Aw," Medina said, "don't they look beautiful?"

Jake smiled. "They sure do. I don't know if I ever thanked you for bringing them into my life, but I want you to know how grateful I am."

Medina sniffled and dabbed at her eyes. "That makes it all worthwhile. Now, if we're all here, I'll take us to the Isle of the Gods then on to Atlantis."

"Actually, I think Marin might like to come with us, too," Jake said.

"Absolutely not!" Caspian reappeared and had obviously heard Jake's comment. "He has no business chasing down sea dragons and getting himself killed. He'll be perfectly all right here until you get back."

Caspian's shout woke Kyle and Finn, who stared about the room in obvious surprise.

"What's going on?" Kyle asked.

"Medina is going to take us to Atlantis," Jake said. "I've spoken to Fabian, and he and Delwyn are going to take care of the house. I'll need to call Malcolm, though, and let him know what's happening. I thought

Fabian and Delwyn might be able to help out at the shop while we're away, too."

"What about the aquarium?" Kyle asked. "I don't think my boss will be happy about me taking off without notice. He moaned enough when Justin did the same thing. I doubt he'll keep my job for me."

"I don't know," Jake said. "You could put some holidays in, but if we don't get back in time, you'd be in trouble."

"I haven't got any holidays left for the year, anyway," Kyle reminded him. "Maybe Fabian or Delwyn could cover for me until we're back?"

"You think your boss will go for that?" Jake asked.

"Maybe with a little persuasion," Caspian suggested. "I'll see what I can do. Between the three of them, I'm sure Fabian and the others can keep your various jobs secure."

"I still think Marin would prefer to come with us," Jake said.

"Marin stays here," Caspian stated, in a voice that made it clear he would not tolerate any sort of argument. "We have more than enough problems to contend with right now."

"Maybe we'll be back before they notice we've gone," Finn said. "If Medina is transporting us, we could be back in a few hours."

"Not if my sister has anything to say about it," Kyle muttered as he took the towel Jake offered him and quickly dried off his tail, restoring his human legs.

"You think this might take some time?" Medina asked.

"She can be stubborn," Kyle replied. "You've met her yourself. Remember?"

"Perhaps there might be another way of getting you there then," Medina said. "A way for you boys to go back and forth without my direct assistance."

"What do you mean?" Jake asked.

"You'll see," Medina said as she swept out of the room, leaving everyone else to follow her.

Jake hoped whatever she had in mind worked. The sooner they got underway, the better, and now he wasn't going to be spending months swimming the distance, he felt much better about visiting Atlantis.

Medina breezed through the house, checking one room after another. She shook her head and tutted regularly, as she opened and closed each door, apparently not satisfied with what she found.

By the time she found a room that met with her expectations, everyone in the house was trailing after her.

"This room should be ideal," Medina announced. "Large, bright and uncluttered."

"We finished clearing out this room last week," Jake said. "We've been thinking about putting a home gym in here."

Medina screwed up her nose. "That won't do at all. No, this is going to be my first new temple of the twenty-first century."

"Temple?" Fabian asked. "Do you need any more? Surely the two in Atlantis are enough?"

Medina waved away his comments as she strolled into the center of the room. "Temples are like lovers. You can never have too many of either."

With a clap of her hands the room sparkled as though a team of cleaners had polished everything from the floors to the windows.

"Can you do the whole house like that?" Kyle asked.

Medina gave him a look that told him quite clearly the answer to that question was a resounding *no*.

"Over there, I think," Medina said as she pointed to the far side of the room.

A moment later a life-size statue of Medina, seated on an elaborate throne, appeared in front of them. The statue appeared to be made of white marble, save for the hair, which was ebony and matched the goddess's own long locks.

Finn stepped a little closer to the statue and cocked his head to one side. His gaze flickered between the goddess and her likeness. "It's not exactly accurate, is it?"

"It's a very precise rendition of myself," Medina stated. "Identical in every detail."

"Not totally identical. The statue seems to have bigger..." Finn gestured to Medina's breasts and Jake smothered a smile.

Fabian grinned outright. "You aren't the first to have noticed that error," he said. "Quite a few of Aunt Medi's priests have picked up on it over the years."

Medina glared at her nephew. "You never did learn how to hold your tongue. As for you" — she pointed a long finger at Finn — "you're a lover of men. You aren't supposed to be noticing women's breasts."

Finn snorted and pointed at the statue. "They're kind of hard to miss."

Even Caspian appeared to find the exchange amusing, but he, like Jake, seemed to want to hurry things along. "Can we get on with this? I *do* have other things to do today."

"You don't *have* to stay," Medina reminded him. "You've sorted out the overly friendly waiter and got him his job back. Your work here is done for now, so why don't you leave if you're so *busy?* Perhaps you could go and arrange cover for the boys' jobs if this is boring you."

Caspian didn't move from where he leaned against the wall. "Just hurry up."

Medina raised her arms and bolts of lightning shot from her fingers toward the foot of her statue. Two columns, about two feet high, appeared to each side of the statue — one with a bowl on top and the other with a large crystal.

"There you go," Medina said. "One fully functioning temple, complete with a transportation crystal, which, when activated, will take you directly to my residence on the Isle of the Gods."

"You touch it to activate it, right?" Delwyn asked.

Medina shook her head. "That's how it works for my priests and those who carry the blood of the gods in their veins. That means Jake and Fabian, of course. The rest of you will need to make an offering for the crystal to work."

"What sort of offering?" Kyle asked.

Medina walked to the column with the bowl and tapped it. "Anything you think I might appreciate will do. Perfume, silk scarves, fresh roses... Whatever you like."

"Cheap wine from the local supermarket," Caspian suggested, earning him another glare from Medina.

"And anyone can use this?" Jake asked. "Not just the mer or Atlanteans?"

"Anyone who you bring here, yes," Medina confirmed.

"And you'd be happy with us talking to others about you?" Kyle questioned with a fair degree of skepticism in his tone.

"Of course," Medina replied. "The more humans who remember me and come to pay homage in my temples, the stronger I become. I'll need all my strength for the coming battle for the city of Atlantis."

"Like you have any intention of fighting," Caspian said.

"I've done my share to assist our cause," Medina snapped at him before turning her attention back to the others in the room.

"I would ask you keep this room as clean as you can," Medina said. "This *is*, after all, a place of worship, just as your modern churches, mosques and the like are. You could even get married before me, if you wished to do so. Couldn't you, Fabian?"

The look Medina gave her nephew and the tone of her voice made it clear the question wasn't rhetorical. Fabian's expression was one of utter horror.

"Married?"

Medina nodded. "You don't think it's about time you settled down with a nice young man? I'm sure Delwyn agrees with me."

"Leave me out of this," Delwyn muttered.

"Aunt Medi, don't start," Fabian warned her.

Medina chuckled. "You can't fool me, Fabian. I know true love when I see it, and I'm waiting for the day you ask me to officiate over your nuptials."

"At least you *can* get married," Finn said. "Try being in a ménage and it's a bit more difficult."

Medina smiled. "Under Atlantean law, there can be more than two people in a marriage. I myself married two men at the same time. If you, Jake, and Kyle wish to cement that bond, all you have to do is ask."

"It doesn't look like a church," Jake said, as eager to change the subject as Fabian. He hadn't thought much about marriage, and while he wasn't opposed to the idea, he didn't want to discuss the possibility in front of an audience. "Shouldn't there be seats or something?"

"Feel free to place some if you wish," Medina said. "But take care not to move the statue, the offering bowl or the crystal. To do so could destroy the magic. You might also note that I'll be able to hear you when you call from here with much greater clarity than anywhere else. If you wish to summon me, doing so from this room is highly recommended. Now, I believe you wanted to visit Atlantis, so shall we go?"

Chapter Five

On their arrival on the Isle of the Gods, they found themselves in a room not unlike the buildings in Atlantis. However, while the sunken city had deteriorated due to the water it was in, this building was in much better condition, although a little neglected.

Finn wandered to the open door and peered outside. The sight that greeted him was like nothing he had ever seen. Having never been to land for the first twenty-one years of his life, he had often wondered about what other places were out there, but even his wildest imagination could not have conjured this place.

The air was cleaner than any he had ever breathed and there wasn't a single cloud in the blue sky.

The ground seemed to be one huge bed of flowers, most of which he had never seen before in his life.

"Welcome to the Isle of the Gods," Medina said. "If you'd like to follow me back inside, I'll show you how to travel to Atlantis by crystal."

Despite the clear blue sky, a crash of thunder roared across the isle.

A strange man, surely a god, appeared directly in front of them.

"How dare you defy my edict," the god raged.

"Cynbel," Medina said. "What a pleasant surprise. How delightful to see you awake again. I don't believe you've had the pleasure of meeting my family."

Cynbel didn't spare a glance for anyone except the goddess. "I banished Atlanteans from Atlantis. You have no right to bring one of them back here."

"Jake is a distant descendant of mine," Medina said. "He and his lovers are here to visit Kyle's family in the city. They won't be staying forever."

"I don't care," Cynbel replied. "That man doesn't set foot in Atlantis — not now or ever."

Medina bowed her head respectfully. "I'll ensure Jake remains on the isle until his lovers have returned from the city. It *is* only temporary."

Cynbel didn't look happy about it but vanished anyway.

"Who was that?" Kyle asked.

"Cynbel, God of War," Medina said. "He can be most disagreeable. He's Caspian's father and the one Caspian inherited his volatile temper from. He's only recently rejoined the world."

Now that she had mentioned it, Finn could see a certain resemblance between the two gods. He didn't like the idea of getting on the wrong side of either of them.

"Come along," Medina urged. "The sooner Kyle speaks with his sister, the sooner we can get you all home."

"What about you, Finn?" Jake asked. "Are you going with Kyle or staying here?"

Finn hadn't thought he would have to make a decision on what to do so soon. He'd imagined having plenty of time to consider things on the long swim from England.

"You don't have to decide right now," Medina said. "We have plenty of time."

"I'll go down with Kyle," Finn said. "I'd like to see Justin and Lucas again, and I don't like how things ended with my father — or I guess I should say, the man who raised me."

Jake pulled Finn into a quick hug. "Remember… No matter what he says, you'll always have me and Kyle, as well as your parents back home."

Finn buried his face in Jake's shirt and breathed deeply. "I love you."

"I know," Jake replied. "I love you, too."

From the corner of his eye, Finn saw Kyle staring at his feet. "Come here," he said, pulling Kyle into the embrace.

"We've got to work on that communication," Jake insisted. "Now, you two take care down there, and return to me soon."

"Come," Medina said as she led the way into another room in the building that seemed to be in a slightly better condition than the previous one. Someone had apparently been doing some repairs here recently.

Finn watched as Medina explained how to open the portal back to England by touching a particular crystal.

"How do you know which one to use?" Kyle asked.

"This one goes to my temple in the palace, while that one on the other side of the room goes to my public temple. If you forget, peer closely into the crystal and you'll see for yourself the place it leads to."

"What about those?" Finn asked, pointing to numerous broken crystals on columns just like the others.

Medina wiped away a tear as she approached the nearest shattered gem. "These used to transport my most loyal priests to various temples around the world. Unfortunately, as the other races waged war on the Atlanteans, jealous of their gifts, my temples and those of my brethren were destroyed. When a temple is leveled to the ground, the crystal here is broken, too. As you can see, only those leading directly to Atlantis have survived the centuries. Had we not sunk the city below the waves, they, too, would no doubt have been broken long ago."

Finn didn't know what to say to that. Medina was a goddess, yet he felt the urge to comfort her. He gave her a small pat on the arm, hoping he wasn't overstepping. She offered him a watery smile before steeling herself and waving at the crystals.

"You're welcome to use whichever you like," she said.

"The palace one is probably most convenient for us," Kyle said. "King Nereus is likely to be there, and my sister works in the palace."

Medina stepped back and tapped the crystal. "Well, here you go."

Finn pressed the crystal and the room shimmered as a bright glow appeared in front of him.

"Just walk into the portal and you'll be in the palace," Medina said. "You'll get your fins back in a few moments and you'll be on your way. You can return here the same way, whenever you're ready."

"We can?" Finn asked. "Don't you need to be with us?"

Medina shook her head. "No. All you need to do is make an offering in my temple and it will activate the portal to bring you back here. If you want to bring others with you—Kyle's sister, for example—you can."

"Could anyone else activate it on their own?" Finn questioned.

"Yes, but only if they know what to do, and those who have evil intentions in coming here will find themselves swiftly and harshly dealt with."

Finn nodded that he understood and stepped into the portal.

Kyle's tail and fins appeared, as Medina had said they would. He felt strange suddenly being back here in the city. It hadn't been his home for long, and when he'd left, he hadn't thought he would one day be coming back.

"Which way?" he asked Finn, who was far more familiar with the catacombs beneath the palace than he was.

"To the left," Finn replied as he swam out of the temple and into the corridor. *"Let's check the kitchens first. If Lynna is still working in the palace, she's probably there."*

Kyle swam after Finn as they quickly navigated the labyrinthine underground levels of the palace.

"The kitchens are that way," Finn said, pointing down a passageway. *"I'm going to head to the king's audience chamber and see if he's sitting. No sense in putting off the inevitable."*

Kyle held Finn back with a hand to his arm. *"I'm coming with you. What if he hasn't calmed down and his forgiveness is a trick to get you to come back here?"*

"*Then it's best I go alone,*" Finn replied. "*If he throws me in the dungeon, I'll need you to come rescue me.*"

"*I don't like the idea of you going to see him alone.*"

"*You* have *to see it makes sense. It's not like Jake can come down and get us if we're both locked up, even if he did know where to go. You go find your sister, keep a low profile and I'll meet you back on the Isle of the Gods before nightfall.*"

Kyle wasn't happy about the decision, but it was clear Finn had made up his mind. And if King Nereus did throw him in the dungeons, Kyle would make sure he got him out of there as soon as he could.

"*Take care,*" Finn called as he swam out of view.

Kyle continued down the corridor, passing a couple of guards on the way. Neither of them was familiar to him or gave him a second glance. They carried tridents rather than the spears Kyle had used during his brief stint among their number. He wished he had brought a trident or spear with him, but it was too late to worry about that now.

There seemed to be a lot more merpeople in the palace now than when he had last been here. If an evacuation of the city should take place, he had no idea where they could all safely go.

As he neared the kitchens he spied a familiar face and sped up to chase after Xane. If anyone knew where his sister was, it would be her mate.

"*Xane!*" Kyle called. "*Hold on.*"

Xane spun around and banged into a nearby guard in surprise. "*S-s-sorry, Otus.*"

"*Watch where you're going,*" the guard snapped.

Kyle hadn't had much to do with Otus during his time in the guards. He'd found the merman to be ambitious and unpleasant and had stayed out of his way as much as he could.

"*Kyle?*" Xane gaped at him in surprise. "*What are you doing here? We thought you were in the land of humans.*"

"*I thought he'd been banished,*" Otus added. "*Maybe we should go pay a visit to King Nereus.*"

Kyle ignored him and focused on Xane. He'd already heard via an old friend who had briefly visited England that he was welcome to return to the city. Were it not for Jake and his life on land, he'd probably have visited long before now. Besides, Finn was already going to speak to his father, and he was sure King Nereus was far more interested in the return of the merman he had raised, rather than Finn's former bodyguard. "*I'm here to talk to Lynna. Do you know where she is?*"

"*She'll be in the nursery with Maurissa and the other youngsters.*"

"*Which way is that?*" Kyle asked.

Xane hesitated. "*You aren't going to upset her, are you?*"

"*Of course not,*" Kyle replied. "*I want to talk to her about coming to live in England.*"

"*The Goddess of Love already came to ask her about that, and we've already told her no.*"

"*Yes, she told me, which is why I'm here to ask myself and try to make her see sense.*"

"*What's so great about the land of humans?*" Xane asked. "*Aren't you always struggling to hide what you are among those who would kill us?*"

"*It's not like that,*" Kyle assured him. "*There are some humans who can be trusted. Not all of them would kill us on sight.*"

"*But some of them would.*"

"*Probably, but we take care not to draw attention to ourselves. There's no more danger from hiding from humans than there is from avoiding shark-infested waters. If you and Lynna came to land with us, you'd see that for yourself.*"

"*I'm not going to leave my family,*" Xane said, "*and Lynna won't either.*"

"I'm *Lynna's family, too.*"

Xane sighed. "*Go talk to her if you want. She won't change her mind.*"

Kyle listened to Xane's directions then left the merman to his work, while Kyle went in search of his sister.

It didn't take him long to find the nursery. He heard the cries of the youngsters at play long before he reached them. At such a young age, the merbabies hadn't yet learned how to focus their voices on speaking to one person. Their shouts were projected for anyone in the vicinity to hear, making the nursery one of the loudest places in the city.

Kyle had thought the nursery was located outside the palace, but it seemed things had changed since the day he'd left.

Watching from the archway, he could see Lynna at the far side of the room. The netting over the entrances prevented the young from slipping away from their minders, and Kyle was careful as he entered, not to let a merbaby escape.

Lynna and the other mermaids seemed to have the young well in hand as they laughed and played.

"*Lynna?*" Kyle called out to her, and she spun around to see him. His sister had put on a little weight since he had last been with her. He guessed that came from her living in the same place and not swimming through the oceans as they had once done before coming to the sunken city. He had enough sense not to mention her fuller figure. His sister could be lethal with her tail when she lost her temper.

"Kyle!" Lynna charged across the room, carefully navigating through the youngsters, then she threw herself into his arms. *"I thought I'd never see you again. When did you arrive?"*

"A few minutes ago. Xane said I'd find you here. Now, first things first, which one of these is my niece?"

Lynna swam back into the fray and returned a few moments later with a blonde-haired mer-girl with green fins the same color as her father's.

"Maurissa, say hello to your Uncle Kyle."

Maurissa giggled and batted at Kyle's nose.

"Can I hold her?" Kyle asked.

Lynna snorted in her typical unladylike manner. *"Good luck with that. She's faster than she looks and is the worst of all the youngsters for slipping away when we're not looking."*

Kyle laughed as he took the squirming child from her mother's arms. *"You know, if you lived on land, you'd only have one youngster to look after, not a whole bunch."*

Lynna frowned and huffed. *"Two whole minutes before you brought that up… As I told Medina, I'm happy here, and I've no intention of putting Maurissa in danger by taking her to land."*

"We'd take care of her…and you," Kyle said. *"We won't let anything happen to her."*

"I won't let anything happen to her," Lynna snapped. *"I know you and other adults can hide what you are from the humans, but Maurissa is too young to understand. She doesn't know that she can never let humans see what she is. I'm not going to put her in danger to ease your mind."*

Kyle had known before they'd made the decision to come here that talking Lynna into coming to land wouldn't be easy. He hadn't thought it would be quite this hard, though. He had forgotten she could be stubborn as a barnacle.

"Perhaps there's another option," Kyle suggested. *"Our mother is still out there somewhere. Maybe we can find her, and you can live with her. I'm sure she'd love to meet her granddaughter."*

"No doubt she would," Lynna agreed. *"Unfortunately, I have no idea which way she went, and I've not seen her since she left. So, unless you know where she's swimming these days, I'd rather not go flippering all over the ocean with a young child, trying to track her down."*

"I wonder if she might have gone in search of her grandmother's clan," Kyle suggested. *"They usually swam in what humans call the Pacific Ocean."*

"You're not listening to me," Lynna snapped. *"I'm not going to put Maurissa in danger. I'm not going to swim all the way to the other side of the world on the basis of a guess that* Mother *might have gone searching for her grandparents' clan. That clan might not even exist anymore. Mother might be dead, for all we know."*

Kyle couldn't think that. Even though he'd had no control over his mother's actions, he felt responsible for her. He *had* to believe she had found somewhere safe to live out her life.

* * * *

Reaching the audience chamber of King Nereus without being recognized had never been particularly likely. Still, Finn couldn't quite hide his groan of annoyance at the sound of *"Your Highness"* in his head as he swam through the palace.

He inclined his head respectfully at the guard who had greeted him then continued on his way.

Word would no doubt spread quickly through the palace. King Nereus would know of his arrival in the city well before Finn reached him. Maybe he would be apprehended by the guards and thrown into the dungeon without even seeing the merman who had raised him.

The queue outside the audience chamber was long, which wasn't unusual. Finn, who no longer considered himself a member of the royal family, no matter how the palace staff greeted him, joined the end of the line, ready to wait his turn.

He hadn't been waiting for more than five minutes before a guard approached him. *"If you'd like to come with me, Your Highness, His Majesty will see you now.*

"I'm happy to wait. There are many here who have been seeking an audience longer than I have."

The guard gestured for Finn to swim ahead. *"Nevertheless, I'm sure they will understand that His Majesty is eager to see his son after so many months apart."*

Finn sighed. He guessed he couldn't put it off any longer. He followed the guard down the line, ignoring the stares of the other mer, much as he had tried to when he'd lived in the city.

Inside the audience chamber, he was relieved to see the room was empty, save for King Nereus himself and his natural son, Justin.

"Hi, Finn," Justin greeted him with a wide smile. *"It's good to see you again — or at least hear you again since, as you can probably tell, I've lost my sight these days. But you don't want to hear about me right now, so I'll leave you two alone, but you must visit my chambers before you leave. I want to hear all the news from England. My adoptive father, Caspian, is terrible at bringing me updates on my football team."*

Finn laughed. *"I don't think I'll be much better. I don't follow it much myself."*

Justin tutted as he passed. *"Still... You come by later and we'll talk more."*

Finn nodded and faced his father. How strange it was to be back here. He felt an odd connection to Justin, whose life had been so similar to his and yet also completely different. Justin was the true son of the man before him, yet had been raised on land by a god. Finn's birth father was a human, but he had been raised by the merman before him. The difference was that Justin had always known he was adopted, while Finn had been lied to his entire life.

He couldn't blame his father for that. The king had been as clueless about Finn's true parentage as Finn himself.

Unfortunately, they hadn't parted on the best of terms and now, swimming before the man who raised him, Finn had no idea what to say.

"Don't you have a hug for your father?" King Nereus asked as he spread his arms wide.

Finn gave a small sob and swam swiftly into his father's embrace, for King Nereus *was* his father, no matter what anyone else had to say on the subject. He still loved his birth father, Malcolm, who had been nothing but welcoming to him since he'd swum to England two years before. But it could not change the fact that King Nereus had been the one to comfort him when he had been stung by a jellyfish, who had told him stories to help him sleep at night and who, if his expression now was any indication, still loved him as though he were his real son.

"I never thought I'd see you again," King Nereus said. *"I'm so glad you've returned. Though from what Justin tells me of your life among humans, I suspect it's only for a visit. Correct?"*

Finn nodded. *"We're here because Kyle wants to persuade his sister to come to England with us."*

"Whatever the reason, I'm glad you came to see me. We have much to talk about. But first, I must apologize for my harsh words when we parted. I was angry with your mother, and you were caught up in that. I'm so sorry, my son."

"I'm sorry, too," Finn said. *"I turned a trident on you, an action punishable by death."*

"You were angry, and you had every right to be. My behavior was inexcusable."

"You never struck me, though."

"Forget it, Finn. As you can see, I survived the sea-fire with just a small burn scar to show for it. I've had a lot of time to think about how I acted that day, and I'm ashamed. Please forgive me."

Finn sobbed in earnest as his father held him.

"You are always welcome here," King Nereus continued. *"You and your bodyguard. I let my pride and my temper rob me of my beautiful young son. Please tell me it's not too late to make amends?"*

Finn couldn't even form a coherent thought. His fear at facing the king had vanished and all he wanted now was to be held and told that everything would work out for the best.

"There's one more thing you must know," King Nereus said. *"Even though I can hear the thoughts of everyone who has sworn allegiance to the city, I don't use the power most of the time. I never intruded in your private thoughts, not until that last day, at least. I wouldn't like anyone else poking into my head without permission, so I have tried not to do so since the day I was crowned."*

"It's okay," Finn said as he managed to get a hold of his emotions. *"You aren't the only one with the power to read my mind these days, anyway."*

"I'm not?"

Finn shook his head. *"Jake, one of the men I live with, can sometimes hear what I'm thinking, too. It's strange, but*

I think sometimes it's better to have things out in the open. Secrets always end up causing trouble."

"They do, indeed."

Finn eased himself out of his father's arms and settled down on the seat reserved for the heir, at the side of the throne. He guessed it was Justin's seat now, but he figured Justin wouldn't mind sharing it for the moment.

King Nereus rose and banged the bottom of his trident on the floor. A guard appeared immediately.

"Audiences are closed for the day. Please take the names of those still waiting so they can be seen first when sessions are resumed."

The guard swam to do the king's bidding.

"Come, Finn. Let's go talk somewhere more comfortable."

Finn breathed a sigh of relief that the 'somewhere more comfortable' apparently wasn't going to be the dungeons. He followed his father to the other side of the palace and the royal family's private chambers. Once there, they sat and Finn helped himself to some of the sea fruits that were always laid out for the king and his guests.

"Hmm, I've missed these," Finn said around a mouthful of food. *"I love lots of the human food, but their fruits don't taste quite as delicious as these."*

"Well, as you know, there's plenty here, so eat your fill."

Finn did as the king suggested, helping himself to another piece.

"Does he treat you well?" King Nereus asked quietly.

"Yes, of course he does – both of them do. Kyle and Jake are the best mates I could have ever hoped for."

"I'm glad to hear it, but I wasn't talking about Kyle or Jake."

"You weren't?"

"I was asking about your real father, the human."

"Oh." Finn hadn't thought his father would want to know about his birth father. He wondered how much he should say. *"He's been great. I've enjoyed getting to know him."*

"I'm glad he's worthy of having a son like you."

"Mother is happy, too," Finn said. The moment the words left his mouth, he realized he had said the wrong thing.

"I don't want to hear about the queen," King Nereus snapped. *"She betrayed me and lied to both of us. She's not welcome here and I've forbidden anyone to mention her name in my presence."*

Finn nodded. *"I understand. I'm sorry for bringing her up."*

The king shook off his bad temper and gave Finn a smile. *"Now, tell me about this human — Jake, did you say his name was?"*

"Yes, Jake Seabrook. He's a direct descendant of Medina, the Atlantean Goddess of Love."

"He is?"

"Yes. According to Medina, she once ruled Atlantis with two other men, one human and one mer. She gifted me with two men of my own when I sought her assistance in finding love."

Finn chatted to his father about Jake and Kyle and the life he had built for himself in England.

"I like it there, but I do miss the ocean sometimes. Thankfully, Medina has created a way for us to travel here without swimming all the way."

"She has?" King Nereus frowned. *"I'm not sure I like that idea. With the immortals waking, having a back door into the city sounds dangerous."*

"I don't think you need to worry about our way of getting here. It involves traveling from our home in England through a portal we have to open by making an offering to Medina,

and it doesn't bring us straight here. It takes us to the Isle of the Gods first. Then we come here from there. If the immortals want to bring an army here, all they have to do is create their own temple and crystal portal, like Medina did. I have no doubt most of the gods and goddesses already have a way of getting into the city."

"I see why your Kyle might want to get his sister out of Atlantis."

Kyle wasn't the only one who wanted the merpeople of Atlantis safe, and the immortals weren't the only problem right now.

"There's more," Finn said. *"Without the sea dragons, the city is visible to all the predators in this area of the ocean."*

"We've already seen an increase in shark attacks since the sea dragons left," King Nereus admitted. *"It's only been a few days, and we've no doubt it's going to get worse."*

"There are human explorers heading this way, too," Finn warned.

"Humans cannot survive at this depth."

"Mankind has made great strides in technology during the last century. I looked it up when I saw some of the amazing inventions they have. Humans can travel right down to the bottom of the ocean in machines built to travel underwater. And they have machines with these things called cameras that can show the humans high above us what is down here, without them even needing to swim down and see it for themselves."

"Are you sure about this?"

"I looked it up on this huge information bank humans call the Internet."

King Nereus smiled softly. *"You always were thirsty for knowledge. You and that young merman Delwyn spent more time reading the stories on the palace walls than any other mer I know. I trust you to tell me the truth."*

"What are you going to do about the humans?" Finn asked. "They can't be allowed to discover the existence of the mer."

"Why not? Your biological father and Jake don't seem to have any trouble accepting us. Perhaps it would be safe for us on land."

"Jake and my dad aren't typical of humans," Finn admitted. "Even Jake took some time to get used to the idea of what we are. He was pretty good about it when I arrived on land, but when he first saw Kyle with his tail and fins, he was really shocked."

"Discovering mythical creatures actually exist would give most people a bit of a fright."

"I know, and like I said, he's been wonderful and accepting. But he's not typical. Other humans, scientists and government agencies... They would take us prisoner and study us if they could."

King Nereus frowned with confusion. "I don't know what a scientist is – or a government agency, for that matter – but if anyone tries to hurt you, I'll raise an army to make sure you're safe and sound, and your captors would regret the day they chose to hurt one of the mer. They just wouldn't regret it for long."

The implied threat of impending death for anyone who dared to mess with him was not lost on Finn. He was glad the king would protect him, but he hoped it wouldn't come to that. He didn't want to see any of the mer in danger. Unfortunately, with humans heading this way and the threat of immortals who were not so accepting of the mer as Medina and Caspian, the sunken city of Atlantis was no longer a sanctuary of safety for their people.

Finn wished he had any suggestions for what they could do to protect the young and vulnerable among the inhabitants. There were few true colonies of mer left in the world. Their numbers decreased every year, and the entire race was on the verge of extinction. Clans could no longer survive in the open waters.

For so many years, Atlantis had been the one place where the mer could truly hide. Now it was visible, a target for every predator in the ocean. Nowhere was safe for the mer of the world, and the time might come when they would have to reveal their presence to the humans. Finn thought he would much rather come out from the ocean on his own terms, instead of ending up captured by those who would do them harm.

The public would be fascinated with them, and many would be supportive. Finn wondered whether it was worth the risk.

A few years ago, he would have said no. Atlantis had been securely hidden and there had been no reason to doubt that would change. Now it had, and they needed to look at all the options, even if some of them involved even bigger risks than staying here, waiting for the sea dragons to come back and finish the job or the human explorers to stumble upon the greatest find of their lives.

Chapter Six

Jake watched his two lovers enter the portal that would take them down to the sunken city. He wasn't sure whether to be relieved or disappointed that he could not go down with them. On the one hand, seeing the legendary Atlantis would be the experience of a lifetime. On the other, he still wasn't comfortable with staying underwater for lengthy periods of time. While his brain told him he could survive because of his Atlantean heritage, there remained a tiny part of him that was determined to panic at the very thought.

Medina hooked her arm through Jake's and led him outside. "You should go explore the island. They could be a while down there."

Jake's stomach growled. "Is there anywhere to find some food on the isle?"

Medina held out her hand and a bowl of fruit appeared. She passed it to him with a bright smile.

Jake wasn't a great fan of healthy eating, but he guessed pizza delivery was out of the question around here. He took a peach instead. "Thanks."

"My pleasure," Medina replied. "Now I must get on. A goddess's work is never done."

Jake wondered what chores she could possibly have to do, but he didn't like to ask. Instead, he decided to take her advice and see what was on the island.

To the left of Medina's home, there stood a similar building, but it seemed to be on the verge of falling down. One of the walls had crumbled away completely, leaving a gap big enough to walk through.

Farther along stood another building, which was much better kept than the rest.

Jake couldn't be sure, but he thought he spotted movement nearby, so he headed in that direction, wondering who else might be on the isle.

When he reached the building, he realized he hadn't been mistaken.

"What about this America place?" a male voice asked.

"It seems quite vast," another man replied. "Whereabouts are you thinking?"

"Maybe we should toss a coin to decide?"

The second man snorted contemptuously. "*You* can leave your fate to chance, but I intend to make an informed decision about where I spend the rest of my life."

Jake didn't like to hover eavesdropping, so he coughed deliberately, drawing their attention.

"Oh my, look what we have here," the first of the men said with a bright smile. He had dark hair and wore old-fashioned robes, as though he had stepped out of ancient Greece or Rome. "Who says our prayers aren't answered?"

Jake frowned, wondering what he was talking about.

"Down, Isander," the second man said. "You don't even know if he's a lover of men."

"Oh, he *is*," Isander replied. "I can tell. He's a man who knows what to do with his cock."

Jake didn't know quite what to say to a comment like that.

"You'll have to excuse Isander," the second man said. "He's rather sexually frustrated. I'm Dolph, former priest of Mariana, Goddess of Sea Creatures. This is Isander, also a former priest. We're what you would call *unemployed* now."

"I'm not sure I understand."

"Unemployed," Isander said. "We need to find jobs, not to mention homes and all the essentials in life."

Jake laughed. "I know what unemployed is. I meant why are you here, on the Isle of the Gods?"

Isander gestured for Jake to take a seat with them. "We're Atlanteans but were saved from being banished by our goddess, Mariana. She transformed us into sea dragons, along with the rest of her priests. When she woke from her long slumber, she freed us, but Dolph and myself chose not to fight with her. We helped to protect the mer from her and her loyal priests instead. Because of this, we've been saved from banishment by Cynbel, but he refuses us access to Atlantis."

"Which means we need to find somewhere else to live out the rest of our lives," Dolph added. "We're allowed to stay here for a limited time but only until we decide where to go. Once we've worked out the details, Caspian is going to set things up for us."

"I'm surprised he didn't dump you on a beach somewhere and leave you to it," Jake commented.

Isander laughed. "I see you've met him. But no, he isn't going do that to us, much as he might like to. It took Cari hours of arguing with him before he'd even agree to help us at all. He isn't exactly fond of Atlanteans."

Jake frowned. Caspian was grumpy and bad-tempered, but he didn't seem to have a problem with him, and according to Medina, Jake was very much Atlantean.

Dolph sighed. "You can't exactly blame him, all things considered. If the rumors about what happened are true, he has good reason to be angry. Besides, he *has* agreed to help us, once we have things decided. He's already given us the knowledge of the modern world and languages."

"So, what's your story?" Isander asked. "I don't recognize you, so I'm guessing you aren't Atlantean."

"Actually, I am," Jake replied, "at least according to Medina. She says I'm a distant descendant of hers. I'm waiting for my partners, who are down in Atlantis. Like yourselves, Cynbel has forbidden me from going to the city."

"Then you're a modern man?" Isander asked. "You can explain to us some of the things Caspian has given us knowledge of that don't make much sense."

Jake shrugged. "I can try."

Isander shifted closer. "And we can get to know each other better, yes?"

"Er…"

"For the sake of the goddess, leave the poor man alone," Dolph said. "You're not the only one who's been celibate for hundreds of years. Anyone would think you didn't have use of your hand."

Isander smirked at his friend. "My hand is getting plenty of action, just like yours. But there's nothing like having another man's hands on your body to get the blood pumping."

"I'll take your word for it," Dolph replied before turning back to Jake. "As you might have guessed, Isander and I have differing tastes when it comes to carnal pleasures. I prefer women, while Isander craves men."

"Like you do," Isander added to Jake. "So, how about it? Do you want to help me break out of this celibate slump?"

Jake chuckled. "Sorry. I'm in a relationship already."

"He's a lucky guy," Isander replied. From his bright smile, he didn't seem bothered about Jake's rejection.

"Guys," Jake said, determined to make good on his promise to Kyle and Finn to treat the two of them the same. "Kyle and Finn, the two mermen down in Atlantis."

"You called them your partners," Isander said.

"Yes, that's a modern phrase that can mean a business relationship, but in my case, it is definitely pleasure."

"Finn, Finn, Finn." Isander tapped his lower lip with a finger. "Not Prince Finn?"

"That's the one, though he doesn't like being called a prince."

Isander roared with laughter. "I don't imagine he does. From what I saw, he never did. I watched him swimming into mischief more times than any other member of the royal family, including his father, who wasn't exactly well-behaved himself. I'm glad he found someone to love him."

"Me too," Dolph said.

"So, two men are definitely enough for you?" Isander asked. "You wouldn't consider taking on a third?"

Jake laughed loudly. "I think I'll have to pass. Two mermen are more than enough to keep me satisfied."

"I'll bet," Dolph commented, "especially during the mating season. They are most energetic. I even bedded a mermaid or two myself, back in the day."

Jake declined to comment on Dolph's remark. He didn't want to admit that he did sometimes have trouble keeping up with the two mermen, not that he let it bother him. He found as much pleasure in watching his two lovers come together as he did participating himself.

"So, I'm guessing this is the home of one of the gods?" Jake asked.

"Yes, this is Cari's temple. She's the Goddess of Prophecy. She's been kind enough to let us stay here."

"You'd be well advised not to enter any of the temples unless you know they belong to a friendly immortal," Dolph warned. "Not all are welcoming of Atlanteans. Cynbel threatened to castrate us both if we dared set foot in his territory."

Jake and Isander simultaneously cupped their groins, the very idea sending shivers down Jake's spine — and not in a good way.

"So, how do I know which are the buildings I can enter?"

"Come on. I'll show you," Isander offered, pointing the way back outside.

Jake stood and followed Isander back into the open. Isander led him to the center of the island and up the hill to the building on the top.

"This is the communal area for all the gods for great celebrations. At least, it used to be. I don't think they're in the mood for a party these days. They're too busy fighting with each other or sleeping. Anyway, this is a safe area. Medina's temple, I guess you know, and we've just come from Cari's."

Jake gazed about the island from the high vantage point and saw dozens of temples scattered about the foot of the hill. He hadn't imagined there were so many immortals. He wondered how many were awake.

Isander pointed ahead of them. "The Isle of the Gods is in the shape of the symbol for infinity. The other half of the island has a volcano in the center. Andaman, God of the Forge, makes his home inside the volcano. He's an ally to the mer, but he doesn't have anything against Atlanteans. He doesn't socialize much, though."

"Which is Cynbel's temple?" Jake asked. "Just so I know to avoid that one completely."

Isander pointed at the building with the hole in the wall. "That's the one."

"Oh… I thought it would be in better upkeep, with him being awake, that is."

"It was until he sent a blast at the wall to make a point."

"Which was?"

"He was demonstrating what he would do to us if he caught me or Dolph anywhere near his territory."

Jake cringed. "Was that before or after he was going to castrate you?"

"Probably at the same time. After all, he is a god," Isander replied. "Anyway, it's better to avoid all the rest of them, to be on the safe side, unless you run across a god who invites you in. Then you'll be safe."

"What about Caspian's place?"

Isander shook his head rapidly. "No one—mer or Atlantean—is allowed to set foot in his temple. Even Cari only goes there when she absolutely has to."

"He's that unsociable?"

"You've met him," Isander reminded him. "Caspian isn't here much anyway, from what we've seen. According to Cari, he lives among humans most of the time."

"Has he always been so bad-tempered?" Jake asked. Caspian was a mystery to him and right from the start Jake had been curious about who and what he was.

"Are my ears burning?"

Jake and Isander jumped and spun around. The god in question stood right behind them. Jake didn't know how long he had been listening, but the conversation was definitely over now.

Caspian didn't wait for a response. "My temple is right before you reach the beach separating the two halves of the island. I would recommend you bypass it entirely on your exploration of the isle."

Jake nodded, quick to reassure the god he wasn't a threat to his peace and quiet.

Caspian disappeared as swiftly as he had appeared.

"As he said, his temple is that way." Isander pointed to the location.

"Are there no other allies?" Jake asked. "There are a lot of temples here, and not many who seem to be on our side."

Isander shrugged. "It rather depends on who you are, as well as what side you are on. Atlanteans who wish to help destroy the mer would be welcomed by Mariana and those gods and goddesses who think like her."

"And those who don't?"

"A few, like Medina and Cari, will tolerate our presence, even if we are Atlantean. Others, like Cynbel, won't."

"And the mer?"

"They have more gods on their side than us peaceful Atlanteans do, but I have no idea if it'll be enough. Many of the most powerful gods still sleep. As sea dragons, we watched the war unfold as the gods turned on each other, each seeking to place the blame for the troubles on another. They wore themselves out, and without the Atlanteans to worship, or even remember them, they could not sustain their powers."

"So gods only exist while people believe in them?"

"Something like that. They *exist* but they can't remain a part of this world. Those who had strong ties with the mer remained conscious. The rest didn't."

"Until now."

Isander sighed. "Until now. The war that started so many centuries ago is about to begin again, and I fear nowhere in the ocean will be safe for the mer."

* * * *

Kyle couldn't visit the sunken city without checking in with Dax. He and his first lover might have moved on, but they were still friends, and Kyle was eager to catch up with his news.

Dax lived with one of the Oracles, and, as such, he was pretty easy to find. The Oracles, three merpeople bound to Cari, the Goddess of Prophecy, were housed within Cari's temple.

"*Dax, how are you?*" Kyle asked as he waved from the doorway, two guards blocking his entrance.

"*Let him past,*" Dax ordered. "*He's a friend.*"

The guards obediently swam to the side, letting Kyle into the room.

"*When did you get here?*" Dax asked. "*Did Finn come with you? Was Jake happy with you coming here? He must be missing you so much.*"

Kyle laughed and shook his head. "*Finn has come with me and we arrived a couple of hours ago. I've been catching up with Lynna.*"

Dax snorted and rolled his eyes. "*And here I was, thinking you'd come all this way to see* me."

"*Well, I did think about heading back without seeing you, but I figured you might sulk if Lynna told you I'd been here.*"

"*Damn right I would,*" Dax replied with a grin. "*So, what does Jake think about you coming all the way here?*"

"*He's fine with it — or he was a couple of hours ago. He's no doubt wondering where we've gone to by now.*"

"*What do you mean? Jake is here, too?*"

"*Not in Atlantis, but he came to the Isle of the Gods with us.*"

"*Are you saying you didn't swim here?*"

"*That's right. Thanks to Medina, we now have a shortcut to the city and can visit here whenever we want.*"

"*Really? So we'll be seeing a lot of you now?*"

"*Probably,*" Kyle agreed, "*if Kai's okay with that.*"

"*Why don't you come through and ask him yourself?*" Dax asked. "*He's in the next room, practicing his fighting tactics with the guards.*"

"*You've let him loose with a spear?*"

"*Like I could stop him.*"

Kyle followed Dax through the archway and found Kai jabbing at one of his guards with a spear.

"*Kai, we have a visitor,*" Dax called. "*You'll remember Kyle?*"

Kai spun around, his opponent taking advantage of his distraction to disarm him.

"Kyle? Why are you back in the sunken city?"

"I'm visiting my family. I hoped to convince Lynna to move to England, but she's being stubborn about the idea."

Kai swam closer. *"I'm glad to see you. I owe you an apology for the way I acted when I visited your home in England."*

"There's no need," Kyle assured him.

"Yes, there is. You were hospitable, and I returned your kindness with rudeness and temper."

"You were jealous," Kyle said. *"I understand that reaction more than you can know. I kissed Dax when you had a prior claim to his affections. I should have been more understanding of your feelings and I'm sorry for my actions, too."*

Dax sighed loudly. *"If we're all done apologizing, how about we turn to more pleasant topics?"*

Kyle definitely agreed with that. *"I've lots of news for you from Delwyn,"* he said. *"He's safe in England with Fabian. They're both staying with us for the moment."*

"Is he happy?" Kai asked.

"Yes, he is."

"What about Marin?"

Kyle sighed. *"He's not doing so well. He's determined to avenge Calder's murder, and I think that's the one thing keeping him going. He isn't eating properly. I don't think he's sleeping more than an hour or two a night, and there's nothing we can do to help him."*

"He loved Calder," Kai said. *"I think they've been together since Marin's first mating season."*

"His heart is broken," Kyle agreed. *"There's no cure for that."*

Kyle wondered whether it might be allowed for Kai to see if he could use his powers to locate Kyle's mother, but he knew having visions of events so far away was tiring for the Oracle. He might also be in trouble with King Nereus were he to discover Kyle had asked Kai to help him without getting the ruler's permission first.

"Is that Kyle I hear?"

Kyle moved aside so Ula and Undine, the other two Oracles, didn't swim into him. Undine, who had replaced Delwyn as the Oracle of the past, was newly blind and struggling to navigate the rooms.

"Undine, I heard you were the new Oracle," Kyle said. *"How are you enjoying your new position?"*

"I love it," Undine replied. *"I especially liked that I could discover what happened to you after you vanished with Prince Finn. I don't need to ask if you're happy in your new life."*

"No, you don't."

"I didn't realize you knew each other," Dax commented.

Undine laughed lightly. *"Oh, Kyle and I are very well acquainted. We once spent a mating season together, didn't we, darling?"*

Dax gaped at Kyle, his eyes wide. *"What?"*

Kyle decided not to tell Dax the truth about his night with Undine, where they had pretended to have sex to fool the guards who were keeping an eye on them. *"Oh yes, it was a lovely night. I'm surprised you remember me, Undine. You were so wonderful. I'm afraid I didn't last very long, did I?"*

Undine played along, as Kyle hoped she would.

Dax stared at her, then Kyle, and back again. *"You had sex with a mermaid?"*

Kyle tried to keep up the pretense, but he couldn't stop his laughter from bubbling up.

Despite the current danger to Atlantis, he was happy to be there, catching up with family and old friends. He might have known Undine for a single night, but she had been kind to him and he was happy for her now. As an Oracle, Undine would have been cursed with infertility, and as such, she would never have to suffer through a pregnancy that might kill her, as her last one nearly had.

All too soon it was time for Kyle to leave. Jake would be wondering where he was, and he was worried that he hadn't heard from Finn since they had parted ways.

Kyle was halfway to the king's audience chamber when he spied Finn swimming toward him, flanked by two guards.

"Finn? Are you under arrest?"

Finn shook his head. *"No. Everything is fine. My father has insisted I have bodyguards while I'm here. This pair have the joyful task for the day."*

Kyle waved the guards away. *"I was Prince Finn's bodyguard when he resided in Atlantis permanently. I'll take over those duties from you now."*

Finn's expression of relief was short-lived.

"I don't think so," the first guard said. *"I don't know you and we have orders from King Nereus."*

"This is Kyle, Prince Finn's lover," the second guard said. Kyle recognized Morgan, a friendly merman from his birth clan and a perfectly capable guard. *"I'm sure he won't let anything happen to his charge."*

"Prince Finn is our *charge,"* the first guard argued.

Finn cringed every time they referred to his title and Kyle had a feeling he might smack one or both of the guards if he didn't get him out of there soon.

"Are you ready to go home?" Kyle asked.

"Definitely. Is Lynna joining us?"

"No, she's digging her fins in the sand. I'll come back again in a few days and see if she's thought things through."

"Is she likely to?"

"Not at all, and now that she knows how easily we can visit, she'll use it as an excuse not to come with us."

"Maybe you should have lied and told her you'd swum here?"

"I thought telling her about the temple would set her mind at ease. Knowing there's a way to get there without swimming all the way should have made her happy. There's so little risk to Maurissa now that I thought she'd agree immediately."

"Some of our people have stronger ties to the sea than others," Finn reminded him. "Not all mer can live on land."

"There are few who can," Morgan added. "Though I never thought Kyle would be one of that number."

"Me neither," Kyle replied. Being in the dark depths of the ocean now made him realize how much he had missed it.

They arrived at the temple and Finn placed a seashell necklace he had bought for Medina at the marketplace into the bowl.

"We'll be back soon," Finn said. "There's no need to follow us through the portal. I'm only to be guarded in Atlantis."

The guards nodded, and Finn activated the portal so he and Kyle could return to the Isle of the Gods.

Chapter Seven

A few weeks later

Kyle sat in his usual seat near the back, during the aquarium's monthly staff meeting. He didn't want to be there at all. He couldn't believe how stubborn Lynna was being about coming to land. That she wouldn't even consider a short visit was something he hadn't anticipated. Her insistence that he would talk her into staying wasn't entirely unfounded, and he hated that she knew him so well.

If Cari's latest prophecy was correct, there wasn't much time before the humans discovered Atlantis, then it would be over for the mer. Unless they were evacuated — and the question was, where to? — the humans would have definitive proof of the existence of merpeople.

He supposed at least Lynna was safe in the palace and close to Medina's temple. She knew where to go and what to do if the worst happened.

The meeting was nearly over when Natalie rose to address the room. Kyle sank low in his seat. Maybe she wouldn't notice him.

"The aquarium anniversary party is all arranged, but we're still missing a few responses from you guys. "Beth, are you going to make it this year?"

Beth laughed. "Yes, and I've managed to convince Rob to stay away from the booze. He's so embarrassed about what happened last time."

Natalie snorted. "The least said about that the better. I think the memory of your husband limbo dancing into the buffet table is one we'd all rather forget. I'll mark you down as a yes. Now, what about you, Kyle? Can you make it?"

Kyle groaned. So much for hiding at the back of the room. He'd avoided the party the previous year, even though he'd have liked to have attended and gotten to know his colleagues in a more social setting.

"Come on, Kyle. You'll have a blast," Natalie urged. "Can I put you down as a yes? Do you have a partner to bring with you?"

Kyle flushed. He didn't hide his sexuality at work, so everyone knew that if he did attend, he would be bringing another man as his plus one, but no one knew he lived with two men.

Some of the staff had met Jake as he dropped him off at work, but no one knew Finn even existed. As much as he hated to admit it, he was as reluctant to draw attention to their unique relationship as Jake and Finn had been. He could tell Jake and Finn were making every effort to ensure he felt secure in his relationship. Now came the opportunity to show he could do the same.

"Can I bring two guests?" asked Kyle, his voice cracking as he spoke. His face heated as everyone in the room seemed to stare at him.

"We usually limit the party to employees and their partners," Natalie replied. "I thought you were seeing that man who sometimes drives you to work?"

Kyle cleared his throat. "I am, but I'm in a relationship with someone else, too." *There!* He'd said it. It was out in the open.

Natalie smiled coldly. "And how exactly do you intend to stop the two men you're cheating on from spotting the other?"

Kyle gaped at her when he realized his words had been misunderstood. "They know about each other," he explained, his face heating even more as his other colleagues continued to gape at him. "We all live together…um, the three of us, that is. We're, er, you know…"

Suddenly Kyle understood how hard it had been for the others to say out loud what it was they shared. He wished he hadn't chosen to reveal their ménage like this. He should have spoken to Natalie alone. Then, if she allowed him to bring two guests, let the rest of the staff draw their own conclusions.

"Oh." Natalie studied her clipboard. "I guess I'll put you down for plus two. Um, yes, well…that's everyone, I think."

Natalie hurriedly took her seat and the manager of the aquarium rose to say a few words of thanks and encouragement, as he did every month.

Bill held a magazine in his hand and waved it at the front row. "I assume you've all seen the reports?"

Kyle had no idea what the man spoke of, and from the shaking heads around him, neither did anyone else.

Bill huffed and opened the magazine to an article that he showed the room. Kyle couldn't even see the title from where he sat.

"As you all know, we've recently installed a new tank at the far end of the shark tunnel. It's intended to be viewed both from above and also from underwater, just as the tunnel itself is. The safety inspectors are due here in a month or two to ensure it meets the specifications for holding our newest arrivals, which are expected before the end of the year. But, until then, I think we can use it to capitalize on this latest discovery by presenting our visitors with their very own mermaids."

Kyle's heart raced. He had to see what was in the magazine.

"But there's no such thing as mermaids," someone near the front pointed out. "I read that article yesterday, and all the experts say it's a fake."

"Yes, yes," Bill replied. "I know what they're saying and I agree. The funds used on the expedition could be put to much better use than trying to convince the world that mythical creatures exist. I'm not suggesting we go out in a boat and try to catch one."

"Then what are you suggesting?"

"I think we should purchase a custom-made tail and fins for one of our staff and she can swim around the tank for the guests. Give them a wave and a smile, maybe even sing the odd song. The public will love it."

Natalie coughed loudly. "Why does it have to be a woman?" she asked. "Isn't that a bit sexist? The picture, if it's real or not, clearly shows a man. Why not have one of the men swimming in the tank."

Bill nodded thoughtfully. "Maybe you're right. Now, who'd like to volunteer for the job? I should warn you, those custom-made tails are quite pricey, so once you've been measured and we've ordered it, there's no changing your mind and backing out."

No one seemed in any rush to put themselves forward.

"What about you, Amy?" Bill asked. "You certainly look the part."

"I can't swim," Amy replied. "I've a fear of going underwater."

"Oh." Bill appeared somewhat taken aback, but quickly recovered.

"What about Kyle?" Doug suggested. "He obviously likes being the center of attention."

Kyle glared across the room. Most of the staff were perfectly pleasant, but Doug was a touch homophobic and had made plenty of snide remarks over the months they had been working together. No doubt this was his way of making Kyle feel uncomfortable for what he had revealed earlier, when, in fact, Kyle felt awkward enough as it was.

"You know, that's not a bad idea," Natalie said. "Kyle, you work out, right?"

"Yes," Kyle muttered. It wasn't strictly true, but he'd done some heavy lifting at the aquarium and that had been the explanation he had offered for his strength. The truth was mermen were naturally strong on land, after spending so much time swimming—the best sort of exercise.

"Perfect. Women will flock to see a merman with a nice six-pack."

Kyle frowned. He didn't like the direction this conversation was going in. He could only think of one way to stop this idea dead in its tracks. "I can't swim either."

"Really?" Natalie asked. "I think you said you could on the forms we had you fill in when you started working here. Since, unlike Amy, your position involves being around the water exhibits, we like to ensure you can swim before hiring."

Kyle was caught and he knew it. "I *can* swim, but I don't think I'm the best person for this job. Who'd want to see me in a tank?"

"I would," Amy piped up with a grin.

"Surely there's someone else?" asked Kyle, frantically scanning the room for anyone who appeared even slightly enthused about the idea. Unfortunately, everyone seemed to be relieved that Kyle was the focus of attention and they were off the hook.

"We'll get you measured by the end of the day," Bill said.

Kyle couldn't think of anything worse than being measured for a fake fish tail. Would the thing be waterproof, or would his real fins tear through the material as soon as he submerged himself? One thing was certain. If that happened, he'd never leave the tank, unless it was to be taken to some horrendous government facility where he'd be tested and chopped up into bait.

* * * *

The rest of the day passed by in something of a daze. Finally, Kyle arrived home, where he immediately tracked down Jake and Finn.

"What is it?" Jake asked as Kyle flew into his arms and buried his face in his chest.

Kyle breathed deep and long, reassured by Jake's calm strength.

"What's happened?" Finn asked as he joined them in the embrace.

Kyle laughed, slightly hysterical at the events of the day. "The manager of the aquarium wants me to play the part of a merman in the new tank."

"He knows what you are?" Finn stared at him, aghast.

"No," Kyle quickly assured him. "There's been a photo of a merman published in some fish magazine. Everyone thinks it's a fake, but now the boss wants to make some profit from what he thinks will be a new mermaid craze. That's not even the worst part."

"What can be worse than that?" Jake asked. "After all, they'll find out what you are as soon as you get in the water."

"I grabbed a copy of the article," Kyle said, producing the magazine. "The picture isn't a fake. This was taken at the far side of the huge cave network, not far from the sunken city. They're practically on the doorstep of the largest colony of mer in the world. Whoever took this picture knows what they saw is real, even if no one else believes them."

Finn stumbled to the sofa and dropped down, reading the magazine in silence.

"What do you think will happen if they actually capture one of us?" Kyle asked.

Jake shrugged. "I don't know. I would think the government would try to cover it up, but if proof had already been made public… I wish I knew what would happen, but no one does. It's like aliens. Lots of people believe they have already visited Earth and the government hides the evidence, but if a spaceship appeared over the Houses of Parliament, there'd be no hiding it."

"Maybe the fake fins will keep your legs dry," Finn suggested.

"I don't know, but I'm going to test them here first, without an audience. I took down the details of the man who makes them and I'm going to email from here and change the delivery address."

"Hopefully, you can *play* a merman and not reveal you're a real one," Jake said. "If the fake tail doesn't work, we'll have to decide what to do."

"You could quit your job," Finn said. "If it looks like you'll be exposed, hand in your notice."

Kyle snorted. "Nice idea, except I have to work a notice period, and I've no doubt I'll be expected to spend it in the tank."

"In the meantime, one of us needs to get to Atlantis and warn them how close the humans are to the colony," Finn said.

"I think it would sound better coming from you," Jake suggested.

Finn scowled.

"Like it or not, when you're in Atlantis, you *are* a prince," Jake said. "You have to speak to your father and see what he suggests can be done to keep everyone safe."

"I guess I'd better go then. Have you got something for me to offer to Medina?"

"Go pick her some flowers from the garden," Kyle suggested. "I'm sure she'll like them."

Finn stood to go do as Kyle suggested.

"Oh, there's something else," Kyle said, halting Finn in his tracks. He cringed as his two lovers looked at him expectantly. "I said we'd go to the aquarium anniversary party."

"All of us?" Finn asked. "I thought the people you work with only knew about Jake?"

"They did," Kyle admitted. "But they shouldn't have, should they? I had no right to feel like I'm on the outside of you two, not when I've put you in the exact same position. I told them about us. They agreed I could bring you both."

Finn grinned widely and kissed Kyle quickly on the lips. "I love you, you know."

"I know," Kyle replied as he kissed him back. "I love you, too—both of you."

He pulled Jake into his arms and they cautiously shared a three-way kiss, bumping noses as they connected, both emotionally and physically, once more.

Chapter Eight

"That looks pretty cool," Jake said as Kyle spread out the fake mer tail by the side of the pool.

The custom-made tail had taken three months to arrive. When Kyle had found out how long it would take, he had considered quitting his job and working his one-month notice before the delivery date. Only the fact that he enjoyed working at the aquarium stopped him from doing just that. The website said the tail was supposed to be waterproof, and Kyle was banking on it keeping his legs dry and his real fins safely hidden. If not, he supposed he could quit on the spot and deal with the consequences. At least Caspian had provided them with enough money to live on for the rest of their lives, as well as deal with any disgruntled employer who wanted to take him to court.

"It looks like it'll be pretty snug," Finn said, "and it feels waterproof. Maybe you'll be able to do the whole fake merman role without anyone suspecting."

"Maybe," Kyle agreed. "There's only one way to find out. If it doesn't work, we'll soon know."

Ten minutes later Kyle eased himself into the pool, his fake tail covering his legs. "Here goes nothing."

Above him, Jake and Finn held their breath.

"I think it worked," Kyle said. "I can't feel the transformation coming on."

"Not at all?" Finn asked. "How does it feel, being in water without your fins?"

"Weird," Kyle said. "I... Er... I'm not sure I can swim in this, though."

Finn snickered. "It might help if you push off from the side of the pool."

Kyle glared at Finn, but did as he suggested, promptly sinking right to the bottom.

Thankfully he could still breathe under the water, but he couldn't seem to propel himself in the direction he wished to go.

Finn splashed into the water beside him, and when he'd stopped laughing at Kyle's dilemma, he pointed to the surface.

After a couple of false starts, Kyle broke through the water.

"You can't communicate underwater as a human," Finn commented. "Or you were ignoring me."

Kyle grabbed Finn and pulled him into his arms. "I'd never ignore you. Now, how about you give me a kiss then we'll start my swimming lessons. Bill is expecting me to start my performance in the tank next week."

"That doesn't give you much time," Jake said. He sat on the edge of the pool to watch.

"You'll do great," Finn assured Kyle with a smile and a kiss. "You're a merman. You're built to swim."

"Yeah, but with an actual tail and fins," Kyle reminded him. "I need to find a way to steer myself without fins."

"The tail has fins," Finn pointed out.

"I can see that," Kyle replied with a roll of his eyes. "But they're not a part of my body, so I can't control them."

"I guess you'd better get practicing, then," Jake said.

Kyle gave him another glare. "Are you just going to sit and watch?"

"Yep. I think this is going to be very entertaining."

"Git."

"I like the colors," Finn said. "It's much prettier than your real tail."

Kyle scowled at Finn, though he privately agreed that the light rainbow-colored tail and fins were beautiful and eye-catching, exactly as Bill intended. In the darkened rooms of the aquarium, Kyle would positively glow.

He hoped when he finally entered the tank, the visitors would stare at him in awe and wouldn't collapse into fits of laughter. From Jake's and Finn's current states of amusement, Kyle suspected he would need to spend the next week in the pool, without his beloved tail, so he could learn to swim as a human. At least it would be a distraction from the increasing shark attacks in Atlantis and the continuing squabbles of the Atlantean gods.

"No, like this," Finn said, the impatience clear in his voice. They were well into Kyle's swimming lesson. "You need to swim with your whole body, like you do normally."

Kyle smacked his hand on the top of the water. "I'm *trying* but this is the hardest thing I've ever had to do."

Finn sighed and swam up to Kyle, wrapping his arms around him. "I'm sorry, love. I don't mean to be sharp with you. I know you can do this, and you'll be the best fake merman the world has ever seen."

Kyle buried his face in Finn's neck. "Thanks, baby. I'm sorry for snapping, too. Now, I'm hungry, so I think we should take a break, get something to eat and start over this afternoon."

Finn guided him to the edge of the pool and Jake helped Kyle get out of the water. Kyle missed being able to swing his tail up and out of the pool with ease. It didn't seem to work when he tried to do the same thing with his legs.

He hoped he got the hang of this soon, because he missed his real tail, and the sooner he got his fake fins under control, the quicker he could get back to swimming in his own pool, with his own tail.

* * * *

Although Kyle still wasn't comfortable with his fake tail, Bill wanted him in the tank and ready to greet the visitors.

Until the long summer holidays started, business was slow, as it always was at this time of year, and they needed something to lure in guests. Hopefully, Kyle, the aquarium's exclusive merman, would be enough.

"Excellent," Bill said as he saw Kyle climbing into the tank in his rainbow fins.

"Is it?" Kyle muttered under his breath.

Natalie hissed at him to keep his voice down. She had helped him get into his tail, much to Kyle's embarrassment, since it wasn't his most graceful of moments.

He landed in the water with a splash. Thankfully, he didn't sink straight to the bottom this time. He trod water, using his legs, snug inside his tail, to stay in place.

"How long can you hold your breath for?" Bill asked.

Kyle shrugged. "I don't know. I've never timed myself." It sounded better than 'forever' and he was grateful Bill had brought up the question, because without the reminder, Kyle might have stayed underwater permanently and drawn as much attention to himself as if he'd transformed into his mer form itself.

"Well, don't overdo it when you get into character," Bill teased. "We can't have our merman drowning now, can we?"

"No, sir," Kyle replied, and to avoid any more questions, he lowered himself under the water, ready to play his part.

Despite his initial horror and later reservations, Kyle actually began to enjoy his time in the tank.

A school trip from one of the local schools was the highlight of his day.

"Look, a mermaid!" a young girl at the head of the group shouted, pointing at Kyle. Even underwater, he could hear her squeal of joy.

He waved back at her and smiled.

As the class crowded around the tank, he twisted and turned under the water, not quite as graceful as he would normally be, but good enough for the delight of the guests.

He pointed to the stairs to the left and followed them to the other side of the tank, ready to greet them properly.

"Well, hello there," Kyle said to the students. "How are you today?"

"You speak English!" The young boy stared at him accusingly. "I thought mermaids spoke fish language."

Kyle grinned. "We do, but I was taught English when I came to land."

"You speak it very well," the teacher said. "Doesn't he, class?"

There were lots of nods from the kids.

"Where did you live in the ocean?"

"Have you met Ariel?"

"What about Sebastian?"

"Can you sing?"

Thankfully for Kyle, Caspian had given him knowledge of the English language, as well as providing him with plenty of pop culture, including the famous Disney movie.

"I'm afraid only the mermaids can sing," Kyle said. "We mermen are pretty tone deaf. You'll meet Sebastian a little later on along your tour. He's around here somewhere."

"Did you live in Triton's palace?"

Kyle grinned. "No, I lived in Atlantis, which is a huge underwater city where lots and lots of merpeople live. We have our own king called Nereus."

"Is he powerful, like Triton?"

"Oh yes. He has his own trident that shoots fire."

"Cool!"

"Very," Kyle agreed.

"Come along, class." The teacher urged the class to continue their tour and they filed away.

The second teacher hung behind a moment. "Great job," he said. "I'm Ivan, by the way."

Kyle smiled at him, noting the admiration in the man's eyes. "I'm Kyle."

"Yeah, I heard. You certainly have the kids fooled. I think they're convinced you're a real merman."

Kyle chuckled and leaned forward. "That's because I am," he teased, knowing Ivan wouldn't believe him anyway. It was freeing somehow, to tell the truth and know he'd be safe from exposure.

Ivan laughed. "Um, so, I've seen you working here the last year, and I was wondering if maybe you'd like to have dinner some time."

Kyle smiled sadly. "Sorry. I'm seeing someone at the moment — two someones, actually."

Ivan grimaced. "Seems like all the guys who work here are cheaters."

Kyle grinned. "I don't know who else you're referring to, but I'm not. I live with my two guys and it's definitely not cheating."

"Oh, sorry," Ivan said. "I guess I assumed…"

Kyle shrugged. "That's okay. So does everyone else. I'm still getting used to telling people what sort of a relationship I'm in. It's not uncommon for us mermen, even if it is for humans."

Ivan laughed. "You do love your merman role, don't you?"

"Oh yes. You could say it's my entire life."

The sounds of children laughing grew fainter and Ivan glanced toward the door the class had gone through. "I should catch up with them before they send out a search party. It was nice to meet you, Kyle. If you ever break up with your men and want to get together, I come through the aquarium quite a lot, with and without the class."

Kyle nodded. "I doubt I will…but thank you."

Ivan went after the rest of his group, stopping at the door to wave. "Maybe I'll meet a merman of my own if I keep my eyes peeled."

"Maybe you will," Kyle replied, waving to Ivan, before sinking back into the water, ready to greet another round of guests.

His boss checked in on him several times throughout the day, seemingly pleased with Kyle's performance. Kyle made sure he was under water every time he spotted the man in the doorway.

Even though he had fun with the children, Kyle found the day rather long and dull. He contemplated whether he should bring a trident to work the next day but quickly discounted that idea. There was no way he could explain sea-fire. He would just have to make the best of things and look forward to the end of the day when he could go home and stretch his real fins, which he had really missed the last week.

* * * *

In July, the day for the aquarium anniversary party arrived and Jake felt quite nervous as he got ready to go out in public with his two partners. Although they had been out together many times before, he knew most of those who saw them together had no idea of the nature of their relationship. Today would be different. Everyone Kyle worked with knew he was bringing two men with him to the large yacht where the party was being held. They also knew the three men slept with each other. Jake hoped there wouldn't be any unpleasantness — if not for his own sake, then for Kyle's and Finn's.

Finn paced the floor, his face pale.

"You don't have to come if you don't want to," Kyle said.

Finn came to a halt. "I want to come to the party. I guess I'm nervous. I'll be fine once we get there."

Jake sat on the edge of the bed and beckoned Finn over. "Are you sure?"

Finn sighed. "No," he muttered as he sat on Jake's lap. "I have a bad feeling about this. I don't know why, but I can't shake it."

"Well, you're not an Oracle, so at least your bad feelings are just paranoia," Kyle said.

"That doesn't help," Finn muttered.

"Is there anything that would?" Jake asked.

"The boat sinking before we get there?" Finn suggested with a grimace.

Jake laughed. "I doubt that'll happen. Come on. We need to get going unless we plan on showing up late and having everyone staring at us."

Finn jumped up quickly, obviously wanting to be the center of attention about as much as Jake did. Jake gave Finn a swift, hard smack on the arse, more to encourage him to hurry than anything else.

"That *didn't* help," Finn muttered as he gestured to his groin. The outline of his rising erection was clearly visible.

"We've no time for that," Kyle said. "Go take care of it in the bathroom and we'll meet you in the car."

Finn huffed as he did as Kyle suggested.

Jake hoped his own nerves would settle as the evening wore on. Soon they were on their way.

When they arrived at the party, everyone from the aquarium was in high spirits. Profits were up from the previous year and much of the credit was going to Kyle for his merman role.

Unfortunately, not everyone was happy about the praise and attention Kyle was getting. Doug seemed determined to try to make Kyle and his partners as uncomfortable as possible. His intentions were obvious from every sneer and snide comment he made.

Despite the fact they were on the largest yacht Jake had ever seen, Doug was a presence they simply couldn't shake.

"So, which one of you is the girl?" Doug asked Finn, who had stuck close to Jake's side for most of the evening. "Is it you, Finn? With all that lovely long hair you have, you could probably pass for a woman if you put on a dress."

Jake had tried to stay on his best behavior, polite and friendly to everyone. He didn't want to make a spectacle of himself in front of Kyle's co-workers, but enough was enough.

"Why don't you go fuck yourself?" Jake asked.

"Oh, have I hit a nerve?" Doug goaded them with every word. "Where has Kyle disappeared to, anyway? Looking for another man perhaps? If one man can't keep him satisfied, it's doubtful two will be enough, either."

Jake's temperature rose and his face heated. He couldn't remember the last time he had met someone as rude and unpleasant as Doug.

Beside him, Finn clung to his hand, which was the only reason Jake hadn't taken a swing at Doug.

"Kyle is putting on his fins," Natalie interrupted with a glare of her own for Doug. "Jake, he's asking if you could go give him a hand. I offered, but he refused because he's not wearing underwear."

"That's probably because he didn't plan on playing a merman this evening," Jake said.

Bill had thought Kyle swimming around the marina would be a great idea. Jake wasn't so sure, but Kyle felt confident in his swimming now, and it was his decision whether to do it or not.

"Come on, Finn," Jake said. "Let's go help Kyle."

"Actually, I wanted a word with Finn," Natalie said. "You go ahead, and I'll take care of him for you."

"I don't need taking care of," Finn told her.

Natalie flushed. "I didn't mean any offense."

Jake leaned down to kiss Finn. "Are you going to be okay, baby?"

"Just hurry back," Finn whispered.

Jake promised he would and went in search of Kyle.

He hadn't even reached the changing room when he heard a splash and a scream. *Finn!*

Turning back the way he had come, Jake sprinted across the deck.

"What happened?" he shouted. "Where's Finn?"

Natalie pointed at the water.

Jake leaned over the railing and saw Finn and Doug treading water below. *Fuck!*

"Doug said something to Finn—I didn't hear what—and Finn hit him. When they started fighting, it was a matter of moments before they tumbled overboard."

Kyle appeared at the side of Jake, fully dressed and without his fake fins. "Jake," he whispered, "what if he *sees?*"

Jake froze with panic. Even now people were calling for the two men to swim around to the dock and climb out of the water. Doug would have no trouble, but Finn would be exposed for what he was as soon as he rose above the waterline.

Even worse, Doug seemed to want to carry on the fight where they were and swam at Finn rather than back to the dock.

Finn darted out of Doug's way, making a real effort to keep from diving.

Jake was still wondering what to do when Kyle suddenly leaped over the rails, the flash of a silver blade in his hand, and dove into the water, as well.

Great, now there are two mermen in danger of being exposed instead of one.

Kyle rose directly behind Doug and put what appeared to be a knife from the cake stand to his throat. "Keep your hands off him or I'll slit your throat."

Jake had always known Kyle was a warrior, but this was the first time he truly appreciated his partner's deadly nature.

He hoped Kyle knew what he was doing.

Kyle held the blade steady in his hand.

"He's a fucking merman," Doug said.

Kyle was thankful the wretched man was too much in shock to shout it out loud enough for everyone to hear.

"Did you hear me?" Doug asked. "You're fucking boyfriend is a fish."

Kyle moved the knife closer. "*He* isn't the one you need to worry about right now. You need to close your mouth or I swear I will slit your throat and leave you for the sharks."

"There aren't any sharks around here," Doug replied.

"You're *really* missing the point. And what makes you so sure there aren't, anyway? After all, ten minutes ago you didn't believe in mermen, either. Now, here's what's going to happen. You're going to forget what you've seen, swim back to the dock and go home, maybe chalk it up to too much alcohol. But remember this… If you tell anyone, it'll be the last thing you ever do."

"But he's a *merman!*"

Kyle sighed. Doug wasn't the brightest of men and right now he was trying Kyle's patience. "I *know.*"

He gave Doug a nudge with his own tail and in a quick, if rather awkward move, he pulled Doug under the water and spun him around.

Then, when he was sure he had his undivided attention, he whacked him good and hard with his tail.

Doug rose to the surface, spluttering and shaking his head.

"They're fucking mermen!" he screamed.

Kyle saw those who hadn't already been drawn to the commotion crowd around the railings. From under the water, he could see Jake and the panicked expression on his face.

Finn swam underwater to Kyle and grabbed him in a tight embrace. *"I think we should swim home underwater. We'll follow the coast to my dad's beach and leave them to it."*

"We shouldn't leave Jake on his own."

"We can't exactly climb out of the water like this," Finn pointed out.

"I know. Damn. I'm so fired after this."

Jake had no idea what to do as everyone craned to see what Doug was shouting about.

"Mermen?" Bill asked. "Is Kyle in the water already? Good lad."

Jake doubted he would be so delighted when he discovered Kyle's custom-made tail was still in the changing room.

Natalie grabbed Jake's arm and pulled him away from the crowd. "Is it true?"

Jake rolled his eyes. "Doug's just playing along for the show."

Natalie snorted. "Doug barely pulls his weight at work. I doubt he'd do anything of the sort. Now, tell me the truth."

Jake gave a small nod.

"I *knew* Kyle was holding his breath too long for a human when he swam in the tank. He almost beat the world record and he didn't seem to be struggling at that."

"Can you help them?" Jake asked.

"By doing what?" Natalie replied. "This is a great opportunity for us."

"What do you mean?"

"Well, until now, we've had Kyle playing the part of a merman, complete with his fake fins. Now we can show the world *real* mermen. Imagine how many visitors we'll have when word gets out."

Jake glared at the woman he had foolishly trusted with his lovers' secret. He put it down to his panic and hoped he could repair the damage. "Kyle and Finn are *not* exhibits in your aquarium."

"I don't think you're seeing the possibilities."

Jake pushed her aside and ran to the far end of the boat. Thankfully, she didn't follow. "Medina!" he screamed, hoping she heard him at such a vital moment.

The goddess appeared before him and smiled. "What has you so frantic?"

"Kyle and Finn are exposed." Jake pointed at the crowd behind him. "You have to do something. Please, can you wipe everyone's memories or something?"

Medina frowned. "I don't have that sort of power, not anymore, anyway."

"What do you mean?"

"Before the Atlanteans were banished, I could have done what you ask. I had priests, devoted to me and me alone, and their loyalty fed my powers. Now I am but a shadow of the goddess I used to be."

"Isn't there anything you can do?"

Medina shook her head and Jake's heart fell.

"Wait… There might be one way," Medina said. "You could become my priest."

"But Kyle and Finn… I can't leave them. They need me."

"Of course they do. Becoming my priest isn't like your modern kind. You can stay with your lovers and carry on as before. You'll just be something more than you are now."

"More?"

"Those powers you struggle to deal with would be amplified," Medina explained. "And you'll have to make an offering at one of my temples—a proper offering, not perfume and flowers."

"What sort of offering?"

"You'll need to prove you know what love is."

"That's all?"

Medina smiled. "It might sound easy, but I think you'll find it harder than you think. So, Jake, do you accept my offer?"

"And if I do, you'll be able to undo what's happened?"

"Faster than you can blink."

"Then I accept."

Medina placed her hand on Jake's shoulder and his knees buckled.

Lightning flashed across the sky and the wind rose, whipping Jake's hair around his face.

He could hear sounds of voices in his head, unclear at first, but becoming louder with every second.

"It'll take some getting used to," Medina said. "What you are hearing is everyone who is praying for love at this exact moment."

"So many voices." Jake's head pounded as the volume rose.

"So many lost souls, searching for their other halves," Medina replied. "Now, let's see about saving your two mermen from stardom."

As Jake struggled to tune out the voices, the crowd at the end of the boat dispersed, no one seeming to have any idea of why they had all congregated in the one place.

"Where are Kyle and Finn?" Jake asked.

"In the car, fully dressed, no fins and ready to go home. They, like you, will remember what has happened. No one else will have a clue. Now, I suggest you go take them home. They've had a bit of a shock."

Jake didn't pause as he hurried off the boat to the nearby car park.

He found Kyle and Finn right where Medina had told him they would be.

"What happened?" Finn asked. "I was in the water and now I'm here."

"Medina," Jake said. "I'll explain on the way home. In the meantime, let's just say we owe the Goddess of Love even more than we already did."

"But what about everyone on the boat?" Kyle asked. "They saw us."

"They won't remember," Jake assured him. "Now let's get out of here. I think I've had enough socializing for one night."

"Me too," Finn said. "That Doug guy made my skin crawl."

"Yeah," Jake agreed. "And Natalie wasn't much better."

"Natalie?" Kyle gaped at him in surprise. "She's always been so nice to me."

"I'm sure she has, but let me tell you, *never ever* let her discover what you are. If you do, you'll never get out of that tank."

"She'd capture us for exhibits?"

"Yes." Jake felt his pulse slow as they put some distance between themselves and the marina. "I think you should give some serious consideration to finding a new job. An accident with your fake fin tearing and you're completely screwed."

It was a testament to how much the incident had shaken Kyle that he didn't argue about giving up the job he loved and merely nodded at Jake's suggestion.

Finn remained quiet.

"Are you two okay back there?" Jake asked.

"Yes. I was just thinking."

"About what?"

"That there isn't anywhere the mer can be safe. Revealing ourselves to the world isn't an option, is it?"

Jake had never truly thought it could be, which left them right back at square one with their original problem. With humans nearing Atlantis every day, there was nowhere left for the mer to hide, and living on land would increase the risk of exposure, until none of the mer were safe.

Chapter Nine

They weren't even halfway home when Jake saw his two lovers were getting a little friskier than usual in the back of the car. It wasn't unusual for Kyle and Finn to pass the time on long car journeys by making out. They claimed it helped to distract them from the travel sickness they both suffered with. They didn't normally get quite this X-rated, though.

"Hey, guys," Jake said. "You want to keep it in your pants while we're on the main road?"

The two of them looked at him as though they had forgotten where they were. He grinned at them. "I don't want you getting arrested."

They settled down, with Finn resting his head on Kyle's shoulder.

They were another half mile along when Jake noticed they were at it again. Finn had his hand firmly inside Kyle's trousers and Kyle had undone at least half the buttons on Finn's shirt.

"Hey!" Jake didn't mind a joke, but this was not funny. "Seriously, guys, you can't do that back there."

Again they blinked at him as though they hadn't realized what they were doing.

One more mile down the road and Jake was starting to lose patience. When Finn ducked his head to take Kyle's cock into his mouth, Jake swore and pulled the car off the road. He didn't want to lose his temper, especially not while driving, but enough was enough.

"What the hell is wrong with you two?" he shouted. "Have you lost your minds? I know you're not drunk because I didn't see you touch a drop at the party, so why can't you keep your hands off each other until we get home?"

Kyle frowned. "I think there might be something wrong with us. I don't know about Finn, but I feel like I am not in control of my own actions."

Beside him, Finn nodded. "It's like when you first got those powers from Medina and tested them on us to see how effective they were. I feel like that, except you haven't told me to do anything."

"Oh, shit." Jake had a horrible feeling this might be a side effect of his recent change in status. *Medina could have warned me.* "Okay, one of you get in the front passenger seat and the other had better keep his seat belt buckled back there, or I swear I'll give the both of you such a spanking you'll think your arses are on fire. And I promise neither of you will be coming, either. Got it?"

They both hurried to obey. Kyle took the seat in the front and Jake continued the drive home, this time without any further incident.

Jake pulled into the long driveway of their home not a moment too soon. The instant Kyle stepped out of the car, Finn was on him, wrapping his legs around Kyle's waist and kissing him thoroughly. Jake had a feeling they would be having sex right there on the doorstep if given half the chance.

Shaking his head, Jake left them to it and hurried into the house. If this *was* something to do with Medina, the best person for him to speak to would be the goddess herself, but since she hadn't come when he'd called her from the roadside, he would have to try to summon her from her new temple.

"Medina!" he yelled as soon as he entered the room. Unfortunately, there was no reply from the absent goddess.

Jake swore. Perhaps Fabian would know what to do. As a former demigod and the nephew of the Goddess of Love, surely he would have some idea what was happening.

He found Fabian in the kitchen, the telephone in one hand and a frown on his face.

"Calling someone?" Jake asked.

"Trying to figure out how it works," Fabian muttered. "Modern technology is not something I have much knowledge of."

"That seems to be a problem with Caspian's knowledge implants," Jake said. "As a god, he probably doesn't need to use most of the stuff we take for granted."

"I can't say I ever thought I'd need to, either," Fabian replied. "Life was much less complicated as a sea dragon."

"You'll get used to it quickly. After all, he gave you the knowledge of what a phone *is*. Using it will be easy once you get the hang of it. Who are you trying to call?"

Fabian tapped the paper. "I've been looking at the properties for sale. There's one here with a pool that sounds like it might be suitable."

Jake smiled, even though he felt a little disappointed that Fabian and Delwyn might be moving out of the house sooner than he thought. He liked having them around, and he knew Finn enjoyed having his best friend so close.

Fabian shrugged. "I have a feeling you didn't come through here to talk about houses, though. Is there something you wanted to speak to me about?"

"Actually, yes." Jake pulled out a chair and straddled it. "What do you know about Medina's powers of making people do things without their meaning to?"

"Why? She shouldn't have that sort of power over you. As one of her direct descendants, you should be immune to that sort of meddling."

"I don't mean her power, exactly, but the ones I have from her. I thought I had it under control, but today, Finn and Kyle have gone nuts. They can't keep their hands off each other."

Fabian laughed. "From what I've seen, that's not unusual."

"I know, but not like this. They would have been fucking in the back of the car if I'd let them."

"Well, your powers will be growing as each new immortal wakes. But unless the whole lot have suddenly started walking among us again, it's unlikely this would come on so suddenly. Has anything else happened?"

Delwyn strolled into the room, his hair wet. It was apparent he had been stretching his fins in the pool. "Did you know Kyle and Finn are having sex in the hallway?"

"Oh, for fuck's sake," Jake said. "You see what I mean, Fabian? It's like they can't even wait to get to the bedroom."

"But you've not told them to have sex," Fabian pointed out. "You've been in here with me."

"I know, but this is what they were like all the way home from the party. Could it have something to do with my becoming one of Medina's priests?"

Fabian gaped at him, but before he could answer, Delwyn crawled onto his lap and began to kiss him.

"Delwyn, darling." Fabian tried to ease Delwyn onto the seat beside him, but he had no intention of moving.

"I swear, I never said a thing," Jake said. "But this is *exactly* what Kyle and Finn have been like since we left the party."

Fabian gave up trying to get Delwyn off his lap, but at least managed to free his mouth to reply. "You said you'd become one of Medina's priests?"

"Yes."

"What did you do a stupid thing like that for?" Fabian asked.

"She needed an increase in powers to wipe the memories of the others at the party because Finn and Kyle ended up in the bloody water, along with another guest, who saw what they were."

"Oh dear," Fabian said. "That's not good at all."

"No, but she seemed to fix it all after I agreed to be one of her priests."

"She could probably have fixed the mess without you taking vows to serve her," Fabian said. "It would have been draining but not impossible."

"Then she played me?"

"I hate to say it about the only one of my relatives that is actually talking to me these days, but Medina can be quite crafty when she wants to be."

"I guess it's too late now. Is all this odd behavior because of me becoming a priest?"

"Oh yes, that's certainly what's happening here. It's not the power to make people do something. It's like some kind of perfume you're giving off that makes everyone around you uninhibited and eager for sex."

"Why isn't it affecting you?"

"Because I'm her nephew," Fabian replied. "I've always been immune to this sort of spell, though I can't say the same for Delwyn, who, as you can see, is very much under the influence while he's in your presence."

"Finn and Kyle aren't in here at the moment."

"No, but they've been in a confined space with you for the drive home, which means it'll be a while before it wears off for them."

"So, what you're saying is, whenever any man is in my presence, they're going to want to have sex?"

"Not just men... Women, too," Fabian said. "Your power will trigger the same reaction in any mortal you meet, though on the plus side, it should only be those who are already in a relationship, not strangers."

"Fuck."

Fabian stood, holding Delwyn in his arms. "The ability to bring love to those around you is one of the strongest gifts bestowed on Medina's priests. You should be able to control it, but it'll take time to learn how."

Jake sighed and followed Fabian and Delwyn into the hallway.

Finn and Kyle were naked on the cold wooden floor, writhing and moaning as they rubbed against each other.

"They didn't even make it to the damn bedroom," Jake said.

The moment the words left his mouth, Finn and Kyle vanished from the hallway.

"What the hell?"

Fabian chuckled. "Try the bedroom. After all, that's where you want them to be, right?"

"You mean I sent them to the bedroom just by saying it?"

"Yes."

Jake sighed. "I wish I had known I could do that back on the drive home. It would have saved me a lot of bother. Are there any more powers I need to know about?"

Fabian shrugged. "Medina's priests had many powers, but not all of them had the same ones. These might be the only ones you'll get, or there may be more to come. It's hard to say. I guess you'll find out over the next few days."

"Are there any more I need to worry about?"

"The permanent erection always sounded kind of painful to me," Fabian admitted, "though many of her priests found it most enjoyable."

Jake didn't think that sounded good at all. He silently cursed Medina for not warning him of the new powers he would get by accepting her offer.

Leaving Fabian to handle the increasingly amorous Delwyn, Jake ran up the stairs to the main bedchamber. He found Finn and Kyle on the bed. Apparently they hadn't even noticed their new location. Somehow, that worried Jake even more than the rest. Their lack of awareness frightened him. What if he accidentally transported them from one place to another in the middle of a fight for their lives?

"Kyle? Finn?" Jake asked as he sat on the edge of the bed. "Can I get your attention please?"

They ignored him, being far too engrossed in each other.

"Oh well, if you can't beat them, join them," Jake said as he undid his shirt.

A couple of minutes later, Jake inserted himself between his two lovers. They accepted him there and turned their attention from each other to Jake, kissing along his chest.

They each took one of his nipples in their mouth and sucked. Jake, who had been half erect since before they'd left for the party, hardened instantly.

Maybe once they'd exhausted themselves, Jake could try engaging them in a sensible discussion.

He closed his eyes and let his two lovers pleasure him with their hands and mouths. Their latest set of problems could wait a little longer. At least, he hoped they could.

* * * *

Afterward, while Kyle and Finn slept, Jake closed his eyes and tried to think about how he might get a handle on these new powers. It might help if he'd ever considered himself to have got the first lot completely under control.

He intended to give Medina a piece of his mind the next time he saw her and he hoped there wouldn't be any more unpleasant surprises.

"Medina, please help me."

Jake recognized the voice of Marin, clear in his head, as though he were speaking to him telepathically under the water.

"Please make the pain stop. I don't want to love him anymore. Please, Medina, make it end."

Jake slipped out of bed, somehow knowing Marin spoke to Medina from the temple in the house. Leaving his lovers wrapped in each other's arms, Jake made his way to the temple.

When he entered, he found Marin right where he expected him to be, sitting at the foot of Medina's statue, tears streaming down his face.

Medina was there, too, much to Jake's surprise. He hovered in the doorway, debating whether to enter the room.

"Hush," Medina said. "Don't cry, darling. You'll find love again. I promise."

"I don't *want* to find love," Marin cried. "I want the pain to stop. Please make it stop. *Please.*"

"The only way to stop the pain is to remove your ability to love," Medina said. "To be cursed in such a way is a terrible thing, and I rarely inflict that punishment on even my worst enemies. I could never curse an innocent to a life without love."

Marin sobbed, and Medina slipped down to sit on the steps beside him. She gathered him into her arms and rocked him tenderly.

"I'm sorry I cannot bring him back to you," the goddess said. "But know this... As long as Caspian lives, there is justice in this world, and as long as there is justice, you will see Calder's murderer pay for what he has done."

"I don't want justice. I want revenge," Marin said. "I want Urion *dead.*"

"I know, darling. I know."

Marin buried his face in Medina's lap as she stroked his hair.

Medina glanced over at Jake. Even from across the room, Jake could see the pain in her eyes. All thoughts of shouting at her for what she had done to him disappeared as he saw her compassion for Marin.

Leaving the two of them alone, Jake returned to his lovers, grateful to have them in his life and willing to pay any price to keep them there.

Chapter Ten

Medina appeared as Jake was devouring his breakfast. He felt a bout of indigestion coming on at the goddess's arrival.

"You wished to speak to me?" Medina asked as she took a seat.

"You didn't warn me about the new powers I would get when I accepted your offer," Jake accused.

"That's because you might not have gotten any," Medina replied. "It's all rather random, I'm afraid."

"How can I stop everyone in my presence from throwing themselves at each other?" Jake asked.

"You can't do anything about that until you've made the offering I told you about."

"You said I need to prove that I know what love is, right?"

"Yes."

"Well, I love Finn and Kyle, so I think that should show that I know the meaning of love."

Medina waved away his words. "Simply declaring that you love someone isn't enough. You have to *prove* it."

Jake sighed. "I presume you have something particular in mind when you say this, so how about you tell me what it is I have to do?"

"I can't."

"Can't...or won't?"

"Can't," Medina confirmed. "Only *you* can do what is needed to prove you know the meaning of love, and it is always very personal to the individual. No two priests have ever proved their love in the same way."

Jake recalled being told about how Justin and Lucas had exchanged vows in Medina's temple in Atlantis. *Could that work for me?* "What if I marry Kyle and Finn in your temple?"

Medina smiled. "That would be a lovely gesture, and a marvelous boost to my powers but not enough to prove you know the meaning of love."

"Oh."

Medina patted Jake's hand. "I'm sure you'll figure it out soon."

"I miss you, Calder. I miss you so much."

Marin's heartbroken voice echoed through Jake's mind.

"I hope so," Jake said. "Because right now I feel trapped in this house, and even that isn't enough. I'm starting to hear the thoughts of the neighbors, too."

"You can't hide from love," Medina said. "And even when you have a handle on your new powers, you won't be able to switch them off entirely. You'll still be able to hear those who are praying specifically to me."

"As long as I don't have to listen to strangers thinking about sex — or even worse, my in-laws — I'll be happy."

"Once you have control of your powers, that'll only happen on my special day."

Jake nodded. "A day I intend to stay in the house for, or better yet, in bed."

"Good choice." Medina chuckled. "Now, there is one more thing you need to know about your offering to me."

"Uh-oh." A feeling of dread settled over Jake at Medina's words. He was too much of a pessimist to consider this 'one more thing' to be anything other than bad news.

"You would be well advised not to fail this initiation," Medina said.

"Why? What would happen if I failed?" Jake shivered with increased dread.

"If you fail to prove you know the meaning of love, you will lose the ability to love, forever."

Jake gaped at her. "You never mentioned that when I agreed to become one of your priests."

"With your lovers exposed as mermen, would knowing this have made a difference to your decision?"

"No, I guess not."

"Then what's done is done."

Jake glanced up as Fabian strolled into the room. He spun on his heel, apparently wanting to make a sharp exit out again, but Medina saw him first.

"Don't rush off, Fabian. I need to talk to you, too."

Jake caught the quick grimace on Fabian's face, but Medina's nephew took a seat at the table.

"I don't want to interrupt," Fabian said. "I only wanted to get a drink."

Medina smiled, and with a wave of her hand, three glasses appeared on the table. Jake didn't recognize the contents, but the aroma tempted him to take a sip. The drink was like nothing he had ever tasted before, delicious and sweet, with a strange fruity flavor he didn't recognize.

"The nectar of the gods," Medina said as Jake finished off his glass. "Now, back to the purpose of my visit."

"You mean there's more bad news about my becoming one of your priests?" Jake couldn't imagine what might be worse than losing the ability to love.

"Oh no." Medina shook her head. "That isn't the main reason for my visit today. I'm here to invite you to attend me at the meeting of the council of the gods today."

Fabian groaned. "You don't think I've suffered through enough of those already?"

Jake raised a brow at him.

Fabian sighed. "It has always been tradition for each god and goddess to have one or two of their priests attend upon them during their meetings. As a former priest and Oracle of Cari, I've attended upon her many times, more than any other priest, in fact, due to my unusually long life."

Medina smiled. "I would have thought you'd be eager to see what is happening now that almost the entire pantheon has woken."

"More have woken?" Fabian asked.

"Yes. Darya, Goddess of the Sea, rose this morning. I'm surprised the quake of her rising wasn't felt here. Atlantis is lucky to remain standing."

"Was anyone hurt during the quake?" asked Jake, concerned for Kyle's family.

"Nothing except a few minor scrapes from falling walls and the like," Medina confirmed. "Thankfully, the previous quakes had encouraged the mer to strengthen the structures of the city as best they could and to move their people out of those buildings that were already precariously close to collapse."

Jake breathed a sigh of relief.

"Why do you want us at this meeting?" Fabian asked. "Is it simply that you want to show your power, or is there another reason?"

Medina blushed. "Having attendants at the meeting will certainly show those who have newly joined us that I am not without supporters. I also thought you might like to know what is happening, since both of you have lovers with strong ties to the city."

"I'm not one of your priests," Fabian pointed out. "And before you ask, I have no intention of becoming one, either."

"You don't need to," Medina replied. "You can attend me as my nephew."

"I expect my mother might have something to say about that."

"No doubt she will." Medina smiled. "She will be in attendance with two of her own priests."

"Of *course* she will," Fabian muttered. "And you don't want to be outdone by your sister, do you?"

Medina scowled at her nephew. "You know as well as I do that Mariana is far more powerful than I am. She always has been and she always will be. She could kill me for talking with you, but you're family, and I won't let anyone stop me from loving my own nephew."

Fabian stood and walked around the table to Medina. He wrapped his arms around his aunt. "I'm sorry, Aunt Medi. I feel as if I've been a pawn of the gods my whole life and I was hoping my new life on land would be the end of that."

"You don't have to come, not if you don't want to," Medina said. "I did think you'd want to."

Fabian stepped back and knelt on one knee. "I would be honored to attend you."

"And what of you, Jake?" Medina asked.

"Um, do I need to kneel down, too?"

Medina chuckled. "No, a yes or no will suffice. Fabian is simply accustomed to being more formal."

"What does attending you involve?" Jake asked. He wanted to know exactly what he was letting himself in for this time, before he agreed.

Fabian retook his seat. "Mainly standing around like a statue watching the gods argue and exchange insults and making sure our goddess' glass remains full and that her drink and plate are not tampered with by another immortal."

"You mean watch out for a potential assassination attempt?"

"Such a thing is extremely unlikely," Fabian said. "But some of the more mischievous and meddling gods have been known to slip other things into an unwatched drink."

"Like what?"

Fabian glanced at his aunt. "Love potions spring to mind, don't they, Aunt Medi?"

Medina wouldn't meet his gaze — the sign of a guilty conscience, if ever Jake had seen one.

"It was only the once," Medina said. "I didn't think you saw me do it."

Fabian snorted. "I didn't think much of it during the meeting itself, but I've had a lot of time to think over the centuries. You slipped Caspian a love potion, he then petitions the gods to make a lover immortal and the world as we know it goes to hell. One might consider these things to be connected."

Jake gaped at Medina. *Did she really given Caspian a love potion? Does she have a death wish?*

Something of his thoughts must have registered with the goddess and she smiled at him.

"Caspian wasn't always the bad-tempered god we know today. In the time we're talking about, he was much more laid back, taking many men into his bed, including all of my male priests."

"All of them?" Fabian asked. "Really? But didn't some of them prefer women?"

"Most of my priests were happy to share their bed with either gender," Medina said. "Caspian made it a particular point to seduce those who had sworn loyalty to me."

Lightning lit up the room and Caspian appeared. "Are my ears burning *again*?"

Medina shifted guiltily and neither Jake nor Fabian would meet the god's gaze.

"The meeting is about to start," Caspian said. "Are you joining us or not?"

"I am," Medina replied.

"Do you need to be searched before you come?" Caspian asked.

Medina gave him an icy glare. "That won't be necessary." She turned to Fabian and Jake. "Will you be attending upon me?"

Fabian nodded.

"Yes," Jake confirmed as well.

Medina clapped her hands together sharply.

A moment later they all stood in a cavernous room with large stone columns. Jake recognized it as the meeting place at the center of one half of the Isle of the Gods. The marble floor appeared to have been cleaned since his last visit and someone had set out tables with food and drink around the edges.

The room was filled with people—no, immortals—and nearly all of them appeared to be dressed in robes of ancient style. Caspian wore his usual modern leather trousers and jacket combination, and one of the goddesses wore what appeared to be a modern skirt and blouse. Other than them, the entire group could have stepped right out of a period film about ancient Greece.

Jake stared about him in wonder until he saw what Fabian was now wearing. He was pretty sure it wasn't called a dress, but since he didn't know the right name for it, Jake couldn't say what it was.

When he took a step toward Fabian, he realized he no longer wore his modern shoes. They had been replaced with sandals that were laced up his shins. His *bare* shins. Like Fabian, Jake's clothes had been changed.

Fabian smiled and leaned in close. "Rather breezy, isn't it?" he whispered. "It's called a chiton."

Jake smoothed down the fabric as he tried to establish whether there was anything under the tunic. There wasn't. "I'm pretty sure I put on underwear this morning."

"Aunt Medi doesn't believe in such things," Fabian replied. "And even if she did, what was worn back then isn't anything like your modern garments. You'll probably be more comfortable without those."

"I feel naked."

"You'll get used to it."

"If my friends could see me now, they'd be in hysterics."

"Modern clothing is very different," Fabian agreed.

A loud horn interrupted their conversation and Fabian guided Jake to the edge of the room.

A few of the others in attendance also remained around the edge, including the woman in modern clothing. The rest of the people took seats at the large oval table in the center.

Jake guessed that those still standing were priests like himself.

Directly opposite him, a man glared over with pure hatred. For a moment Jake thought the venom was for him, before he realized the man stared at Fabian.

Jake wanted to ask who it was, but he didn't dare break the room's silence. The meeting was about to begin, and now that he was here, he had no intention of leaving.

The god at the far end of the table rose from his seat. "I'm sure you all know why we are here," he said. "Our pantheon has been all but forgotten in the centuries while we have slept. We need to take urgent action to ensure our continued survival."

"All the pantheons are in the same position," Caspian said. "Times have changed for all immortals."

A goddess with hair the color of living flames stood and leaned on the table. "I say *we* cause the next change. For months now we've done nothing but mourn for what we have lost and *talk* about the problem. I say we've done enough talking. We must *act* if we're to ensure our survival. The Atlanteans must remember who they are and where they came from. Only then can we regain what we have lost."

"The Atlanteans will never return to Atlantis," another god said. "I banished them for their crime and that is the end of the matter."

"Cynbel, in case you haven't noticed, centuries have passed, and those responsible are long dead."

"I've noticed," Cynbel said. "But I could not reverse the banishment, even if I wished to do so."

"Why not?" asked the first god.

"Because to do so would send me right back into stasis."

The goddess smiled. "A small price to pay for the good of the pantheon."

Cynbel banged his hand on the table and the entire room seemed to shake.

Fabian nudged Jake's arm. He nodded at a nearby table.

Jake glanced at Medina and saw she was gesturing to her glass.

Fabian led Jake to the drinks and showed him which one Medina preferred. Jake followed Fabian's silent instructions and went to the table to fill Medina's glass once more.

As they returned to their place at the wall, their paths crossed with the glaring priest Jake had noticed earlier.

"Traitor," the priest hissed as they passed.

Jake raised a brow at Fabian, who mouthed 'Later'.

The priest gathered a plate of food and took it over to the table, placing it before a goddess who bore a slight resemblance to Medina. He nudged Fabian. "Your mother?" he murmured.

Fabian nodded and the goddess appeared to notice them for the first time.

"How *dare* you show your face here?" she shouted as she jumped from her seat.

Fabian didn't even flinch at her fury.

The various gods and goddesses turned to see what the commotion was that had interrupted their meeting. Jake tried not to cringe at their scrutiny.

"Fabian is here to attend me," Medina stated calmly. "As my nephew and a former priest of Cari, he is the ideal person to show Jake, my new priest, what to do at these meetings."

"You stay out of this," Mariana snarled. "I stripped that treacherous creature of his powers."

"While he was at the bottom of the ocean," Caspian chimed in. "You tried to murder your own son."

Mariana glared at Caspian. "*You* stay out of this."

"*Silence!*" Cynbel roared.

Everyone in the room immediately obeyed.

"Mariana, I couldn't care less about your personal grievances against your son. Such trivial matters are not the reason we have gathered. There are more important issues to be resolved."

Jake gaped at the god who called the attempted murder of another human being 'trivial'.

Medina nodded. "I agree, and as the first to rise from slumber, I have had more time than the rest of you to take in this new world we find ourselves a part of. I see an opportunity for us to bring this pantheon greatness once again."

"What do you suggest?" Cynbel asked.

"Look at how many people there are in the world today. There are over seven billion humans out there. They also have the technology to communicate across the globe as quickly as we can travel it. All it would take is one god or goddess to be caught doing something miraculous in front of a modern camera, and the whole world would know about us again."

"What is a cam-er-a?" one of the gods asked.

"It's a wondrous device that can make a record of anything you point it at."

Most of the gods at the table appeared confused.

Jake wondered if he should tell them he owned a camera and offer to demonstrate it, but he quickly dismissed the idea. He had no idea what these beings were capable of, and until he had a better idea of that, he would stick to watching and listening.

Cari cleared her throat and shook her head. "The problem with Medina's suggestion is what she calls miraculous, people today would barely take note of. There are magicians who can appear to fly, walk through walls and make entire buildings disappear. Anything we do would be explained away by the humans as a trick."

"Cari is right," Caspian said. "Many humans today don't believe in the existence of gods at all, or they practice new religions that have grown in popularity over the centuries."

"Then we need to *make* them believe in us," another god said. "We have to show them who we are, so they can worship us again."

Jake rolled his eyes. Believing in these gods was one thing. He had seen too much to dismiss them. That didn't mean he had any intention of worshipping them, as this arrogant god seemed to suggest.

"And how do you suggest we do that?" Caspian asked. "The gods of every pantheon you can name are mostly forgotten—Greek, Norse, Egyptian, Roman, all of them. Yes, there are some who still pray to them, but few truly believe they are being heard. They merely follow traditions that have been passed down from generation to generation. If a god appeared before them and they told someone, they would think him a lunatic and call the authorities to have him arrested."

"We have an additional disadvantage over the other pantheons," Cari said. "While Egypt, Greece and the other countries still exist, and relics and artwork of the old gods have survived the centuries, Atlantean culture has not been so lucky. Our images are at the bottom of the ocean in a place few humans even believe existed."

"What do you mean?" Cynbel asked. "Are you saying Atlantis itself has been forgotten?"

"Yes, that's exactly what I'm saying. There are texts and stories about the island, and some humans search for proof that it existed, but for most people, Atlantis is nothing more than a mythical place with no real substance in the actual world."

"It cannot be!" A goddess with long blue hair that whipped around her as though she were in the middle of a hurricane shook her head in disbelief. "Atlantis is as real as we are."

"Yes, but if you were to suggest such a thing among the humans, they would think you a fool."

"If that is truly the case, there's one obvious course of action open to us." The goddess stood and a long trident appeared in her hand. "We show them Atlantis once more."

"Oh, fuck," Fabian muttered beside Jake.

"What is it?" Jake asked quietly.

"She's talking about raising the island again."

"What?" Jake's question came out louder than he had intended, and he hurriedly schooled his expression into one of quiet observation.

"We don't have the power to raise Atlantis," Caspian said, "so it's rather a moot point anyway."

"I believe we do," the goddess replied. "If we are all in agreement and if we combine our powers, we could raise the island, revealing Atlantis to the world. The humans would have to accept the evidence of their own eyes."

"I agree," Mariana said. "It would also ensure the current occupants of the city will leave the place they have no business being in."

"The mer have every right to live in Atlantis," Cari argued. "It's their home."

Mariana sneered across the table. "The waters where Atlantis lies are their home. We raise the city and they can go live wherever they wish. I will not stop them from seeking new waters to reside in."

The sneer in her voice was evident as she spoke of the mer. Jake leaned toward Fabian to whisper. "What is her problem with the mer? Why is she so prejudiced against them?"

"Does prejudice need a reason?" Fabian murmured back with a sad sigh.

"I suppose not."

"It's about power," Fabian explained. "My mother has control over every creature of the oceans, from the smallest fish to the largest whale. She can summon them to do her bidding. Even true sea dragons, if any still exist, can be bent to her will. The mer, despite being creatures of the sea, are immune to her powers and always have been."

Jake nodded in understanding of what Fabian told him, even if he didn't understand how someone could hate an entire species simply for being who they were.

He turned his attention back to the immortals, who continued to argue.

"Atlantis is the safest place for the mer," Cari argued against Mariana. "Mankind has polluted much of the oceans of the world and explores many of the places where the mer were once abundant."

"Then the mer will need to be careful, won't they?" Mariana said. "I say we raise the city."

"If we were to do this, it would send most of us right into stasis," Caspian pointed out impatiently. "None of us has the number of followers we had when we first sank the island."

"Perhaps we raise only part of it," Cynbel suggested. "The city and surrounding environs, rather than the entire continent."

The blue-haired goddess nodded. "I agree. The raising of the city may take a lot of powers, but when the humans see Atlantis is real, their belief will restore what we lose ten times over. I say we vote on this now."

Cynbel banged on the table twice. "All those in favor of raising Atlantis, speak now."

The roar from the gods shook the walls. Jake noticed Caspian, Cari, Medina, as well as several others, didn't call out.

"I believe the ayes have it," Cynbel said. "I suggest we raise the city at midnight tonight."

"Why not now?" Mariana asked.

"Because the mer deserve to be given time to leave safely," Cynbel replied. "I trust those who have the ears of the mer will warn them of what is to come."

Jake watched as the gods and goddesses slowly departed. Medina was one of the last remaining and she approached them with a sad smile.

"Jake, Fabian, you'll want to warn your lovers to get their families to safety. I suggest you hurry."

"Can this be stopped?" Fabian asked.

Medina shook her head. "The vote is final."

"But don't they need your powers to help raise the city?" Jake asked. "I got the impression it would take everyone to do this."

"It will."

"Can't you refuse to help?"

"My consent is not required," Medina explained. "Darya, Goddess of the Sea, will be the one to raise Atlantis. She will syphon power from all of us, no matter which way we voted."

"She was the one with the blue hair," Fabian added. "I don't recall her having any issues with the merpeople, but the outcome will be the same, regardless."

"This isn't about the mer," Medina explained. "Not for her, anyway. Her twin brother is the God of the Sea and is one of the few still sleeping. The raising of Atlantis could wake him, as well as the others in stasis."

"I don't understand," Jake said. "How can she take your power without your consent?"

"Because we each had an equal vote," Medina said. "It's the way our system works."

"Can't someone try to talk Darya out of this?"

"Even if we could, another god would be the one to take her place. Each of the oldest gods — that is the gods and goddesses of the sky, land and sea — has the power to syphon from the rest of us. Even if you could convince Darya, the others all voted the same way she did. The best thing you can do is warn those you love of what is to come."

Fabian nodded. "I'm sure Cari will be getting her Oracles out of the city, but Delwyn also has other family there."

"Kyle and Finn will want to bring their relatives to safety, too," Jake said. "I need to get back to them."

The words had barely left his mouth when he found himself standing in his kitchen once more.

"Kyle! Finn!" he shouted at the same time as Fabian called for Delwyn.

When his lovers didn't answer him immediately, Jake ran from the room. He knew he'd find them in one of two places, the pool or the bedroom.

Since the swimming pool was nearest to the kitchen, Jake tried there first. At the glimpse of silver fins, he thought for a moment he had found Finn, but he caught sight of the brown head of hair.

"Delwyn's through here," Jake yelled.

He nearly crashed into Fabian as he raced back out of the room and headed for the staircase.

Predictably, he found Kyle and Finn still wrapped in each other's arms. A glance at the clock showed him barely five minutes had passed during the time he had been on the Isle of the Gods.

"Wake up, guys," Jake called as he opened the curtains wide.

"What time is it?" Finn mumbled.

"Too early," Kyle replied. "Jake, come back to bed."

"We have an emergency," Jake said, knowing if he took Kyle up on his offer, they'd lose at least an hour of valuable time.

"What is it?" Finn asked as he rubbed sleep out of his eyes.

"Atlantis is about to be discovered," Jake said. "The mer need to be evacuated, right now."

"Lynna won't come here," Kyle said. "I've already told her about the human explorers in the area. She won't leave."

"I'm not talking about the explorers," Jake said. "The gods are going to raise the city."

"What?" Finn stared at him in utter shock. "Can they do that?"

"Apparently they can," Jake replied. "The mer have until midnight to get away from the area, otherwise they'll be brought to the surface of the ocean with the island itself. If that should happen, they'll be exposed to the world, because it'll be a matter of hours, if not even less, before Atlantis is on every television set on the planet."

"We need to warn King Nereus," Finn said.

"I agree," Kyle said. "We'll go to the city at once."

"Delwyn may wish to come with you," Jake said. "Fabian says he has family there."

Finn nodded. "His parents live there, as well as the Oracles."

"Cari will be warning her Oracles," Jake said.

They hurried from the bedroom, Jake explaining as quickly as he could what had happened at the council meeting. They met up with Fabian and Delwyn, also on their way to Medina's temple.

Jake took a moment to be relieved that whatever powers caused those in his vicinity to become overly amorous seemed to be dampened by the state of emergency.

"You should stay here," Finn said to Jake when they had opened the portal. "The gods don't want you there, and you've not swum at such depths before."

"I agree," Kyle said. "Time isn't on our side, not when we have an entire city to save."

Jake agreed. "I'll stay here with Fabian."

Fabian grimaced. "Curse my wretched mother for taking away my ability to survive underwater."

Jake had a feeling the two of them would be spending a lot of time pacing the temple that day.

Chapter Eleven

As soon as they arrived in Atlantis, the three mermen swam their separate ways.

Finn headed straight for the king's private quarters. It was too early for him to be holding audience. Hardly any merpeople were up and about at this early hour. Even the servants were largely absent. He recalled his father had always been grumpy and irritable first thing in the morning.

Reluctant to disturb the man who had raised him, Finn instead detoured to Justin's chambers, hoping he and Lucas were early risers.

Luckily for Finn, Lucas was already awake. The guards let him into the chambers without any question.

"Finn, what brings you here so early?" Lucas smiled in greeting. *"If you're looking for Justin, he's asleep. We had a late night and we've just returned. I was about to join him."*

Finn wished he didn't have to disappoint Lucas, who appeared tired and ready for his sleeping sponge. *"You need to wake him, immediately. We have to evacuate the city."*

"What's happened?"

"There's no time to explain, at least not more than once. Go fetch Justin, then we need to talk to the king."

Lucas didn't question him again. He swam into the adjoining chambers to rouse his lover.

Justin grumbled as he swam into the room. *"What can possibly be so urgent?"*

Finn didn't reply as he led them to the king's chambers.

They found King Nereus already awake, much to Finn's surprise.

"Finn, what a pleasant surprise. Come have breakfast with me. You too, Justin and Lucas, of course."

Finn grabbed a piece of fruit, having skipped his own breakfast. *"Father, we need to evacuate the city."*

"Is this about the human explorers again?" King Nereus asked. *"I have guards hidden all around the perimeter of the sunken city. They have orders to report back immediately if they see any humans in the area. I've not had any such reports."*

"It's not the human explorers," Finn explained. *"The gods are going to raise Atlantis again."*

"Raise?" Justin asked. *"You mean* literally *raise it from the bottom of the ocean?"*

"Yes. We have until midnight to get everyone out of the city."

"But the entire world will see the city if they do that," Justin pointed out. *"Humans have satellites that can see the entire planet from space. I think they'll notice a bloody great island appearing out of the ocean."*

"That's what the gods are counting on," Finn replied. *"If humans see Atlantis rise from the sea, the gods think it will increase their powers, because they'll believe in them again."*

"They're more likely to put it down to some massive geological disaster," Justin said.

"It doesn't matter what they think about the appearance of an island," Lucas interrupted. "The important thing is that they don't discover the existence of us merpeople, which means we need to get everyone out of the city as fast as possible."

"I agree," King Nereus said. "The question is, where do we move everyone to? The oceans are no longer safe for our people and many will not wish to follow Finn's example and live on land. We are, first and foremost, creatures of the sea."

"I think our people should be given a choice," Justin said. "Finn, how many people can you and your men accommodate in that mansion of yours?"

"I don't know," Finn said. "But we've room for many."

"Perhaps the most vulnerable should go to land via Medina's temple," Lucas suggested. "The youngsters and the elderly, those who would be in the most danger in the open waters. The rest of us can search for a new home in the seas, and when we've found one, the others can join us if they wish to."

It sounded like a good idea to Finn.

"I'll summon all the guards to my audience chamber immediately," King Nereus said. "We have no time to spare."

* * * *

Kyle found his sister wide awake and swimming far too fast for so early an hour, thanks to his young niece, who was apparently an early riser, unlike the rest of the family.

"It's rather early for you to be up and about, isn't it?" Lynna asked with a smile. "How would you like to watch Maurissa while I make us some breakfast?"

"*There's no time for breakfast,*" Kyle said. "*We need to leave the city at once. I've come to take you to England.*"

"*Not this again.*" Lynna turned her back on him and put Maurissa down on her sponge, passing her a shell rattle to play with. "*I'm not going to leave the city or my mate.*"

"*I'm not suggesting you leave Xane. He needs to come too. Everyone needs to leave the city and we only have until midnight to get everyone out.*"

"*Midnight?*"

"*Yes, so you see the urgency of the situation?*"

"*Not really, no. Why must we leave? We're safe and settled here. It's our home.*"

"*The Atlantean gods are going to raise the island from the bottom of the ocean. Any mer still here when they do this will be trapped on land and exposed to the whole of the human world. We must go immediately. Where's Xane?*"

"*He's working the early shift this morning.*"

"*Go find him. I'll watch Maurissa while you're away.*"

Lynna still didn't appear entirely convinced, but she swam out of the chambers, leaving Kyle to spend some quality time with his niece.

An hour later, Kyle was wondering what had happened to his sister to keep her from returning.

Shouts from outside drew Kyle's attention and he picked up Maurissa and swam toward the cries.

"*What's happening?*" a mermaid carrying a net of fruits asked.

"*Everyone to the palace audience chamber,*" the guards called. "*Everyone to the audience chamber immediately.*"

Kyle, unlike the rest of the merpeople, knew what was happening, but everyone else appeared confused as they swam through the palace.

He had never seen so many people crammed into the audience chamber at once. He'd had no idea the population of the sunken city was so large.

Not everyone could fit into the room, and mer crowded in the archways and down the corridors. Some swam near the floor, others near the ceiling and many more in the space between, yet still there wasn't enough room.

The guards were placed strategically around the room and the expressions on their faces told Kyle they had already been briefed by the king.

"*My people, we are in grave danger.*" King Nereus' voice echoed throughout the chamber and beyond. "*This city, which has been our home for so many years, is no longer safe. I have received word that the Atlantean gods intend to raise this city from the ocean floor this very night.*"

A murmur of dissent reverberated through the crowd.

"*His Highness, Prince Finn, offers shelter in a safe location on land for those who are most vulnerable. The elderly and the children, together with the nursing mermaids and those heavy with child, are to follow Prince Finn to the place known as England.*"

"*What of the rest of us?*" called a merman in the middle of the room.

"*When we've judged how much space remains in His Highness' home, more will be invited to go through the portal to join them, starting with the older children. The rest will need to swim from this place. The cave network to the east is outside of the boundaries of what was once the continent of Atlantis. I suggest those who do not wish to go to land at all gather as many supplies as you can and head there. It will be from there we will begin our journey in search of a new home.*"

The crowd began to disperse. Kyle remained in the audience chamber, searching for Lynna's face among the mermaids. He couldn't see her.

"You're not going to land, are you?" an unfamiliar mermaid asked. *"Surely the mother of your child should be the one to take her?"*

"This is my niece," Kyle said. *"Her mother is who I'm searching for. She seems to have disappeared."*

"Ah. I thought for a moment you intended to go to land. You'll forgive me, but you look strong enough to take care of yourself in the water."

"Kyle will be coming to land," Finn said as he swam up behind the mermaid. *"It's his home, as well as mine, that we're inviting you to."*

"Oh." The mermaid flushed. *"My apologies, Your Highness. I didn't realize this merman was a friend of yours."*

"He's my mate," Finn said. *"One of them, anyway. Kyle, where's Lynna?"*

"I don't know, I thought she might have come here. She left me to go find Xane more than an hour ago, and I've not seen her since."

Maurissa chose that moment to scream for her mama.

"I was going to suggest I take this little one to England while you go search for Lynna, but now I'm not so sure." Finn chucked Maurissa under her chin.

"We have plenty of time," Kyle said. *"It's still early morning. I'm sure Lynna can't have gone far. I'll keep hold of Maurissa for the moment and meet you back at home later."*

"If you're sure?"

"Yes." Kyle kissed Finn briefly. *"I love you, Finn."*

"I love you, too. Be careful and hurry home."

"I'll be there by lunchtime."

Finn swam back and waved to the waiting mermaids and youngsters. *"If you'll follow me, please."*

Kyle watched his lover lead his people through the palace. This is what Finn had been raised for — to be a leader, a ruler and a merman loved by those he protected.

As soon as Finn was out of sight, Maurissa began to squeal again.

"Hush," Kyle encouraged. *"We'll find your mama soon."*

Deciding the best thing to do was to trace the route Lynna would have taken earlier, Kyle made his way to the palace kitchens. He found them bustling with activity as the staff filled their net bags with everything they could find. Without the gathering fields, they would need all the provisions they could carry in the weeks ahead.

"Have you seen Xane or Lynna?" Kyle asked.

"Xane was here earlier," one of the mermaids replied. *"I've not seen him since we were summoned to hear King Nereus, though."*

"Was he in the audience chamber?"

"I don't know. I can't remember."

Kyle growled in frustration. *"What of Lynna?"*

"I've not seen her all day."

Kyle wondered what had happened. What had kept Lynna from reaching Xane?

"Maybe she's gone to land?" one of the mermaids suggested.

"She wouldn't leave for England without her daughter," Kyle said. *"Maurissa means the world to her."*

"I don't mean she'd have gone to England, I meant the birthing island."

"*Birthing?*" Kyle gaped at mermaid. "*Lynna's with child?*"

"*Yes, didn't you know?*"

"*No. She never mentioned it. Why wouldn't she tell me?*"

The mermaid gave him a sympathetic glance. "*Lynna, like many of our women, lost her last babe. She isn't due for a few more weeks, but sometimes that's how it happens.*"

Suddenly his sister's weight gain took on new meaning. "*Where's the birthing island?*"

"*It's about the same distance as the mating islands, but in the opposite direction. It's smaller, but has many mossy clearings, which are much more comfortable for those mermaids who choose to give birth on land rather than in the water. If she's there, you should find her easily.*"

Kyle nodded and began to swim away.

"*Wait! You're not taking Maurissa there, are you?*"

"*Well, I can't exactly leave her on her own,*" Kyle pointed out.

"*Take her to the nursery,*" the mermaid suggested. "*My sister is watching over our own youngsters in there while we're packing supplies. She'll be happy to mind Maurissa while you go search for Lynna.*"

"*I thought all the youngsters had gone with Finn?*"

"*His Highness has taken the very young first. Those who remain are over five years and are still here. Maurissa will be much better off in the nursery than seeing her mother in pain.*"

Kyle agreed, and after thanking the mermaid for her assistance, he detoured to the nursery, where he left Maurissa then swam for the birthing island as fast as he could.

* * * *

Jake guided the refugees through the house while Fabian remained in the temple to greet the new arrivals.

He wasn't sure even this place would be big enough to accommodate everyone who was about to descend on them. He gave another silent thank you to Caspian for gifting him with the language of the merpeople. He didn't know how he would have managed without the ability. It was hard enough trying to explain basic functions of the bathroom with it. Apparently there was no word in the language of the mer for a toilet.

As he returned to the temple, he ran into Finn.

"Hi, baby, how's it going?" Jake pulled Finn into his arms and hugged him tight. "Is Kyle with you?"

"He's tracking down Lynna. I'm going to go back shortly for the next group. What time is it?"

Jake checked his watch. "Just after ten."

"It's mid-morning already?" Finn sighed. "This is taking longer than I thought it would."

"Is there going to be enough time to get everyone out of the city?"

"I hope so."

They hurried back to the temple, and after tossing another rose from the garden into the offering basin, Finn disappeared through the portal again.

"Not everyone is going to make it through," Fabian said. "There are too many mer to bring here."

Jake had no idea what the population of Atlantis was, but he trusted Fabian had a fair idea of the numbers. He had watched over the city for centuries.

"Is Delwyn back yet?" Jake asked.

Fabian shook his head. "No."

"I'm sure he's okay," Jake reassured him. "Those who have arrived seem to be pregnant mermaids and youngsters."

"The most vulnerable," Fabian said. "I hope he and his parents don't leave it too long before they come through the portal. I won't survive without him."

Jake patted Fabian's arm. "I'm sure he'll be here long before midnight."

"If he isn't, there's nothing I can do about it," Fabian replied.

"Let's not start worrying yet."

The portal glowed, a sign that someone was about to come through. They cut their conversation short as the second group of evacuees began to arrive.

* * * *

Kyle found the island without any difficulty. As small as it was, he still couldn't have missed it.

He swam to the beach and dragged himself onto the sands as quickly as he could. As soon as he had his legs, he ran into the trees.

"Lynna? Are you here?"

The sound of a baby crying came from somewhere to his left. Kyle picked up his pace and followed the sound.

"Lynna?"

"Kyle? Is that you?"

"Yes, Lynna, hold on. I'm coming."

Kyle stumbled through the foliage, tripping on roots and scratching himself on brambles.

Lynna was on the ground with a newborn babe in her arms. The tiny young merbaby was the smallest child Kyle had ever seen in his life.

"Why didn't you tell me?" Kyle asked.

"Superstition," Lynna replied with a sheepish grin. "They say the curse that prevents the mermaids from delivering healthy children isn't as strong if the mermaid doesn't tell anyone she's with child."

"The mermaid who told me where to find you knew," Kyle said.

"Because she figured it out for herself, no doubt. I wanted you to say something. You must have seen my weight gain since we last saw each other."

"Well, yes, I noticed, but I thought it was fat."

"Fat!" Lynna glared at him. "You thought I got *fat?*"

"I would expect you to *tell* me if you were with child."

"But the curse…"

"I don't believe in such things."

Lynna gave him a wide-eyed look of disbelief.

"Very well, I *might* believe in curses, but if there is a curse, I doubt it can be changed by keeping secrets from those you love. Did you tell Xane?"

"He figured it out for himself," Lynna said.

"Where is he now?"

"I'm not sure. The pains started before I found him, and I came here alone."

"We should go back to the city. He's probably searching for you and Maurissa."

"Wait a moment. Kyle, where *is* Maurissa?"

"I left her in the nursery before I swam here."

Lynna breathed a sigh of relief.

Kyle stood and held his hand out to his sister. "Come on. Let's head back."

Lynna shook her head. "The babe can't go into the water yet."

"Why not?"

Lynna patted the moss beside her. "Sit down, Kyle, and learn a few things about merbabies."

"I know as much as I need to about them," Kyle replied, though he sat as Lynna requested.

"Merbabies who are born on land are born with closed gills," Lynna explained. "It takes up to twelve hours for them to open."

Kyle touched one of his own gills, hidden behind his ear where no human could see it, at least not unless they were nuzzling him there, as Jake was prone to do since his discovery of how sensitive they were.

"Twelve hours?" Kyle asked. "Are you sure?"

"Yes, of course I am. It doesn't always take so long. It was around ten with Maurissa, but rumor has it males always take longer."

"Bloody hell, Lynna, why did you come to land to give birth if you knew that?"

Lynna rolled her eyes, mumbled something about idiot mermen and gave a heavy sigh of impatience. "Kyle, *you* told me the gods are going to raise the city out of the water. What if I'd still been in the city, in labor, when they raised it?"

"I'd have made sure you weren't," Kyle argued. "I'd have got you to England where you had the choice of the pool or a comfortable bed."

"I wasn't going to go to England without Xane. I didn't have time to track him down, return to you *and* go to England. I was in *labor*."

There was no point in arguing with Lynna when she was in this sort of mood. The fact of the matter was, it was too late now to complain about how they could have done things differently.

Kyle tried to judge the time from the position of the sun, but he had got out of the habit during his time with humans. He could tell it was still morning, but not much more than that. Twelve hours waiting for the merbaby's gills to open, then the swim back to the city... It was going to be cutting things very fine indeed.

"You should go back to the city and get Maurissa to safety," Lynna said. "I'll be fine. If you find Xane, tell him where I am."

"I can't leave you here."

"Yes, you can. You *must*. Take Maurissa to your England and look after her until Xane and I can come and collect her."

Kyle stood. "I'll come back for you as soon as I can."

"Don't be a fool, Kyle. You need to take care of Maurissa. If I don't make it, I want you to raise her as if she were your own."

"I won't need to bring her up, because I'm coming back for you and my nephew. Have you decided on a name for him yet?"

"I thought perhaps I might name him Xane, after his father, but his papa isn't too keen on the idea. He suggested Lamar, after our father, but with Maurissa already named for our mother, I wanted to pick a name from the other side of the family. Xane wants to leave the choice to me and I've not decided yet."

"Hopefully, you will by the time I get back."

Kyle didn't give Lynna time to argue with him again. He ran back to the beach, determined to get Maurissa to safety as quickly as he could. The sooner she was in England, the faster he could return for his sister and nephew.

* * * *

Kyle arrived in England with Maurissa and found a house filled with more people than he had ever imagined possible.

"Where's Jake?" Kyle asked Fabian.

"I think he said something about ordering food for lunch. Finn's downstairs, too."

Kyle went in search of his lovers, knowing they would take care of Maurissa while he returned to Atlantis.

The house had never been so noisy. Babies were crying and toddlers were shouting. As for the adults, the sounds of frustrated confusion were almost drowning out the youngsters. Kyle had a great deal of sympathy for them all. He had found it difficult to navigate this strange land himself, even after Caspian had given him knowledge of the modern human world. He wondered if the god would be stopping by to assist the mer again or whether he would stay away this time.

He found his lovers in the kitchen with King Nereus and Justin, who were arguing about Justin's sight.

"You do remember you're supposed to be blind on land as well as off," King Nereus reminded his son.

"Yes, I remember, but I think getting our people to safety takes priority here, Father."

"What are we supposed to tell people when they realize you can see when you're in human form, just like the Oracles can?"

Justin held out his arms. "It's a *miracle*," he declared with a wide grin.

The king sighed impatiently. "Can you at least try to take this seriously?"

Justin snorted. "I'd rather take the current emergency seriously and worry about everything else later. I won't pretend to be blind when doing so could endanger the lives of others."

"Very well," King Nereus said. "We'll discuss this later. Now, let's get back to work."

The two of them turned back to something they were studying on the counter, but Kyle couldn't see what it was.

"Kyle!" Finn shouted across the crowded kitchen. "Did you find Lynna?"

"Yes, but we have a slight issue," Kyle replied as he joined them.

"What sort of issue?"

"She's on the birthing island."

Finn stared at him in disbelief. "You never mentioned she was with child."

"I didn't know."

"How's that possible?" Jake asked as he poured drinks into every glass, mug and beaker they owned. "You've been visiting her recently. Surely you noticed."

"I just thought she'd put on some weight," Kyle muttered. "I didn't want to say anything to her, and apparently she thought by saying nothing it would help fend off this so-called curse."

"Actually, there is a curse," Justin piped up from where, Kyle could now see, he and his father were studying a crudely drawn map.

"There is?" Kyle asked. "How do you know that?"

"My father told me," Justin replied.

Everyone stared expectantly at King Nereus.

"Not that one," Justin clarified. "Caspian, my adoptive father. I asked him about it once, and he told me it was something to do with his mother, though he didn't say what exactly."

"I still don't see how Kyle can see his sister so recently and not *notice* that she's pregnant," Jake teased.

"Mermaid pregnancies are five months long," Finn reminded him. "They don't get quite as large as human women."

Kyle nodded. "That isn't the real problem, though. According to Lynna, it can be up to twelve hours before the babe's gills open and he can enter the water."

Finn immediately turned to the clock on the wall. "How long ago did she give birth?"

Kyle answered the unspoken question. "There should be enough time for me to get her back to the city and here. I just brought Maurissa to land to make sure she's safe. Have you seen Xane?"

"No, isn't he with Lynna?"

"She hadn't seen him since before our arrival this morning. I'm going to go try to find him before I fetch Lynna. Let's hope the babe's gills open quickly."

"Males tend to take a little longer than females," King Nereus added, unknowingly reiterating Lynna's words of earlier.

"Not always," Finn said. "My mum told me mine opened pretty quickly, just six hours after I was born."

"Let's hope Lynna's new babe is equally eager to reach the water," Kyle said. "Now, who wants to look after Maurissa while I head back to the city?"

Suddenly the men in his life went quiet. It seemed no one was eager to volunteer for babysitting duties.

"Bring her here," King Nereus said. "I'll take her through to the pool, where the mermaids have set up a temporary nursery."

Everyone breathed a sigh of relief and Kyle headed straight back to the temple.

Finn glanced at Jake as he quickly ate his sandwich. He could tell something was bothering his lover, but in the midst of the current crisis, he didn't have time to ask him what was wrong.

"We've evacuated all the vulnerable from the palace and to the west," King Nereus said. "I think we need to look to the south now, which is the most densely populated part of the city and very close to the old nursery. Justin, can you and Lucas cover that area?"

Justin nodded. "Sure. I'll go fetch Lucas and we'll head back there immediately."

"Excellent. Finn, I need you to swim north and spread the word that they'll be next."

Finn stuffed the last of his sandwich into his mouth and mumbled his agreement around a mouthful of food.

"Otus." King Nereus waved over the temporary leader of the guards.

"Your Majesty?"

"I want you to ensure the guards are transporting all the weapons and armor they can carry from the barracks to the cave network. If you need more mer to assist with this, recruit anyone who doesn't appear busy. You'll need to ensure the gatherers are being adequately protected as they harvest as much as they can from the fields to the north and west. Most of the gatherers should be in the fertile lands in the west. You should also check the fruit gardens in the south, though I believe those have all been harvested this year already."

"Yes, Your Majesty."

Otus bowed and spun on his heel to leave, walking right into Finn's birth father, who had chosen that moment to visit.

Finn tried to imagine how the scene would look to his human father. Lots of naked men and women wandering around the house as if nothing was amiss. Only Jake was clothed at all.

"I take it you two aren't coming into work today?" asked Malcolm, his eyes fixed on Jake as though if he looked away from him, he might suffer some horrendous fate.

"Sorry. I forgot to phone in," Jake said. "Can you manage without us for a few days?"

"Yes, of course. I just wanted to check you were okay. When you didn't come in this morning and Finn never arrived for the lunchtime rush, I thought I'd better stop by. Alex is holding the fort, along with May. Alex says you owe him a huge favor for making him work on his day off."

"Tell them thanks," Jake said. "As you can see, we're in the middle of a bit of a situation."

"So I see. Is there anything I can help with? More sandwiches, perhaps?"

"If you can spare any, that would be great, Dad," Finn said. "We've got more mer arriving throughout the day and we're already running short of food."

"Dad?" King Nereus suddenly seemed to realize who had entered the room. "This is Malcolm?"

Finn nodded as the man who had raised him stared at his natural father. *Should I introduce them or flee from the room?*

"Yes, I'm Malcolm," Finn's father said. "And who might you be?"

King Nereus straightened his spine and stood straight and tall, towering over everyone else in the room. "I am Nereus, King of Atlantis."

Malcolm paled. "Oh. Er... It's nice to meet you."

Finn didn't think his dad sounded pleased to meet his father. Even though Finn had been mending bridges with King Nereus in recent weeks, he hadn't talked to his parents about his visits. They knew he had been visiting the city and how he had been getting there and back, but other than that, Finn had kept his discussions with King Nereus to himself.

Malcolm faced Finn and he could see the questions in his dad's eyes.

"It's fine," Finn said. "We've talked things over and you don't need to worry."

"You're sure about that?" Malcolm asked.

"Very sure," Finn replied. He took his father to one side and lowered his voice. "You'd better warn Mum not to come around here until the coast is clear."

"Will do," Malcolm said. "Now, I'd better get back to work. I'll send Alex over with some sandwiches when it slows down later. Is there anything else you need? Clothes, perhaps?"

Finn shook his head. "Maybe later, but right now food is a priority."

Jake finished his own lunch and jangled his car keys. "I'm going to head to the supermarket and pick up some baby stuff. We need food suitable for babies, nappies and goodness knows what else."

"Take Summer with you," Malcolm suggested. "She's already stocking up and she knows what to look for."

Jake nodded. "Good idea, because I've not had any experience with babies, mer or otherwise."

Finn kissed Jake goodbye, grabbed a quick drink of juice and headed back to the temple…and the portal.

* * * *

The sunken city was in chaos when Kyle returned. Mer were swimming in every direction, shouting and yelling for family and friends as they tried to ensure their loved ones were safe.

Kyle searched every face for Xane, but he could find no trace of him. He suspected the merman was searching for Lynna and that they were simply missing each other. It also occurred to him that Xane might have figured out that Lynna was on the birthing island and gone there himself.

After a full circuit of the city, Kyle decided that was almost certainly the case and swam for the birthing island once more.

"Lynna? Xane?"

"I'm over here," Lynna called.

Kyle ran in the opposite direction to where he had found his sister earlier. He found her in a shallow rock pool, her babe in her arms.

"Have his gills opened?"

"Not yet," Lynna replied. "I needed to transform to ease the pain from giving birth. As you can see, he has his fins. Aren't they pretty?"

The pure black scales of the youngster's tail were as unusual as they were beautiful.

"His great-grandfather on Xane's side of the family had the same coloring," Lynna explained. "You never had chance to meet him and we lost him last year. I think perhaps Xane might like to name our son after him."

"What was his name?"

"Cian."

Kyle smiled as he considered his nephew. "I think I like that one."

Lynna sighed. "I take it that you didn't find Xane?"

"No. I've not seen him. I thought maybe I'd missed him and that I'd find him here with you."

"I wonder if he's escorting his family to the cave network," Lynna suggested.

"He should be caring for his mate," Kyle replied.

"His great-grandmother is very frail and lost her sight many years ago. She isn't the strongest swimmer, either. She dotes on Xane. He's probably been helping her get to safety because he knows I can take care of myself."

"You've just given birth."

"Yes, thank you for reminding me." Lynna rolled her eyes. "I managed it perfectly well on my own, like every other mermaid does. Xane will return for me when he knows the rest of his family is safe."

"He would have been better off taking them to the portal," Kyle pointed out.

"Xane and his family won't live among humans, and I don't want to, either. As soon as we're settled, wherever our people end up, we'll come for Maurissa, too."

"What about Cian?" Kyle asked. "Don't you think it would be safer for him in England?"

"Merbabies can't survive the first few weeks if they're parted from their mother."

"Then you should come to England," Kyle stated. As far as he could tell, this was the obvious solution to all their problems. He didn't understand why Lynna couldn't see this too.

* * * *

Finn swam from house to house, calling as loudly as he could for all youngsters and the elderly to make their way to the palace. There were few mer left in the area, and most of them did as he suggested. Unfortunately, there was a handful who were reluctant to leave their homes. Finn tried to explain the danger they were in, but his pleas fell on deaf ears.

Knowing he couldn't waste too much time and that there was still a huge area of the city where word might not have yet reached, Finn carried on swimming and calling out to anyone who might hear.

Those who were reluctant to travel to England, Finn directed to the cave network. Since the caves were relatively close by, some of the mer agreed to go there, to err on the side of caution, in case the city truly did rise to the surface that night.

Finn could tell some of the mer didn't believe what he told them about the gods and their plans for the city. Luckily, most of the inhabitants had witnessed the previous altercations between several immortals, so at least knew they existed, even if they didn't accept the rest of his warning.

"Sea dragons!"

The cry of terror came from outside the city but was loud enough and came from so many at once, Finn could hear it from where he swam.

He gripped his trident tightly and tore through the ocean toward the shouts.

He met the fleeing merpeople swimming in the other direction.

"Sea dragons are burning the gathering fields to the north," one of the mermen shouted when he saw Finn.

Finn nodded and swam for the fields. They were quite a distance from the city and past the boundaries the dragons used to protect. If they were attacking the fields, then they were doing so on the orders of Mariana. The Goddess of Sea Creatures despised the merpeople, despite her supposed love and protection of those of the sea.

The mer had only recently discovered the truth about the sea dragons, in that they were Mariana's priests, transformed to sea dragons hundreds of years ago. Now they were no longer collared, and instead of protecting the mer, they were helping their mistress drive them out of Atlantis.

When Finn arrived at the gathering fields, there were no merpeople in sight. There was also nothing left of the fruits the mer had been growing in the area. The two sea dragons had destroyed every last plant with sea-fire.

More worrying than that, they appeared to be heading to the lands to the west, no doubt intending to bring about the same destruction there.

Finn didn't hesitate. He aimed his trident at the nearest of the two dragons and summoned the sea-fire with his thoughts. He was glad he had been practicing in recent months.

Unfortunately, his bolt of sea-fire had little effect on the sea dragon it hit. The animal clearly felt the shot, but it didn't so much as mark the creature's thick hide. The sea dragon turned on Finn, breathing more sea-fire than a dozen tridents could conjure.

Finn darted out of the way and tried to fire another shot from his trident. He couldn't summon so much as a spark.

Ducking behind a boulder, he tried to calm his nerves. Concentrating as hard as he could, he attempted to bring forth the sea-fire again. It took several minutes of concentration before the prongs of the trident glowed blue.

Finn crept out slowly from his hiding place, intending to fire on the sea dragons again, hoping to aim for a more vulnerable part of the body this time, like the eyes or the mouth. To his dismay, the sea dragons had disappeared while he'd been trying to work his weapon.

With a curse of frustration, Finn swam after them, hoping to catch up before they reached the gatherers. With a bit of luck, he could at least distract them long enough for the gatherers to swim to safety.

With his trident poised and ready to fire, Finn sent a strong blast right at the head of the largest of the two sea dragons.

It was a direct hit and the sea dragon howled in pain.

On the far side of the creatures, Finn could see the gatherers fleeing the fields.

The second of the sea dragons sent flames down on the harvest, callously burning them. Finn hoped the mer had gathered enough food for them to survive the coming weeks.

For the first time, Finn wondered where exactly the boundaries of the city of Atlantis were. Would the gathering grounds rise with the city, or was there a chance some of them could stay on the bottom of the ocean, where the mer might continue to harvest them?

Finn hoped some of the fertile lands would stay underwater, because the rest of the surrounding area was barren. If they couldn't harvest the land here, they would have to swim for many miles before they found somewhere else.

While the mer fled, Finn continued to send bolts of sea-fire at the dragons. None of his blasts were as effective as the first one. Now that they knew he was there, the sea dragons ducked and dodged his attempts to hit them, while at the same time sending their own fire at him as well as the gathering grounds, burning everything in sight. Pain shot through his shoulder as a burst from the nearest sea dragon winged him before he could avoid it.

When he thought the gatherers had swum safely away, Finn sent one final blast at the sea dragons before swimming back to the city. He should probably get back to England and get his wound tended, but he couldn't return without the next group of evacuees.

He knew the sea dragons probably wouldn't follow him to the city. They weren't dumb animals, and their attacks on the gathering grounds were tactical in nature. He wished he knew what their next move would be. He hoped it would be to retreat, now their job was apparently done, but he couldn't say for sure.

In the meantime, the best thing he could do was return to his task of making sure the next group of evacuees was packed and ready to leave as soon as the word was given.

* * * *

When Jake returned from the supermarket with Summer, he found the house even more crowded than when he had left it. He had no idea where he was going to put everyone that night. Many of the rooms were still completely unfurnished and the pool could only hold so many merpeople at once.

He opened the front door as he juggled his bags. Summer stood right behind him.

"Er…"

"What is it?" Summer asked.

"I should warn you that the mer don't seem to be too bothered about things like clothing."

"Yes, I know," Summer replied. "Can we go in now? These bags are quite heavy."

"You should have left them in the car," Jake said. "Alex won't be pleased with me if you overdo things."

"I'm not an invalid."

Jake knew better than to argue with her and opened the door to let her in.

"Ah, there you are." Caspian stood at the foot of the staircase.

Jake hoped the god had some good news for them. "I've been out to stock up on supplies for the youngsters," he explained.

"Good idea," Caspian said. "I've furnished the rest of the rooms of the house for you. I know you and your men have enjoyed renovating this place, but time has run out."

"We didn't realize we were on a timer," Jake said.

Caspian shrugged. "I don't think anyone thought time would run out this quickly. Of course, it might have helped if you, Kyle and Finn hadn't spent quite so much time in bed."

Summer snorted and Jake glared at her.

"What other news have you brought us?" Jake asked, in an effort to change the subject. "Are the gods still intending to raise the island?"

"Yes."

"Have you given the mer the ability to understand English and the knowledge of the modern human world?"

"No, they won't need it," Caspian replied. "This is temporary. Cari has already seen where they will be relocating to. I don't see the point of confusing them with a lot of useless information that they won't need this time next year."

Jake wondered whether it was worth pointing out that they might not need the knowledge next year, but they certainly appeared to right now. He'd already had two bathtubs overflowing and several burns in the kitchen to contend with.

Before he could say anything, Caspian vanished, leaving them to get on with distributing their shopping to those who needed the items.

Justin and Lucas returned with another group of merpeople and Jake updated them as to what Caspian had told him.

"It would be nice if one of my foster parents could tell *us* where they see us living," Justin complained.

"The gods don't tend to work that way," Jake replied. "I'm still rather surprised that they interfere quite as much as they do."

"Me too," admitted Justin, even though he had been raised by Caspian and Cari and should have known better than anyone how the Atlantean gods operated.

Jake left Summer with the mermaids who had the youngest children and joined Justin and King Nereus as they updated their map.

They were still contemplating their next move when Finn returned, looking tired and disheveled. A burn on his left shoulder looked nasty and painful.

"Finn, what happened?" Jake rushed across to his lover and guided him into a nearby chair. "Justin, pass me the first-aid kit. It's under the sink."

"The sea dragons aren't letting us leave unhindered," Finn explained. "They've destroyed the gathering grounds to the north and the west of the city."

"Was anyone hurt by them?" King Nereus asked. "Besides yourself, of course."

"I don't think so," Finn said. "I distracted them as much as I could while the gatherers swam to safety. But we've lost the rest of the harvest."

Jake tended to Finn's arm, causing his lover to hiss with pain. "Sorry, baby."

Finn ignored him and pointed at the map. "They were here last time I saw them. The gatherers have gone to the cave network now."

"Whereabouts is that?" Jake asked.

Lucas pointed at the map. "Too close to the dragons, unfortunately."

"I only saw two of them," Finn said. "I don't know where the rest are."

King Nereus frowned as he studied the map. "I think we need to move quickly to get everyone out of the city."

"Not everyone wants to leave," Finn said. "Some of the mer I've spoken to didn't believe me. They want to stay in their homes."

"Lucas and I found the same thing," Justin agreed. "I think it's safe to say that no matter how hard we try to evacuate everyone, when the gods raise the city, there *will* be some mer on the island."

King Nereus shook his head. "We can't waste time trying to force those from their homes who don't wish to leave. I suggest we at least try to persuade them to take refuge in the palace. The highest floor and balconies should be the safest and easiest to swim away from when the time comes."

"Perhaps a small group of guards should stay behind, too?" Justin suggested.

"No," King Nereus said. "While it would make sense for some guards to stay there to protect those who refuse to leave, the more people who remain behind, the harder it will be to avoid the exposure of our people. Unless there are guards who are refusing to leave, as well, anyone who wants to be out of the city before it rises should be allowed to leave."

* * * *

Kyle paced along the beach as he watched the moon rise above the ocean. "Any sign yet?" he asked Lynna.

"Not yet," Lynna replied. "I told you I'd tell you the moment they open. I don't want to be stuck here any longer than you do. I want to find Xane."

Kyle was more worried about Xane than he wanted to admit. Xane seemed devoted to Lynna, and Kyle couldn't understand why he hadn't come here to find her. He wished he knew his sister's mate better, so he could try to figure out where he might be.

Despite two brief visits back to the sunken city, Kyle could find no sign of the missing merman. He had even resorted to calling for Medina and the other immortals he knew, but they weren't answering his calls.

"Maybe we should wait here until after the island is raised?" Lynna suggested. "The city isn't directly below us."

Kyle gave the idea a few moments thought before dismissing it. "I don't know how the gods intend to raise the island, exactly, but we suspect it'll cause great waves. This island, and the ones used by the mer during the mating seasons, are likely to be flooded completely."

"Are you sure?"

"No, I'm not sure, but we can't risk it. I want you safe in England well before midnight."

"I don't want to go to England. I want to head to the cave network with the rest of our people."

"The most vulnerable, which includes the new merbabies, have been evacuated to England."

"I don't care. I don't want to live with humans."

Kyle sighed. "Where did you get this prejudiced view about humans from? I know you've never met a human in your life."

"I don't *need* to meet one," Lynna replied. "I've heard more than enough about them from those who have sought shelter in the sunken city. Humans are selfish creatures, polluting our waters without a care for those of us living here. I don't know how you can live with one of them."

"Jake isn't like that," Kyle said. "If you could meet him, you'd see how kind he is."

Lynna sighed. "I know you're happy with him, and I'm glad he treats you well, but I don't *want* to live with humans."

"It won't be for long, just until the mer are relocated safely to a new home in the ocean. Wherever you're all being relocated to, it's going to be a long and dangerous journey, which won't be good for your newborn son."

Lynna gave another long sigh. "I'll come to England, but only because I don't seem to have another choice."

* * * *

Finn kept glancing at the clock, willing time to slow down long enough for Kyle to return. He had suggested to Jake that he go to fetch him, but after Finn's encounter with the sea dragons, Jake was reluctant to let Finn out of his sight again.

"You're injured," Jake said. "Your wound might get infected."

"Merpeople don't get infections," Finn argued. "The seawater will help me heal."

"I still don't like you going back there. You said yourself, everyone who was willing to come here has already arrived. Those who are left are the ones who refused to leave for either here or the caves."

"Apart from Kyle, Lynna and the babe."

Jake sat on the edge of the bed and pulled Finn onto his lap. "Kyle will bring them back here as soon as he can. He wouldn't want you to put yourself in danger for him, would he?"

"No, I guess not." Finn closed his eyes and rested his head on Jake's shoulder.

"Tired?" Jake asked.

"No," Finn replied around a wide yawn. "I won't be able to sleep until Kyle is safely home."

"Hmm?"

Finn thought he heard Jake chuckle as his lover eased him down onto the bed. Maybe he would just shut his eyes for a few minutes. It had been a long and tiring day.

Chapter Twelve

"Cian's gills have opened," Lynna called.

"At last!" Kyle pulled his sister to her feet and they ran into the surf. "Hurry, Lynna. We don't have much time to get to the city."

They swam as fast as they could. Atlantis had never seemed as empty as it did when they finally returned.

The normally busy city appeared deserted.

"*Xane!*" Lynna's call halted Kyle immediately. "*Xane, over here.*"

Kyle watched his sister change course and swim toward the marketplace. "*Lynna, we have to hurry.*"

Lynna ignored him as she swam in the direction of her mate.

"*Xane, where have you been?*" Lynna called.

"*I've been searching for you,*" Xane replied.

"*I've been on the birthing island all day,*" Lynna explained. "*You have a new son.*"

"A son?" Xane peered at the new baby with a wide smile. "*But you weren't due for another month.*"

"I know, but I guess he wanted to meet us a little sooner."

"If I'd known, I'd have checked the birthing island, but in the panic, I didn't think of that. I thought you'd already gone to this England place with Maurissa, but as I'm not one of the vulnerable, I've not been able to go there to check."

"Kyle took Maurissa there earlier," Lynna explained.

"I searched for you, too," Kyle added. *"I guess we must have kept missing each other."*

Xane nodded. *"I must have swum through the city and back and forth from the caves a hundred times today. In all the chaos, we probably passed each other more than once."*

"Well, let's not waste any more time," Kyle said. *"We must hurry if we're going to get to the portal before midnight."*

"You go ahead. I'll be right behind you."

"Where are you going?" Lynna asked.

"I have to tell my family where I'm going."

"You haven't time to get to the caves and back," Kyle said.

"They aren't at the caves," Xane replied. *"Father refuses to leave, and my mother won't leave him."*

"What of the others?" Lynna asked.

"They're in the caves," Xane confirmed. *"It's Father who's being stubborn."*

"Hurry after us," Lynna said.

Xane nodded and swam for his family's home.

Kyle urged Lynna on to Medina's temple on the main street. The building was nearer than the palace, and the portal there should take them to the Isle of the Gods just as efficiently as the one in the palace.

As they reached the building, the ground began to shake.

"It's started," Kyle said, even though there wasn't any need to state the obvious.

A crack spread along the ground and the temple collapsed into the ravine that appeared.

"We'll have to use the palace temple instead," Kyle said. "Hurry, Lynna."

They swam for the palace and darted through the corridors, traveling down into the levels below the ground floor, where the palace temples were located.

The whole building shook around them and the ground rose, even as they swam lower and lower.

"We aren't going to make it," Lynna shouted. "The whole place is coming down."

"We have to reach the portal," Kyle insisted. "Don't stop and don't look back. Just swim as fast as you can."

As the island rose, Kyle knew they weren't going to make it in time. Water churned around them as it poured out of the building, carrying Kyle, Lynna and Cian away from their destination.

When the water had gone, Kyle and Lynna were left on the stone floor, waiting for their fins to dry out so they could use their legs to continue their flight to safety.

Around them the building continued to shake and the sounds of stones falling echoed through the corridors.

"Kyle, I'm scared," Lynna said.

"Me, too," Kyle admitted. "Me, too."

An almighty crash brought the walls around them crashing down.

Kyle felt crushing pain on one of his newly restored legs, then he didn't feel anything at all as his vision darkened and he slipped into unconsciousness.

* * * *

The news was all over the television and Jake, like everyone else in the country, was glued to the screen.

"We're reporting here from the middle of the Atlantic Ocean where, overnight, an island three times the size of the State of New York has suddenly appeared. We'll be bringing you our exclusive report at the top of the hour, but here are a few of the amazing pictures already taken of the island that some are saying could be the mythical Atlantis."

Jake groaned. They didn't know how right they were.

The gods were mysteriously absent, and Jake was sorely tempted to make an offering to Medina and travel to the Isle of the Gods to see what was happening.

The refugees who had made it to England via Medina's temple filled the house. Jake had a feeling Caspian had known this was coming all along, and that this was why he had provided them with such a huge mansion. Cari must have warned him of these events long before they transpired.

Finn and King Nereus entered the room as the adverts before the news report began.

"Has Kyle shown up yet?" Jake asked.

Finn shook his head. "I've checked the entire house and neither he nor Lynna are here."

"I hope he's safe in the ocean. If anyone is in the palace or other buildings, they aren't going to be able to get back to the water without the whole world watching."

Finn sat beside Jake and took hold of his hand. "If one of the tunnels still exists, he might be able to get out of the main city that way. The tunnels all lead to various points on the island, and quite a lot of them end near what appears to be the edges of the new island."

"Do you think any of them could have survived the rise?"

"I don't know. I hope so."

The adverts on the television ended and Jake chewed on his lip as he watched.

"Welcome back to News Twenty-Four Seven, where we're coming to you live from above the island that has mysteriously appeared in the Atlantic Ocean overnight. We'll be bringing you live pictures as well as updates about the tidal waves that have hit the various coasts bordering the Atlantic. But first, we have an interview with world-renowned geologist, June Moffett. June, you must be as surprised as the rest of the world at the appearance of this island in the middle of the Atlantic Ocean. What's the official word in the scientific community?"

"Officially, we have no comment to make at the present time."

"And unofficially?"

"Unofficially, I can't wait to get down there and explore."

The presenter laughed. *"I have no doubt that will be quite an experience. Unfortunately, that may have to wait a while. In an official statement issued this morning, the island has been declared off limits to civilians by the United States military, whose vessel passed by the island in the early hours of the morning and noted the new land mass. We are receiving reports, however, that other governments may declare the territory to be theirs and that the US has no jurisdiction over the island. We'll have the latest on these reports later."*

Jake wondered who would end up claiming the island. Technically, the Atlanteans were no longer a people. They had been scattered throughout the world centuries ago when their gods had banished them. It wasn't as if they could claim their land back.

The report continued, showing some distance shots of the island while the presenter lamented the fact that the military restrictions meant they could not fly any closer.

It was close enough that Jake could make out the buildings, and in particular, the spacious palace in the center of the city. Unfortunately, the helicopter was too far away to tell if anyone might be in the buildings.

Jake hoped all the unevacuated mer were safely in the ocean and that the divers in the area had been safely swept away by the rising of the city.

"Could it be that the island has simply remained undiscovered all this time?" the presenter asked.

Jake rolled his eyes as the geologist did likewise on the screen. "Yeah, right, all the satellites up there and you think they somehow missed it?"

"Not seeing it might sound more believable than the truth," Finn pointed out. "Most modern-day people don't even believe Atlantis existed. Now it has risen from the waves again. It doesn't exactly sound likely. And they haven't even found the merpeople yet."

"We hope," Jake muttered. "Once the military gets involved, it's merely a matter of time before the mer are at their mercy. We have to hope any on the island can make it to the sea before they're found."

"We won't let them be discovered," King Nereus said. "I have a duty to protect my people, and I will do whatever is necessary to ensure the survival of each and every one of them."

"There's not much we can do from here," Justin said as he entered the room. Jake saw he had taken a few moments to borrow some clothes and dress. Unlike the rest of the merpeople, Justin had been raised on land and wasn't accustomed to walking around naked.

"I need to return to Atlantis," King Nereus replied. "I won't leave my people to face the humans alone."

"I'm coming with you," Justin said.

"Me, too," added Finn.

King Nereus shook his head. "One of you should stay in this England place to help those who have sought shelter here. This land is strange, and many will find the transition difficult."

Justin and Finn stuck out their chins, both equally stubborn.

"I want to see if I can find Kyle," Finn said. "He was searching for his sister and hasn't made it back."

"Very well," King Nereus said. "Finn, you come and search for your mate. Justin, I'll leave you in charge of rounding up anyone who is in the palace. I'll speak with these humans on their arrival on the island."

Jake coughed pointedly. "You might have difficulty with that. You don't speak English, do you?"

King Nereus frowned. "But you speak mer?"

"Yes, I do," Jake agreed, "thanks to Caspian giving me that knowledge. But I think it's highly unlikely that anyone who lands on the island will. You'll need either Finn or Justin—or someone else with the ability to translate for you."

"Who else speaks mer and English?"

Jake struggled to think who might be able to do so. "Kai and Dax can, thanks to Medina. Lucas and Fabian were given the gift by Caspian, too. Kyle, as well, though Finn would need to track him down first."

"I think Lucas should stay here and help with the refugees," Justin said. "The people love him and respect him. Since the city is now above water, I'll be able to keep my sight, so I don't need him to guide me."

"I'll help Lucas," Jake agreed.

"We're interrupting our coverage of the discovery of this new island to bring you this exciting footage from the island itself from video posted on the Internet earlier today. We can

now take a closer look at the island that might be the mythical Atlantis."

Jake and the others turned their attention back to the television. The screen showed what appeared to be mobile phone footage of two young men, who alternated between talking into the camera and showing their surroundings.

"We're here in Atlantis," the younger of the two men said. His accent was American, but neither of them wore military uniforms. *"I'm Richard and this is Pete, and we're on the west coast of the island. The navy vessel is on the east coast, and while the governments of the world argue about who owns this land, we've decided to come and say hello to the locals."*

The second man poked his head into shot. *"Yes, you heard Rich correctly. This island is already inhabited and we're going to find out by who."*

"How the hell are they getting a signal for their phones out there?" Finn asked. "I can't even get mine to work in the supermarket."

Jake chuckled. "That's because you're technologically challenged."

"They're close to the barracks," King Nereus said. Even without understanding the language, he could follow what was happening on the screen.

The two men entered the building a few moments later.

"Check out these weapons," Pete said as he picked up a trident. *"Wow, this is heavy. No match for guns, of course, but still, it must have taken some strength to fight with one of these."*

Rich picked up a spear and there followed a few shaky shots of the two of them sparring together for fun.

They didn't stay in the barracks for long, quickly leaving and moving toward the palace.

"When we arrived last night, we saw lights in the building ahead," Pete said. *"They didn't last long, but it was enough for us to spot there was someone here."*

"Someone or something," Rich said in a spooky voice. *"Other than a few birds, there's not a single animal on this island. There isn't any vegetation, either. The ground is soaking wet, even though there's been no rain. I don't care what the scientists say, this island has every sign of spending hundreds of years under the ocean."*

"Look there!" Pete interrupted, and the camera angle changed again.

"What is it? What did you see?"

"Someone ran into that building." Pete pointed at the palace.

"Was it a man or a woman?"

"A woman and she was completely naked."

"And you didn't get it on camera?" Rich glared at Pete and they hurried up what used to be the main street.

"I'm going back immediately," King Nereus said as he stalked out of the door.

Finn jumped up. "I'm coming with you."

"Me, too," said Justin.

Jake hugged Finn. "Be careful. Whatever you do, don't get caught by the government."

The footage on the screen came to an end and the reporter reappeared. *"There you have it, the first pictures taken from this new island. We understand that the two men who took the footage are now wanted for questioning. Please call the number on the bottom of the screen if you can help identify them."*

Jake had no idea who they were. He hoped they were decent-enough men who hadn't harmed the merpeople. For their mobile phone footage to have found its way on to the Internet, they must have made it on and off the island without being spotted by the military, who would no doubt be striving to secure the island as soon as possible, making it much more difficult for the merpeople to return to the water.

Chapter Thirteen

When they arrived in Medina's temple on the Isle of the Gods, the goddess was absent.

Even more worrying, the crystal that would take them to her temple in the palace was broken, as was the one to her temple on the main street, though if they'd had used that one, they would have been risking being seen by the watching humans, anyway. From what Medina had said before, it seemed both her temples had been destroyed.

Isander stood in the doorway, looking outside. He didn't appear to have noticed their arrival.

"What's happening out there?" Finn asked.

"The immortals are all congregated in the large meeting place at the top of the hill. It's quiet at the moment, but there have been quite a few bolts fired. There are a lot of very pissed off gods up there."

"Are they all awake now," King Nereus asked.

"I think so," Isander confirmed. "Somehow, the raising of the island has generated enough belief in the immortals to bring the rest of them out of stasis."

"That's probably because the whole world is watching," Justin explained. "A few reporters speculate it might be Atlantis, even if they don't know for sure."

"The whole world knows?" Isander asked. "How is that possible?"

"Modern technology," Justin replied. "It's hard to explain, and we don't have time. We need to get back to the city."

Finn pointed at the crystals. "We need to access a temple in the palace. Can you help us?"

Isander shook his head. "Medina's temple must have been buried in rumble from the collapsing walls when the island rose. The other temples were all under the palace, too. I suspect most are in a similar state, and even if the temple itself survived, it would be impossible to get out."

"Then how can we get to Atlantis while avoiding the cameras?"

"I don't know what a camera is," Isander said.

"They're what the world is using to watch the island," Finn explained. "We don't want to be seen."

King Nereus stepped forward. "I don't care if I'm seen or not. I intend to speak with these humans who seek to claim my city for their own. There must be a way to get back there. If the temples in the palace are inaccessible, what of the ones of our allies on the main street?"

"Father, do you think that's wise?" Justin asked. "The soldiers might shoot you on sight."

King Nereus held his head high. "They can attempt to do so, but they will not succeed."

"Father, your trident is no match for bullets. Sea-fire can't stop them."

"The trident can protect as well as fight," King Nereus said. "It hasn't been required since my great-grandfather's time, but each king is taught how to produce the shield of the gods when he takes the throne. One day, you will learn how to do that, too."

"Are you sure it's safe?" Justin asked. He sounded doubtful, and Finn had to admit he felt equally skeptical about King Nereus' shield.

Bullets were fast and powerful. Did the trident have the ability to shield him from them? It had never been tested before and Finn didn't like the idea of his father relying on this now.

"Cari's temple is probably the nearest one to the palace," Isander suggested as he led them to her home on the island.

Finn breathed a sigh of relief when he saw the crystal Isander approached remained intact.

"You need to make an offering to return from the city," Isander warned them as King Nereus stepped toward the crystal and activated the portal.

Justin walked through first, Finn following behind him, with their father at the rear.

The temple appeared strange from the ground. Finn had swum through it several times in the past and hadn't appreciated how high the ceiling was or how tall the columns were.

The building appeared to be in a poorer condition compared to the last time Finn had seen it. "Are you sure this is Cari's temple?" he asked.

"Yes," Justin replied. "It's been undergoing repairs after part of the building collapsed during one of the quakes. The reinforcements are probably why it has survived the rising at all."

Finn guessed that explained it. There was no time for sightseeing and King Nereus walked out of the temple into the morning sun.

"Maybe we should have made him wear clothes," Justin suggested.

Finn wore a pair of baggy shorts and flip-flops. Looking at the state of the ground, he had a feeling he should have chosen more sensible footwear. He gazed longingly at Justin's sensible trainers.

Justin could pass for another civilian sneaking onto the island, with his jeans and T-shirt combination.

King Nereus, on the other hand, had declined the offer of clothes and Finn had no intention of raising the subject again.

"Where are we going?" Finn asked as he hurried to catch up with his father.

"The pictures on the talking box showed the human vessel was anchored off the east coast, so that is where I intend to go. Which of you wishes to translate for me?"

Finn wanted to search for Kyle, but he knew Justin needed to do his duties as the heir to Atlantis and calm the people who remained. "I'll come with you."

Justin nodded. "I'll try to find out who is here, how many there are and what the interior of the palace is like."

They went their separate ways, Justin racing up the street to the palace, perhaps hoping that if he ran fast enough, he could escape detection.

Finn followed his father in the opposite direction. He had not realized quite how large the environs of the city of Atlantis were. Even though the city itself was only a small part of the original island, they had a long walk to the coast.

The sea was still nowhere in sight when one of the immortals finally decided to appear. Cari stood directly in their path, along with an unfamiliar man.

"King Nereus, I must advise against your current course of action," Cari said.

"What do you know of my intentions?"

"You hope to negotiate with the humans," Cari said. "You believe you can convince them to allow you and your people to leave the island."

"Yes."

"They will not agree to this."

"We haven't even spoken to them yet."

Cari sighed. "I'm the Goddess of Prophecy. I have seen what is to come. You must turn back from this road."

"You aren't always correct in your predictions of the future," King Nereus pointed out.

"Because the future is not a set path," Cari replied. "You'll recall that my Oracles foretold that if Prince Finn were to leave the city, the Atlanteans would return. Your son *has* left the city and Atlanteans are heading this way. The call of the city is too strong to be denied. Two of them have already walked this land today in their quest for the truth about what happened to the land of their ancestors."

"So we saw."

"Then believe me and listen now," Cari begged. "You must leave the city at once."

"I am Nereus, King of Atlantis -"

"You were king of the sunken city," Cari corrected. "The city is no longer at the bottom of the ocean. It is no longer a suitable location for the mer to live."

"I can see that," King Nereus snapped. "Unfortunately, what I can't see is somewhere else we can go, instead. If I speak to the humans in charge, I can try to negotiate the resettlement of my people."

Cari raised her hand to stop their progression. "I can see you are going to need more convincing. Here... Let me show you what the future holds if you continue with your plans."

Finn gasped as the world around him changed. The island vanished and he found himself standing in a strange room with lots of odd instruments.

"This is what humans call a science laboratory," Cari explained.

Finn had guessed as much.

"Take a look around, King Nereus, and after you've seen the type of people you'll be dealing with, you can decide whether it is worth the risk of speaking with the humans."

Finn took a step after his father, but Cari raised her hand to stop him. "You don't need to see through there, Finn."

"Why? What is it?"

"Nothing you should ever have to see."

Finn had to see for himself what was so bad. Even though he knew he should follow Cari's advice, curiosity got the better of him.

When he rounded the corner, he bumped straight into his father, who quickly tried to send him back the way he had come. He wasn't fast enough to stop Finn from seeing what Cari wanted him to avoid.

Finn's own body lay on the lab's table. He was in mer form and his stomach and the top of his tail had been sliced open. Several scientists were cutting him open, studying him and making notes on what they found.

He had no idea how he had died, but from the look of his body, Finn guessed his death was imminent.

His father dragged him, stumbling, back to Cari.

"I tried to warn you, Finn," Cari said.

The world changed again and they found themselves back on the island. Finn collapsed to his knees as his stomach revolted against the sight of his own dead body. His father held his hair out of the way as he vomited, tears streaming down his face.

"I won't let them hurt you," King Nereus assured him.

Finn gave a shaky nod and let his father help him rise. *What are we going to do?*

"Negotiating with such monsters is not an option," King Nereus said. "But how can we evacuate the island when it is already discovered?"

"Can you transport us all to the ocean?" Finn asked.

Cari shook her head. "No, I'm afraid not."

"Why not?"

"My powers were syphoned to raise the city, which means I'm much weaker now than I would normally be."

"I thought raising the city was supposed to increase all your powers?"

"It was, but those of us who opposed the decision to raise the city found that our powers were taken first for that purpose and drained almost completely. As such, it will take longer for them to be restored, even with the boost from the world seeing Atlantis. I could transport the two of you, as I did just now, but not everyone.

There are several hundred mer on this island, and even if we combined the powers of all the immortals who would see you safe, it would not be enough."

"You mean there's nothing you can do to help us?"

"No, I believe my grandfather can assist," Cari said as she gestured to the man beside her. "This is Antar, God of Space and Time. He has the power to stop time for the humans here, to give the mer a chance to escape back into the ocean."

Antar nodded. "My powers are not what they used to be. The time I can give you is limited."

Cari pointed back to the city. "I would suggest you head to the palace, where the remaining mer are gathered, and lead your people back to the water. We'll stay and watch for the humans, and when we see they are too close for your safety, Antar will stop time."

"I'll be able to give you about an hour," Antar said. "I would recommend you hurry."

Finn and King Nereus ran back the way they had come, hoping Antar could give them enough time to get all their people to the water.

* * * *

Kyle's head ached and one of his legs hurt even more. He wondered if he had broken a limb. He couldn't imagine the pain of a bone breaking could be much worse than how he felt right now.

"Kyle? Are you awake?" Lynna's voice came from his right, but he couldn't see her from where he was and he couldn't move.

The room they were in was dark, though he could see pretty well, as all mer could, thanks to their naturally

L.M. Brown

enhanced vision, enabling them to swim in the darkness of the deep oceans.

The wall ahead of Kyle had collapsed, and the doorway was blocked by a heap of rubble outside in the corridor. Even if he could move, they were completely trapped.

"Yes. Are you okay?"

"I think so."

"What about Cian?"

"He's sleeping on my chest. Apparently that earthquake didn't faze him a bit."

Kyle would have laughed, but he hurt too much. "I think it's safe to say that what happened was more than an earthquake. In case you haven't noticed, there's no water in here now, which means the gods did as they said they would and raised the city from the bottom of the ocean."

"Oh, I noticed," Lynna replied sarcastically. "Things were a lot better before all these immortals started waking up. Why couldn't they leave us in peace? We never hurt them. We're peaceful."

"I know, but you have to remember, not all of them want us out of Atlantis. Some wish to help us, they *have* helped us. Without Medina and Caspian, I'd not have two amazing men in my life."

"But the ones who want us to leave seem to be the ones winning this battle," Lynna pointed out. "We mer can't live on land, not and be happy."

"*I'm* happy," Kyle said, "and you could be, too, if you lived in England with me."

"I want to live in the ocean and nothing you can say will ever change my mind."

Kyle could tell Lynna meant every word. His baby sister was all grown up, and whether he liked it or not, he had to let her make her own decisions. "We'll find you somewhere safe to live as soon as we get out of here. I think you have to agree that Atlantis is no longer an option, not for any of the mer."

Lynna sighed loudly. "But if the sunken city is no longer safe, where is?"

"I don't know," Kyle admitted quietly. "The oceans aren't what they used to be."

* * * *

Finn and King Nereus arrived at the palace to find Justin gathering everyone into the king's audience chamber.

"Father?" Justin frowned at him in obvious confusion. "What are you doing back here? I thought you were going to negotiate with the humans."

King Nereus strode into the center of the room. "I have it on the authority of the Goddess of Prophecy that such a course of action will endanger us even more."

"Not us," Finn argued. "*Me.*"

King Nereus shook his head. "It's clear that if the humans were to find out about our existence it will endanger *all* of our people. You might have been the one in the vision, but I have no doubt there would be more. The humans would hunt us down, one by one."

Finn hadn't thought about it like that.

"We need to get everyone off the island and into the water before the humans arrive," King Nereus said.

"What about the cameras watching?" Justin asked. "If a large group of people suddenly disappear into the ocean, even the dimmest reporter will figure out the truth."

"The Goddess of Prophecy and the God of Space and Time are watching the humans. Antar can freeze time for us, but only for an hour."

"An hour?" Justin sucked in his breath through his teeth. "It'll take twice as long just to reach the edge of the island. We'll be spotted by those helicopters before we ever make it to the water."

"What about the tunnels?" Finn asked. "Are any of them still functional?"

Justin shrugged. "I don't know. The ones we've checked have all collapsed, but I know there must be more I'm not familiar with. You probably know of dozens that I've never used."

"I'll go check the ones I know about." Finn took two steps toward the corridor before he remembered he hadn't checked the room for Kyle. He guessed he was more upset by the vision of his possible future than he had thought. A quick glance around the room revealed no sign of Kyle, his sister or her mate.

"Kyle isn't here," Justin said, accurately guessing who he searched for. "We believe there are mer trapped on the floor between this one and the lower ones where the temples are located. If Kyle was trying to get his family to England, chances are, that's where they are."

Finn was torn. He wanted to search for Kyle. He needed to hold him in his arms, but he was one of the few mer who knew where many of the secret passages were located. Delwyn had had an uncanny knack for finding the tunnels, and the two of them had explored them for hours. As a prince, Finn had access to every area of the palace and he had made the most of it.

For the first time Finn understood what it meant to be his father's heir and to put the good of the people before his own needs. Even though Justin would now take over the position of King from their father, Finn had been raised to rule Atlantis.

"I'll be checking the tunnel from the kitchen to the gathering grounds, then the ones leading from the royal family's chambers. If you find Kyle, send word to me."

"I will," Justin assured him.

Finn ran through the palace, wishing he could move as fast as he did when he swam.

The tunnel from the back of the larder in the main kitchen appeared to be in good shape at first. Finn opened the door easily and stepped into the darkness. He quickly navigated his way down the winding tunnel, hope flaring with every step he took. A third of the way into the tunnel he found himself face-to-face with a wall of rock. This route was impassable, and he backtracked, eager to move on to the next tunnel.

Four routes later, and Finn was no further on in finding a way out of the palace. The raising of the city had caused major damage to the foundations of the building. He suspected it was only a matter of time before the entire roof collapsed on top of them. The sooner they got out of there, the better. He needed to find a safe way to lead everyone to the ocean.

When he had run out of tunnels to check from the royal family rooms, he headed to the staff quarters. There weren't as many routes out of that part of the palace, but he hoped one of them might have survived.

The first one was completely inaccessible. The room it was accessed from no longer existed. A heap of stone blocked both the room and the tunnel.

"Prince Finn?"

Finn nearly barreled into the man standing in his path. He didn't recognize him, although he gave off an aura of authority.

"I have a gift for you," the man said.

"What sort of gift?" Finn backed away a little. He wasn't sure whether to trust the stranger or not.

"You can trust me," he said, almost as if he had read Finn's mind. "My name is Andaman and I am the Atlantean God of the Forge."

Finn recognized the name from Delwyn's reports of recent events in Atlantis. "You gave the mer their armor for the battle against Mariana, didn't you?"

"Yes. I have always been a friend of the merpeople and am grateful for their continued acceptance of my gifts. It is what helped me remain in this world when so many of my people slept. But there is no time for such talk. You must lead your people back to the water before the humans discover your presence."

"I know, but the tunnels are all blocked."

"Yes, which is why I've brought you this." Andaman held out a large hammer. "I would recommend the tunnel leading from the kitchens to the gathering grounds will be the quickest to clear. Only twenty yards of the tunnel is blocked. The rest, on both sides, is undamaged."

"It'll take hours to remove the rubble."

"Not with the hammer of the gods," Andaman replied. "Give it a swing on the pile through there."

Finn took the hammer and found it surprisingly light in his hand. He struck the tool on the pile of rocks and watched a huge chunk of it disappear in a cloud of dust. "Whoa, did I do that?"

"You did, indeed," Andaman said. "Now, go clear the route to the sea. The gathering grounds as you call them, were farming lands for the Atlanteans. The fields are currently located about five miles from the ocean. Tell your people to wait at the far end of the tunnel. When you're all there, call out for Antar and he will appear and freeze time for one hour, which should give you all time to reach the water, providing you run."

"What if the humans arrive here before we get everyone through the tunnel?" Finn asked.

"That is why you must hurry."

Andaman vanished, leaving Finn alone with the hammer.

"Well, don't just stand there." Andaman's voice echoed through the corridor and spurred Finn into moving.

Finn raced back through the palace to the kitchens and into the first tunnel he had tried. When he reached the collapsed roof, he swung the hammer at the rock, and like before, the hammer destroyed everything it touched, as though the stones were no more substantial than dust.

He worked his way down the tunnel with ease, occasionally glancing up to check that nothing else was about to fall in on him. Thankfully, all he could see above him was the empty rooms of the floor above. There was nothing left to drop down into the tunnel.

In a relatively short amount of time, Finn had cleared the whole tunnel, and he headed back to the audience chamber to start directing the merpeople towards the way out.

He sent three guards into the tunnel first, warning them not to go out into the open until Antar had declared it safe to do so. Then he headed down to the underground chambers, in search of his father, Justin and most importantly, Kyle.

Justin's report about the floor below appeared to be accurate. The rooms were in a far worse state of repair than those above.

Guards were carefully lifting away stones, trying to gain access to the stairs leading down.

"Here... Let me handle that," Finn called as he pushed his way to the front. He swung the hammer at the stones and they vanished instantly.

Everyone in the room gasped in astonishment and Finn made short work of opening the stairway.

"Kyle?" Finn shouted as he obliterated the last of the rubble. "Lynna? Are you down here?"

No answer came, and Finn hurried along the route that would lead him to Medina's temple. He hoped Kyle hadn't been in the temple when it was destroyed.

Finn hurried around the last corner and discovered the entrance to Medina's temple blocked by another collapsed wall. "Kyle?" he screamed.

"Through here!"

It wasn't Kyle's voice, but the fact that someone had survived down here gave Finn hope that he would find his lover soon.

With a speed that would probably have been dangerous with a regular hammer, Finn quickly cleared the debris and half a dozen merpeople emerged from the room. He directed them back the way he had come, and they left him to continue his search.

This section of the building was in terrible shape and Finn spent considerable time clearing rocks from his path.

He called for Kyle repeatedly until finally he heard the voice he longed for.

"Finn? Is that you?"

"Kyle?"

"Yes, we're through here."

"Who's with you?"

"Lynna and my new nephew."

"Where's Xane?"

"I don't know. We've not seen him since before the city began to rise. His parents refused to leave."

"From what we've seen, only those in the palace weren't swept off the island when it rose. If he wasn't here, he'll be in the ocean with the rest of the mer."

Finn swung his hammer at the pile of rubble separating him and Kyle. A few minutes later, a gap wide enough to crawl through had been opened.

"Come on. Let's get out of here," Finn called.

A few moments later, Lynna emerged with her baby safe in her arms.

Finn pointed the way he had come. "You need to go back that way. Is there anyone else down here besides you and Kyle?"

"We called out, but no one answered until you came."

"Then I suggest we get moving."

Finn peered into the gap, wondering what was keeping Kyle. "Are you coming, Kyle?"

"He's hurt," Lynna replied.

"What?" Finn hurried through the debris and into the next chamber. "Why didn't you say you were injured?"

Kyle struggled to sit up. "I was getting around to it."

"Sure you were," Finn muttered as he dropped to his knees beside Kyle. One look at Kyle's twisted limb told him it was bad.

"I think it's broken," Kyle said.

"I think you're right," Finn replied. "Come on. You can lean on me until we get you to the water."

Kyle made no effort to move. "I'll slow you down. You need to get Lynna and Cian out of here."

Finn glared at Kyle. "If you think I'm leaving you, you can forget it."

"My leg's broken," Kyle argued. "It's not like a sprained ankle. Even leaning on you, it'll hurt to move."

"I know, but it'll hurt you a whole lot more if the humans find you down here."

Kyle paled. "Humans?"

"Atlantis is discovered. There's an American military vessel off the east coast and news cameras watching from the air. We need to get everyone off the island, into the ocean and well away from this place."

"Fuck."

"Yeah, so you see why you're going to have to put up with the pain until you get to the water. Once you have your fins, you'll be fine."

Kyle sighed. "Finn, I need you to get Lynna and my nephew safely to the water."

"We're *all* going to the ocean," Finn insisted.

Kyle grabbed Finn's hand. "Do you love me?"

"You know I do. That's why I've no intention of leaving you here."

"If you love me as much as you say you do, then I want you to take my sister and the babe and get them to safety. Will you do that for me, Finn?"

Finn could barely see through his tears. *How can Kyle ask me to do such a thing as leave him here?*

Kyle struggled to sit up and pulled Finn into his arms. "Take care of Jake for me," he whispered, right before he kissed Finn.

Finn could taste the salt of his tears as Kyle made love to his mouth with his lips and tongue.

By the time they parted, Finn wept without restraint, his heart aching. "I'll come back for you. I swear it."

Kyle opened his mouth, no doubt to argue, but Finn put his finger over Kyle's lips, halting his words of protest.

"I *am* coming back to get you, and you can't stop me. As soon as Lynna and the babe are safe, I'm going to get you out of here."

Finn gave Kyle one last kiss, light and chaste this time, before he hurried back through the opening. He returned a moment later and thrust his hammer into Kyle's hand. "Take this. I hope you don't have to use it though."

Kyle nodded, and Finn left him again.

Lynna stared at Finn as he grabbed her arm and steered her away.

"What about Kyle?" Lynna asked.

"I'm going to come back for him as soon as you're in the water," Finn explained.

"I'm not leaving my brother," Lynna argued.

Finn tugged her to start moving. "You have to think of your son. Now, come on. The sooner we get you to the ocean, the quicker I can come back for Kyle."

The reminder about getting her new baby to safety spurred Lynna into action and they ran through the chambers and corridors.

It didn't take long for them to reach the tunnel leading out to the gathering fields, where the rest of the merpeople waited for the sign to leave.

Finn made his way through to the far end of the tunnel, Lynna close at his heels. He found his father and Justin at the head of the queue.

Justin frowned as Finn approached. "Didn't you find Kyle?"

Finn nodded. "I'm going to go back for him when everyone else is safe. His leg is broken."

"We can only shield you from the humans for a limited amount of time," Cari said as she appeared in front of them. "It should be long enough for everyone to reach the ocean. There won't be time for a return trip."

Finn didn't care whether he was shielded or not. He had no intention of leaving Kyle behind. "Can you help Kyle?" he asked. "Can you heal his leg?"

"I shouldn't," Cari replied.

"I didn't ask whether you *should*. I asked whether you can," Finn snapped.

"Yes, we can," Caspian said as he too appeared.

"Caspian, you know we're not supposed to interfere so directly," Cari scolded.

Caspian glared at his sister. "I don't care. It's not Kyle's fault this has happened. The blame lies entirely at the feet of the immortals. Besides, we're already interfering by doing far more than healing Kyle."

"It's not the same thing," Cari argued. "Antar is using the power he was given to help the mer, just as I use mine and Andaman has used his. You are the God of Justice. Your power is to bring about justice, not to go around healing random mermen. If you help him, you'll be punished. You know the older gods are far stricter than the rest of us when it comes to tampering with fate. If it wasn't for the more pressing issues, they'd have had something to say about your meddling long before now."

"I took a vow to help all mer who come to land. The whole pantheon knows this — or they certainly should by now. Kyle is a merman, on land, who requires assistance. To deny him this would be to break my word."

"You're bending the truth quite a lot there," Cari said. "I'm not sure all the other gods would agree with your interpretation."

"They can disagree if they like. It makes no difference to me. Now, where is Kyle?"

Finn stepped forward. "He's trapped in a chamber near Medina's temple. His leg is broken."

Caspian gave him a grim smile. "I'll go help him."

Cari gestured out at the ocean. "You don't have much time. Look at the clouds. Antar has already started the magic."

Finn looked at where Cari was pointing and saw the clouds building up quicker than he had ever seen before.

"I'll go find Kyle," Caspian said. "Everyone else needs to get ready to run."

"Is it safe to go now?" King Nereus asked after Caspian had vanished.

Cari raised her hand. "One, two, three," she counted under her breath.

Lightning struck out at sea. The wind picked up so quickly that it howled as it blew down the tunnel.

Then it was quiet. Too quiet. The silence was eerie and Finn shivered with unease.

"Run to the water," Cari said. "As fast as you can, run!"

King Nereus, Justin and Finn stepped out of the tunnel and into the open. They stood to the side as they waved the rest of the merpeople past, pointing in the direction of the water.

"Go with Lynna," Justin said.

Finn yearned to linger, to wait for Caspian to return with Kyle, but to do so would be breaking his word to Kyle. He ran with Lynna, taking the squalling baby boy from her arms as they raced through the burned gathering fields, the few untouched sea fruits already beginning to wilt in the air, away from the salt water that nourished them.

There must have been a few hundred merpeople making their way to the sea. Finn wondered how many were already in the ocean, and how many hadn't survived the raising of the island.

The merpeople were so few in number that to lose any was a tragedy. Finn knew many of his people didn't believe in the curse, but he had seen too much to scoff at the idea. *Are we being punished, and if so, what for?*

Chapter Fourteen

Kyle watched Finn disappear through the gap in the rubble. It took every ounce of his willpower not to call him back, telling him he had changed his mind.

He closed his eyes and gripped the hammer Finn had left him. He concentrated on pleasant memories of his two lovers to try to distract himself from the pain.

Then, suddenly, his leg no longer hurt. He opened his eyes to see Caspian towering above him.

"You might want to hurry to the sea," Caspian said.

"Did you fix my leg?" Kyle asked as he scrambled to his feet.

"Yes. You need to head to the tunnel from the kitchens."

"Thank you."

Caspian rolled his eyes. "*Now* someone thanks me. Kyle, listen to me. You need to *run*."

Kyle nodded and hurried past Caspian, hoping he remembered the way to the kitchens. Everything appeared so different traveling on foot.

He ran through the palace, the kitchens and into the tunnel. He couldn't see anyone around.

Kyle rested a few seconds when he reached the open air. At least he was no longer in danger of having a building collapse on him.

"The sea is that way," Caspian said. "What are you standing around here for?"

"I needed to catch my breath," Kyle replied.

"You're a healthy young merman in peak physical condition. Run now and catch your breath later."

Kyle had no intention of arguing. He raced across the land, cursing as he tripped and stumbled on the uneven ground. His bare feet hurt as the sharp stones cut into his soles.

Caspian appeared ahead of him. "My grandfather can't keep time frozen much longer. You only have a few more minutes."

Then suddenly Caspian disappeared. Kyle heard a loud 'fuck' from him, but he hadn't time to worry about what had happened to the god.

It wasn't enough time. No one could run as fast as that. When time began to move, the cameras would almost certainly pick him up, running naked across the island and disappearing into the ocean. The thought spurred him on, even though he knew it wouldn't be enough.

* * * *

Jake had stayed near the television in the kitchen all morning, watching the news channel as they reported from the newly discovered island, while at the same time keeping up a steady supply of meals for his guests.

The two men who had been exploring earlier were identified and taken in for questioning by the military. It seemed they had had their fifteen minutes of fame and now had to pay the price for it.

As Jake watched the news, his worries increased. How in the world were the mer remaining on the island going to escape without being caught on camera?

"We interrupt our interview to bring you breaking news."

Jake drew in a sharp breath as the reporter disappeared from the screen and an aerial view of the island appeared.

"It appears that despite the military presence and the warnings to stay away from the island, yet another person has been spotted on the western side of the land mass. We now go live to our reporter on the scene."

Even from the distance of the helicopter, Jake recognized Kyle immediately. To avoid offending the viewing public, Kyle's privates were pixelated, but there was no hiding the fact that he was completely naked as he raced toward the distant water.

Jake couldn't see anyone else, and the reporter referred to a single man. What had happened to Lynna, the baby and Finn? *Why is Kyle on his own?*

He watched in horror as the news crew changed the camera angle to show a second helicopter swooping down. Even Jake could tell this one belonged to the military.

"Run, Kyle," Jake begged, even though his lover couldn't hear him.

The camera zoomed in, showing a clear view of Kyle's face.

A few moments later Kyle's mobile phone, sitting on the dresser, rang persistently. Jake checked the screen and saw it was Kyle's colleague, Natalie. He ignored the call and switched off the phone.

Back on the television, the two helicopters circled Kyle, one filming while the other appeared to be coming in to land.

With a final burst of speed, Kyle sprinted along the newly created beach and into the water.

By the time the helicopter had landed and the soldiers were on the ground, Kyle had disappeared below the waves, thankfully without showing a trace of his fins.

Jake's own mobile rang, and he saw it was Natalie again. She must have gotten his number from Kyle's employee file, where Kyle had him listed as his emergency contact. He let it go through to the answering service, but when she immediately rang again, he decided to get it over with and answer. He could brazen it out.

"Natalie, what can I do for you?" He kept his voice as polite as possible, while at the same time gritting his teeth.

"Is Kyle with you?" Natalie asked. "Can I talk to him?"

"He's out with Finn at the moment," Jake said. It wasn't entirely a lie. Jake hoped Finn was already in the water and Kyle had gone to join him.

"He's not answering his mobile," Natalie said.

"That's because he left it here," Jake told her. "I'll ask him to give you a ring when he gets in."

"Do you know when that'll be?"

"No. They left before I woke up this morning. I'll get him to call you."

"Do you know where he's gone?"

"No. What's this all about?" Jake didn't even bother to hide his annoyance. *Why can't this woman take a hint?*

"Have you been watching the news?" Natalie asked.

"Some of it, why?"

"Are you watching it at the moment?"

"No, I'm talking to you on the phone," Jake replied sarcastically. "Do you have a point? I've got to leave for work soon."

"Oh, I have a point," Natalie said with a light laugh. "You might want to check the latest news about this mysterious island that appeared, because if I'm not very much mistaken, our friend Kyle is running around that island, stark naked, for the whole world to see."

Jake forced out a laugh that he hoped sounded convincing. "Kyle was here this morning. I assure you, he's not running around some island, naked or otherwise."

"Are you sure about that?" Natalie asked. "Because if it's not him, it seems your man has a twin brother."

Jake sighed impatiently. "I don't have time for this. I'll tell Kyle you called."

He hit the End Call button and crossed his fingers that Natalie wouldn't phone back. Thankfully, she didn't.

Back on the television screen, the news showed a still close-up of Kyle's face. Natalie wouldn't be the only person to have recognized him. It wouldn't be safe for Kyle to return here, not right now, maybe not ever. The risk of him being taken in for questioning was far too great.

Jake's stomach churned as the implications of what had happened hit him. *What the hell are we going to do now?*

* * * *

Kyle caught up with the rest of the merpeople on the way to the caverns.

Finn saw him approach, and after passing Cian to Lynna, he swam back to meet him. Kyle threw his arms around his lover and held him close.

"*Time began to move again before I reached the water,*" Kyle said. "*My face may have been caught on camera.*"

"*That's not all that they'll have caught if it was,*" Finn teased.

"*I'm less worried about being arrested for exposing myself as I am for being outed as a merman,*" Kyle replied. "*What are we going to do?*"

"*Let's get to the caverns first. If the humans start searching the waters for you, we'll have bigger problems than your cock being shown to the world.*"

Kyle agreed, and they quickly joined the rest of the merpeople as they swiftly sought sanctuary in the caves.

Lynna found Xane and his family, who had indeed been swept from the island when it had risen.

Leaving his sister in the safe hands of her mate's family, Kyle and Finn found a small cozy cavern in the network and Finn curled up in Kyle's arms. Kyle knew exactly what Finn needed, because he yearned for the same thing. He wished Jake were with them. He desperately wanted to feel the safety and security of having both of his lovers close by.

"*What are we going to do?*" Finn asked quietly. "*If you've been caught on camera, someone will probably have recognized you already.*"

"*I know.*"

"*We need to get a message to Jake, but I don't know how. We can't go back to the city, which means the only way to return to England is to swim there again.*"

"We can't risk it while they're so many humans watching the island," Kyle pointed out. "They'll be studying the entire island, including the surrounding waters."

"Do you think the gods might help us again?" Finn didn't sound very hopeful, and Kyle didn't blame him. It was thanks to the immortals they were in this predicament to begin with.

"I'm going to try to get some sleep," Kyle said. "I don't know about you, but I didn't get much last night. My leg hurt way too much."

"How is it now?"

"As good as new, thanks to Caspian."

"I'm glad," Finn said as he rested his head on Kyle's chest. "But I would have come back for you, you know?"

"I know," Kyle replied. "After all, you already did come back for me. I know you could have stayed safe in England after the gods raised the island."

"I couldn't leave you there. I love you so much. I loved you from the moment you swam into my father's audience chamber, and I've never stopped. My feelings for you have only grown stronger over the last few years."

"Mine, too. I don't know that I'd survive without you and Jake in my life."

"Me neither. I hope Jake isn't too worried about us."

"He's probably frantic."

Finn grimaced. "What if we can't go home?"

"I don't know, Finn. My home is with you and Jake, so wherever you two go, I'll be there."

"It might be a little difficult if Jake is on land and I'm in the ocean," Finn pointed out.

"We'll find a way. We have to."

Chapter Fifteen

Medina appeared in Jake's bedroom with her usual flurry of robes and perfume.

"I assume you know Kyle has been seen on the island?" Jake asked.

"Yes, but they don't know what he is. I'm sorry. Caspian tried to transport him out of there when time started again, but Mariana stopped him by pulling him off the island with a rather obnoxious summoning spell."

"She did?"

Medina nodded. "Such a spell should only be used in genuine emergencies. Caspian is furious that she prevented him from transporting Kyle to safety. Unfortunately, many of the immortals are angry that Caspian interfered to such an extent at all."

"What happens now? If Kyle comes back here, he'll be taken in for questioning, and it'll only be a matter of time before they figure out he's a merman."

"Yes," Medina agreed. "Cari has had several visions of the future over the last few hours and many of them have included the brutal exposure of the mer."

Jake cringed at the confirmation. "It's not safe for Kyle to return here, is it?"

"No."

"What are my options?" Jake asked as he began to pace the floor again. He suspected he'd be wearing a groove in the carpet soon.

"You need to decide," Medina replied.

"Decide what?"

"How much you love your two men, of course."

"Is this what I need to do to prove I know the meaning of love?"

"Yes."

"Then tell me what to do and I'll do it."

Medina smiled. "Only you can make this choice. I know you'll choose wisely."

Jake wasn't so sure. He didn't want to lose either of his lovers, but was he strong enough to let them go?

When he turned on his heel, Medina had disappeared.

Jake sighed and decided to go talk to Malcolm. Finn's father had been like a surrogate dad to Jake, and he knew he would give him the best advice he could without holding back, even if his words weren't the ones Jake wanted to hear.

Malcolm was rushed off his feet in the sandwich shop and Jake felt a twinge of guilt at leaving him in the lurch.

"You look like you have the weight of the world on your shoulders," Malcolm commented as he served a customer. "What's happened now?"

"You've not been watching the news, have you?" Jake asked. If he had, Malcolm wouldn't need to ask what the problem was.

"No. I barely had time to grab a coffee this morning. What have I missed?"

"You've not seen the news?" the customer on the other side of the counter asked. "A whole new island has been discovered in the middle of the Atlantic Ocean. It's been on all the news channels."

Malcolm gasped and stared at Jake. With the customer listening intently, Jake was limited on what he could say. Alex, at the other end of the counter, looked at them questioningly.

"Can I borrow Malcolm for a bit?" Jake asked.

Alex shrugged. "Sure. It's pretty quiet at the moment. But don't forget you already owe me for working on my day off."

Jake grinned and steered Malcolm into the house at the back of the shop. "I won't forget with you reminding me," he called back.

Once they were alone, Jake sat beside Malcolm. "The gods raised Atlantis from the bottom of the ocean."

"I take it from the influx of mermaids in your house yesterday that you had advance warning of this?"

Jake nodded. "Yes, but not enough to get everyone out of the city. Kyle was there with his sister when the island was lifted from the ocean floor."

"Is he all right?" Malcolm asked. "What about Finn?"

"Finn was here at the time, but he went back to Atlantis this morning to find Kyle. The island is all over the news and so is Kyle. He was filmed running from the city to the ocean."

"Did the cameras pick up his fins when he entered the water?"

236

"No, thank goodness, but it's not going to be safe for him to come back here. I've already had one of his work colleagues phone to ask to speak to him. She'd obviously seen the news and was trying to figure out whether it was Kyle or not."

"You think it'll be safer for Kyle to stay in the ocean, don't you?"

Jake struggled to speak. "Yes. The thought of losing him kills me, but I'd rather him be safe in the water than in some government laboratory."

"You watch too much television," Malcolm teased, "but I can't blame you for being cautious."

"I won't risk Kyle's life, even if it means losing him."

"But you wouldn't just be losing Kyle, would you?" Malcolm said. "You're here because you believe Finn will stay with him, don't you?"

Jake hadn't even wanted to say the words, but Malcolm was absolutely right. "Finn can still return here, but he won't leave Kyle alone."

"Are you sure about that?" Malcolm asked. "He might choose to come back to you instead."

"Finn's a merman. He belongs in the sea and we both know it. He and Kyle might have made a life for themselves on land, but they've never truly become part of this world."

"They've stayed here for you," Malcolm said quietly.

"And you and the rest of the family," Jake added.

"But mainly for you," Malcolm insisted. "Finn adores you and so does Kyle. I have no doubt they are on their way back to you, even as we speak."

"That's what worries me," Jake replied.

"There isn't much you can do to stop them," Malcolm pointed out.

"I could ask one of the immortals to warn them not to return," Jake said. "I'm sure Medina would pass on my message if I asked her to. But I don't know if that's the right thing to do, and it isn't only me who would miss them. You and Coral would be losing a son, and Alex would lose his brother."

Malcolm took hold of Jake's hand and squeezed it tight. "I never thought I'd be reunited with Finn at all. To have had him for even this short amount of time has been more than I ever hoped for. Yes, I'd miss him, but it's not as though he'd be dead. He could return to visit, as could Kyle, when things have died down."

Jake hung his head. "But I don't want them for just a visit. I know I'm being selfish, but I want to keep them in my life."

"You're not being selfish," Malcolm assured him. "You love them, so of course you want them to stay here."

"There's something else, too."

"What's that?"

"Recently I agreed to become one of Medina's priests, so she could generate enough power to wipe the memories of some of Kyle's work colleagues who had seen him and Finn in their merman forms."

"They were exposed?"

"Yes. It was an accident. Medina fixed everything, but I found out the price of her help later."

"And what is that price?"

"I have to prove I know the meaning of love or I lose the ability to love forever."

Malcolm chuckled. "I'm fairly sure no one could ever doubt you know what love is."

Jake grimaced. "Medina told me I have to prove my love by making the right choice now."

"I know you'll make the correct one."

"That's what she said, but what is the right choice? If I selfishly keep them here, it could be dangerous for Kyle, and I might lose the ability to love them at all."

Malcolm shook his head firmly. "No one can stop you loving your men, but if you give them up, you'll end up with a broken heart, from which you may never recover. Have you thought that maybe that is what Medina meant?"

"I hadn't thought about it that way," Jake admitted. "So you think I shouldn't give them up?"

"I think you'll find a way to be with them, even if it means leaving us again. After all, you *are* Atlantean, which means you can survive underwater, just as safely as your mermen can."

"I'm not sure I'm a good enough swimmer to live at the bottom of the ocean. I get tired doing laps in the pool."

"You'd manage, and Kyle and Finn would help you. It's at least an option to consider."

"Yes, it is," Jake replied quietly. He hadn't even thought of the possibility of living in the ocean with his lovers. Atlantis might be off limits to him, but since that city was equally unsuitable for the merpeople now, maybe he could live underwater.

With a whole new dilemma to mull over, Jake thanked Malcolm for his advice and returned home.

* * * *

Kyle woke early, having spent a restless night in the cavern. He hadn't realized how spoiled he had been during his time in England. He missed having a comfortable bed and the warm body of his human lover beside him.

Finn had been equally fidgety all night, his fins flipping this way and that as he tossed and turned.

The sounds of movements outside their nook woke Finn, and the two of them emerged, wondering what the new day would bring.

King Nereus had declared they should allow some time for any mer who had been caught in the tidal wave to swim to the caverns. Unfortunately, they couldn't wait forever, because the humans were far too close for the safety of the mer.

Kyle swam to the back of the gathering crowd with Finn at his side.

King Nereus hovered in the center of the group. Justin and Lucas were at his side. A few of the nearby mer stared at Finn, clearly wondering why he didn't take his place by the king's side, too.

Kyle wrapped his arm around Finn's waist and kissed him on the cheek. *"You can go stand at your father's side if you want."*

"I don't," Finn replied sharply. *"I never wanted to be a prince and it's bad enough with everyone calling me Your Highness again. The sooner we're on our way back to Jake, the better."*

Kyle smiled. *"We'll be home before you know it."*

"I hope so. I don't know what I miss more, Jake or our bed."

Kyle chuckled. *"After last night, I'd say definitely the bed."*

"I'll tell him you said that," Finn teased.

King Nereus stared straight at them and Kyle remembered the ruler of Atlantis could read the thoughts of every mer person who had sworn allegiance to him and Atlantis. The king was the one man in the cavern who could tell they weren't listening to what he had to say.

"*Atlantis is no longer a suitable home for us,*" King Nereus said. "*The guards have reported that the island is completely surrounded and there are divers searching the waters on every side. We don't know if they are searching for us or studying the island itself. Either way, these caves are too close to the humans, so we must leave immediately, before we are discovered.*"

"*Where are we to go to?*" someone asked.

"*As you know, the most vulnerable of our community are safe in the land of humans. This includes the Oracles, who are, as you know, blind when they are in their mer forms. While in England, they were most aware of how important their visions are and stayed in their mer forms as much as possible. Before I returned here, Ula was gifted with a vision of our future home. It is located on the other side of the world, in the largest body of water on this planet. We will swim south, then west, until we find the place Ula saw.*"

"*How will we know when we arrive, if the Oracles aren't here to tell us?*"

A bright glow of white light appeared beside the king. A moment later, Cari appeared.

"*I will guide you on your journey,*" the Goddess of Prophecy said. "*I, too, have seen your new home and will help ensure you reach it safely.*"

"*We leave today,*" King Nereus announced.

Kyle glanced at Finn. The plan for their people was to go in the opposite direction to where they needed to head, if they intended to return to Jake. It seemed they must part company with the rest of the merpeople sooner than expected.

As the rest of the crowd dispersed to gather their belongings, Finn and Kyle swam over to the king.

"*Father, I think you know what I'm going to say.*"

King Nereus sighed. *"Yes, Finn. You and Kyle intend to swim back to your home in England, don't you?"*

Finn nodded. *"Our place is there now."*

Cari raised her hand to interrupt Kyle's own words. *"Kyle, before you make your decision, there's something you must know."*

"What is it?" Kyle asked.

"When you ran for the water, you were caught on the human cameras. Your face has been shown throughout the world."

It was exactly what Kyle had feared.

"I would suggest you travel with the rest of your people to your new home."

"What about Jake?" Finn asked. *"He'll be worried about us."*

"Jake is well aware of the danger posed to Kyle, and to you, by association, if Kyle were to return to England too soon. It will take quite some time for you to reach the caves in the southern waters of the Pacific. Perhaps, by then, it might be safer for the two of you to travel back to England."

Kyle nodded. *"It seems we have no choice. Can you tell Jake what we're planning on doing?"*

"Of course." Cari vanished, leaving Kyle and Finn to begin what would surely be a long journey to an ocean where even Kyle, who had lived a nomadic life until traveling to Atlantis, had never swum.

* * * *

Caspian tapped his foot impatiently as Jake rounded up all the merpeople who had taken up residence in his home. The god apparently had an announcement to make and was eager to get on with it.

When everyone had been assembled in the pool room, Caspian shouted for silence.

"I bring you news of the rest of your people," the god said. "They have now begun their journey to what will be the new home of the merpeople of Atlantis. Jake, I know you're concerned about Kyle and Finn, and I assure you they are safe and traveling with the rest of their people."

Jake inclined his head to acknowledge he had heard. He'd suspected that might be the case, but it still hurt to hear that his lovers had chosen not to return to him. He didn't blame them at all and knew they had made the right decision, but his life was lonely without them.

"The journey will take four-to-five months," Caspian continued. "They travel through dangerous waters and have no wish for you, the most vulnerable of the community, to share those dangers. It is therefore decided that you will all remain here until the rest of your people have reached your new home. The gods who are allies will then transport those of you who wish to return the ocean. Anyone who wishes to stay on land will be given the opportunity to do so, but I suspect most of you are eager to return to the waters."

All around him the mer nodded and voiced their agreement.

"Can I ask a question?" Jake asked.

"What is it?"

"Why not have Medina or one of the other gods build a new temple in the colony? The mer could travel that way and any who find their families split between the land and the ocean could visit back and forth with ease."

"Like your own."

"Well, yes, and any others," Jake said. "In light of Kyle's exposure to humans, it would be too dangerous for him to come back here permanently, but I'm sure he and Finn would welcome the opportunity to visit."

Caspian gave a grim smile. "No doubt they would. However, each time a crystal portal is activated, it acts as a beacon to every other immortal. While this one here on land isn't likely to draw in Mariana and her sea dragons, any on the floor of the ocean are. The fact that the dragons set out to destroy the mer harvests during the evacuation tells us that it isn't just about Atlantis for that particular goddess. While the new colony is a great distance away from the location of the formerly sunken city, sea dragons can cover the distance in a fraction of the time to the merpeople. Keeping the new colony secure is our first priority, and the fewer who know the exact location, the better."

"How do you know the sea dragons aren't already on their way to the colony?" a mermaid with a youngster at her hip asked.

"We're monitoring them closely," Caspian assured her. "They remain in the Atlantic and relatively close to Atlantis. They are currently tormenting the human explorers for their own amusement."

"I haven't seen any reports of that on the news," Jake commented.

"That's because they at least have the sense to remain invisible while they're doing so."

Jake nodded and tried to quell his disappointment in not having an easy way to maintain his relationship with Kyle and Finn, while staying here in England. He knew they would be equally frustrated, Finn especially, since the rest of his family was here in England, too.

"I'll return when we're ready to move you back to the waters," Caspian said. "If you need anything in the meantime, speak to Jake."

Jake raised his hand, in case there was anyone present who didn't yet know who he was.

Most of the mer appeared quite relieved to hear that they wouldn't have to stay on land forever.

Caspian waved Jake to one side as the mer returned to whatever they had been doing before the god's arrival. "I sense you have something you wish to ask me?"

"Yes. I want to know whether I can truly survive under the ocean at great depths."

"I see no reason why you can't," Caspian replied. "The gift bestowed on all the Atlanteans was hereditary, and no matter the number of generations between you and those who first swam the oceans, the magic should work exactly the same way."

"Then I could live in the ocean with Kyle and Finn?"

"If you wished, but I don't think you'd be happy there."

"I'd be happy as long as I had Kyle and Finn at my side."

Caspian rolled his eyes. "Spare me from the sappiness."

Jake flushed and Caspian vanished from the room. He supposed at least he had the answer to his question.

He had no idea what the hell he would do on the bottom of the ocean, but no doubt Kyle and Finn would be happy to show him the ropes, just as he had introduced them to the world of humans.

Chapter Sixteen

Jake should have known Natalie wouldn't give up her quest to track down Kyle. Two days after the raising of Atlantis, she arrived on his doorstep.

"I want to speak to Kyle," she stated as soon as Jake opened the front door, cautiously, in case a naked mermaid passed by at precisely the wrong moment.

"He's not here. I told you he'd been called out of town on a family emergency." Jake considered shutting the door in her face, but she seemed to anticipate his move and put her foot in the way.

"I've been calling his mobile for two days. He's not answering."

"That's because he left it here," Jake said. "I'll have him call you as soon as he's back home."

"That's not good enough," Natalie argued. "I need to speak to him on a matter of vital importance. You *must* have a contact number for him."

Jake sighed, stepped out onto the stoop and closed the front door behind him. "What could *possibly* be so urgent you need to bother him at such a time?"

"I'm afraid that's confidential."

"Confidential and urgent?" Jake snorted and rolled his eyes. "You work at an aquarium and Kyle's current job description is pretending to be a merman. I'm sure you can manage without him for a few more days."

Natalie brightened considerably. "Then he'll be back before the end of the week?"

Jake cursed his bad choice of words. "I doubt it."

"But you said a few more days," Natalie pointed out. "That would imply that he'll be back very soon."

"I don't know when he'll be back, but he said he'd call before the weekend and let me have a number to contact him on." Jake crossed his fingers behind his back as he lied through his teeth. Maybe he could get one of the immortals to help out by getting Kyle to a phone somewhere. "I'll ask him to contact you as soon as I speak to him."

"We need him back at work," Natalie insisted. "No one else can wear the fish tail. It was custom made for Kyle."

"Well, Kyle's not here," Jake snapped. "Now if you'll excuse me, I'm very busy right now."

Without giving her chance to argue further, Jake went back inside the house. He hoped they could find some method of getting Kyle to a phone soon, because he could tell Natalie wasn't going to give up her mission to track him down.

"She is most persistent," Fabian commented when Jake had closed the door behind him. "Is Kyle going to get in trouble at work?"

Jake shrugged as he took Maurissa from Fabian and headed to the kitchen. "I don't think the aquarium is real high in Kyle's priorities at the moment."

Fabian smiled. "I don't imagine it is. I'll ask my aunt if she can put some sort of repellent on the house here. It should keep any unwanted visitors away."

"Can she do that?"

"Yes. She used to use it to keep people away from her temples during private ceremonies. Back when the Atlanteans were a thriving race of people, many would visit the temples in the hope of seeing the gods in person. The immortals were the world's first celebrities."

"And she'd do that for us?"

"I don't see why not. The more people coming here, the more likely it is that the mer will be discovered. It's in everyone's interests to keep them hidden."

Jake hoped Medina could assist with keeping snoops like Natalie away. If she could, it would be one less headache for him, and he could concentrate on more important things, like looking after Kyle's niece and the rest of the refugees.

* * * *

Although he tried to remain a part of the crowd, there was no escaping the fact that everyone from the sunken city still viewed Finn as a prince.

Kyle, armed with a trident, fell into his former position as his bodyguard with ease.

His father appointed a second merman to guard him, as well, for the duration of their journey, much to Finn's annoyance.

"Your Highness, perhaps you might like to stay in the middle of the group," Keshet suggested.

Finn sighed as he swam back where he was told, instead of exploring the shipwreck to the east. *"I can take care of myself,"* he grumbled. *"I've managed perfectly well without a bodyguard since I left the city."*

"I'm sure you have," Keshet agreed. *"But you've been living on land, where the danger from sharks and squids is probably rather minimal."*

Finn didn't bother arguing. Even though Keshet was a guard who had joined the ranks after Finn's departure from the city, their short acquaintance made it clear he was as immovable as every other bodyguard who had been appointed to protect him.

He glanced at Kyle. Or *nearly* every bodyguard, he amended. Kyle had been much more open to the idea of mischief in the form of slipping away for some time alone.

Finn watched Keshet as the guard divided his attention between Finn and another merman who Finn didn't recognize.

"He's very handsome," Finn commented when he caught Keshet gazing longingly at the orange tailed merman again.

"He is, indeed," Keshet agreed.

"Maybe you should approach him," Finn suggested. *"See if he might enjoy what you have to offer?"*

Keshet chuckled. *"Nice try, Your Highness, but I'm not going to neglect my duties."*

"You'd risk losing your chance with him, just to babysit me?"

Keshet smiled and shook his head. *"Gilad and I have been lovers since before we came to the sunken city. I'm not leaving your side until another guard takes over for the next shift. And I doubt you'll want me to encourage my replacement to take over any sooner than necessary."*

"Why?"

"Otus has the next shift."

Finn groaned. Of all the guards to be lumbered with, Otus was the worst. He'd been insufferable as a regular guard, but since the unfortunate death of the leader of the Atlantean guards, he had become even more pompous. It wasn't as if he had been officially appointed to the role, either. From what Finn had heard, he'd taken over without any formal appointment being made, and in the ongoing chaos, no one had bothered to challenge him.

"I didn't think so," Keshet teased. *"Now, are you going to behave, or am I going to have to call Otus to take over watching the unruly prince?"*

"I'll behave," Finn replied. *"You're much better company than Otus."*

Kyle laughed from his other side. *"And here was me thinking I was His Highness' favorite bodyguard."*

Finn smacked Kyle on the shoulder. *"Oh, you're definitely my favorite, but not if you call me that again."*

"Of course, Your Highness."

"Kyle!"

"What's the matter, Your Highness?"

Finn stuck his tongue out as Keshet roared with laughter.

"Poor baby," Kyle teased. *"Come here."*

Kyle pulled Finn into his arms and kissed him softly. Finn whimpered with pleasure as their fins tangled together.

"I hate being a prince," Finn said as they continued swimming, hand in hand. *"I never wanted that, not ever."*

"I know, but no one can help the position they are born to."

"I wish we were swimming the other way, back to England where I'm plain old Finn Mitchell."

Kyle squeezed Finn's fingers, rubbing his thumb over Finn's inner wrist. *"I'm sorry I wasn't quick enough to get to the water without being seen."*

"It wasn't your fault. You couldn't help being injured."

"But if I'd not been caught on camera, we could go home to Jake."

"We'll find a way to return to him. I promise."

Finn nodded, though he didn't know how they could manage such a feat. The sudden appearance of Atlantis was worldwide news. Kyle would be recognized wherever he went.

* * * *

Although many of the merpeople who were staying with him chose to spend a lot of time in the water, Jake noticed that the Oracles were much happier walking around on two legs, enjoying being able to see the world around them.

"Ula, do you have a minute?" Jake asked as he approached the Oracle of the Future and Undine, the Oracle of the Past. They were giggling like a pair of teenagers over one of the magazines Summer had left in the living room the previous week. Jake knew neither of the Oracles could read English, but apparently the fashion disasters on the red carpet needed no translation.

Ula looked up from the article and nodded. "What can I do for you?"

"I was wondering whether you might have had a vision of the future of myself and Kyle and Finn."

Ula sighed. "I'm sorry, but I can only have visions when I'm in my mermaid form. With the increase in our powers in recent weeks, I'm rather relieved to take a break from them."

Jake couldn't say he blamed her. "That's okay. I just thought I'd ask. I guess I'm worried that our futures no longer coincide."

Ula patted his hand consolingly. "I have had many visions of Prince Finn, and I have never seen him happier than when he is with you and Kyle. I don't need to see the future to know you three are meant to be together."

"That doesn't necessarily mean we will be," Jake pointed out. "Look at Marin for the proof of that. From what everyone has said, he and Calder were perfect for each other, but fate has torn them apart."

Ula gazed out the window to where Marin sat, alone with his thoughts in the garden. "Sometimes I truly *hate* my visions. Especially when, with all the power I have, I can't save someone as strong, kind and loving as Calder. I consider myself blessed to have known such a merman, and my heart breaks for Marin."

Undine nodded, her eyes watery. "The Goddess of Sea Creatures has a lot to answer for. She should be protecting the merpeople, not bringing about our demise."

Jake hadn't gotten the answers he wanted, but the Oracles *had* helped him. They had made him see that there were worse fates than being separated from his lovers by distance.

Leaving the two mermaids to chuckle over the magazine once more, Jake walked outside to see if he could take his mind off his own problems by helping Marin. It also had the added benefit of getting him out of the house and away from all the inhabitants who spent way too much time thinking about love and sex, thoughts that resounded in Jake's mind all too often, despite his best efforts to shut them out.

"Mind if I join you?" Jake asked.

"If you like," Marin replied with a shrug.

"How are you holding up?"

Marin sighed. "It's too crowded in there for me to risk training with the trident. Every room in the house is filled. Since I can't practice, I'm going out of my mind with boredom, when all I want to do is swim right back to Atlantis and kill that murdering bastard."

"I doubt the sea dragons are on the island now," Jake pointed out.

"I don't care where they are. I'll swim every body of water on this planet until I find him."

"Is that what Calder would have wanted you to do?" Jake asked.

Marin glared at him. "You never even met him, so don't you dare tell me what he would have wanted."

Jake held up his hands in a gesture of surrender. "I'm sorry. I'm not trying to change your mind or anything. If it had been Finn or Kyle, I've no doubt I'd want to tear apart whoever was responsible."

Marin stood and stared down at Jake. "One way or another, I'm going to return to the ocean and track him down, and not even those gods who think they can control our lives will stop me."

Jake believed him. There was a steely determination in Marin's eyes. Shame washed over Jake again at the strength he saw in the young merman before him.

"I'll help you, if I can," Jake offered.

"Thank you," Marin replied. "I may take you up on that offer."

Jake rose and held out his hand to Marin, who shook it briefly.

When Marin had returned to the house, Jake lingered in the garden a little longer, walking the paths as he searched his soul for answers. The arrival of Caspian, who had never been one for frequent house calls, worried him more than he wanted to admit.

"Marin is not to return to the ocean," Caspian declared without preamble.

"Isn't that his choice?" Jake asked. "Everyone else here is going to be able to choose whether to stay on land or go join the rest of the merpeople. What makes Marin so special?"

"If Marin returns to the ocean, he'll swim right for Atlantis, where he'll die at the hands of Calder's murderer," Caspian said. "My sister Cari has seen his future and if he continues to seek his revenge, his life will be woefully short."

"He wants justice for Calder's murder," Jake said. "You're supposed to be God of Justice. Why aren't you helping him?"

"I'm *helping* him by keeping him alive," Caspian snapped. "And if you care about him, you'll discourage him from this suicide mission he seems determined to go on."

Caspian vanished, leaving Jake staring at an empty space.

"You'll have to forgive my brother," Cari said.

Jake spun around, swearing under his breath at the way these immortals kept popping in unannounced.

"He took a vow to help all of the merpeople who come to land. Unfortunately, his way of helping Marin isn't want Marin wants."

"Is Marin really going to die if he goes after Urion?"

"Yes."

"Is there any way to change what will happen? If Marin knew beforehand where the attack came from, he might be able to avoid it."

"Fate cannot be avoided."

"Then why try to keep him on land?" Jake asked. "Isn't that the same thing?"

"Yes, it is," Cari agreed. "But I'm not the one trying to alter the future. That would be my brother."

"Why?"

"Because he's stubborn as a mule," Cari muttered, right before she vanished into thin air too.

"Immortals," Jake muttered. All he needed was Medina dropping in with some more bad news, and right now he didn't think he could take much more.

Deciding to stay outside for a little longer to enjoy the peace and quiet, Jake sat back down and tried to concentrate on blocking out the voices in his head. Maybe he should try to make the house a sex-free zone, ban the lot of them from any form of intimacy. Perhaps then he might get a few minutes alone with his thoughts.

Chapter Seventeen

The luminescent foliage lining the outside of the caverns could be seen from a mile away.

"Is that it?" Lynna asked.

Kyle nodded. *"I think so. It's as Cari described it."*

"It looks rather exposed," Lynna said. *"Not safe like the sunken city was."*

"Compared to an invisible city, everything is exposed," Kyle replied. *"We'll be doing what we can to secure the safety of everyone in the colony."*

"I know." Lynna sighed. *"I thought once we'd arrived in the sunken city, we'd not have to be swimming all over again, especially not with a new baby."*

"At least we're nearly there," Kyle told her, *"which means you'll be reunited with Maurissa again."*

"I hope she's well."

"I'm sure she is. Jake wouldn't let anything happen to her."

"You trust him?"

"Of course. He'll be treating Maurissa like she's his own family, because in a way, she is."

King Nereus gathered everyone together at the edge of the caverns. "*Guards, I want you to search the caves, clear out anything dangerous and report back here once the area has been secured.*"

Kyle swam forward to join the guards, but King Nereus halted him. "*You and the other bodyguards are to stay here. You're needed to protect the rest of the mer while we're exposed.*"

Kyle nodded and, along with the rest of the bodyguards, took up a position around the edge of the group of mer. Finn stuck close to his side.

"*What are we going to do now that we're here?*" Finn asked. "*Do you think it's safe to return to England?*"

"*I don't know. I wish I did.*"

"*I miss Jake.*"

"*I know, baby, so do I.*"

"*What if it's still not safe to go back?*"

"*Then I'll stay here with the colony,*" Kyle said.

Finn wrapped his arms around Kyle's waist and rested his head on his lover's chest. They hadn't been to land once during their journey to the new colony. King Nereus hadn't believed it safe to swim to islands unnecessarily. Finn hoped they could make up for lost time soon.

"*What about you?*" Kyle asked. "*What have you decided?*"

"*I haven't,*" Finn admitted. "*I love you both so much. How can I be expected to choose between you? I can't even split my time between the two of you because we're so far away from England now.*"

"*I'm not sure any of us would be happy with that arrangement,*" Kyle admitted. "*Despite our problems, we are a ménage, and I only feel completely content when I'm with the both of you.*"

"*Me, too.*"

Kyle hugged Finn close, ignoring the occasional stares from the rest of the mer. Sometimes he forgot that it was so recently that the laws of the mer of Atlantis had been changed to allow them to love openly.

"*I don't want to leave you,*" Finn said.

Kyle stroked his hand down Finn's spine. He didn't want Finn to leave him, either, but he felt saying so would be selfish. If Finn had to choose, Kyle couldn't bear to make it harder for him.

"*I'll think about what I'm going to do after the solstice,*" Finn said. "*If I'm swimming back to England, the last thing I want is to be stuck in the middle of nowhere with no land in sight when the mating fever arrives.*"

"*If you're swimming back to England, I'm coming with you,*" Kyle replied. "*I may not be able to go to land, but there's no way I'm letting you make the journey alone.*"

"*You don't have to do that.*"

"*I'm your bodyguard,*" Kyle reminded him. "*And we both know the king would never let you leave alone.*"

"*I know. Oh, Kyle, how did we get in such a mess?*"

Kyle felt guilt wash over him. *He* was the reason Finn was in this predicament. If he hadn't hurt his leg, he'd have been with the others, safely in the ocean, instead of getting caught on camera and ruining all their lives.

The spent their waiting time talking and swimming around an area that Kyle felt was much too confining. It took several hours for the guards to confirm the caverns were safe, after which the rest of the mer slowly made their way to the main entrance.

The guards put up thick netting across the large entrance. It wouldn't keep out the biggest and most dangerous of predators, but it would slow them down until the guards could send them on their way. They would need at least three guards on the entrance at all times.

Kyle stared about the large cavern, brightly lit with the fluorescent plants, and saw many tunnels off the main room. It didn't seem very comfortable, but he had certainly lived in worse during his nomadic life before seeking sanctuary in Atlantis. Finn, on the other hand, had rarely lived in such conditions. Raised in Atlantis, he had then swum to England where they had the luxury of human houses and furniture. The journey to the colony had been the longest and harshest of Finn's life, not that his young lover had uttered a word of complaint.

"There are larger caverns over there," one of the guards who had searched the place said. *"One might be suitable for an audience chamber, and the others off that one for the royal residences."*

"Shall we take a look, boys?" King Nereus asked.

Justin snorted. *"Somehow I suspect this time I'm not going to be missing much while I'm blind."*

Finn patted Justin's arm. *"One cave is pretty much like another, I guess."*

Justin nodded. Until the evacuation of Atlantis, he had pretended to be blind on land, so no one knew he was actually blind because he was part Oracle. Now that secret had been revealed, as well, and he was being treated as reverently as Cari's serving Oracles, who were safe in England at the moment. Finn had confided in Kyle that he was pretty sure Justin was as frustrated with the attention as Finn himself. Neither of them truly relished being heirs to Atlantis, though they both did their duties these days.

Looking around the cavern, Kyle wondered what King Nereus would do now. Still a leader, the King of Atlantis could no longer call that city his home.

"*Come on,*" Finn urged. "*I'm tired. Let's find somewhere quiet and get some sleep.*"

Kyle could see that no one was standing on ceremony and many of the mer had already disappeared into the network of caves. He took Finn's hand and they followed their example, eventually finding a cozy little cave where they could curl up together.

"*Tomorrow we look for a sponge bed,*" Finn said.

Kyle laughed. "*You can go look for one if you like. I intend to sleep for at least a week.*"

Finn chuckled and burrowed closer to Kyle. "*I love you.*"

"*I love you, too.*"

* * * *

Finn heard the chattering and caught his name, but he couldn't see who was talking in the cave next door. Whoever it was, they were making no effort to keep their conversation private and probably didn't know the subject of their gossip was so close.

The mer had been in the cavern for a couple of days now. Everyone had been working hard to make the place secure and safe, so their families could join them. Finn knew his time to make a decision was running out. He thought he had considered every aspect of his life, but the discussion next door, clearly not meant to be heard by him, highlighted something he hadn't even considered.

"*I'll bet the king won't let him on land again,*" one of the mermen said.

"He lets Prince Justin go to land."

"Prince Justin was married in the Goddess of Love's temple. Prince Finn and his bodyguard aren't joined in any way. I heard they refuse to be officially bound together because they have another lover."

"Still, the king won't let him suffer through the mating season without relief."

"I heard he did before."

"Where did you hear that?"

"One of the guards told me after Prince Finn disappeared. Apparently, that was why he left. His father had demanded he remain untouched."

Finn sighed as he realized his ears should have been burning quite a lot following his departure to England. He had been forbidden from going to land, but his mother had been the main one holding him prisoner, and she'd had good reason to do so.

Still, his father had always expressed a wish for Finn to be officially joined to a mermaid. Obviously, that was out of the question, but would his father want him and Kyle to make things official before they were allowed to go to land?

Finn didn't know where the mermen had heard about Jake, but neither he nor Kyle had exactly kept it a secret. They hadn't actually discussed any form of marriage or bonding, even though Medina had indicated that, in her temples, the union could involve all three of them. Whether they made things official or not, Finn had no intention to doing so without all three of them being present and in agreement. He had no idea when they would see Jake again, but he didn't want Jake to rejoin them to find they had taken such a huge step without him.

No, we aren't going to be making anything official, no matter how much my father might wish it otherwise.

He hoped the king wouldn't try to stop him from going to land during the mating season. If he did, he was in for a nasty surprise, because Finn had every intention of going to land and helping Kyle break his fever. He hoped they could find somewhere secluded and private so Kyle could return the favor.

There was only one way to find out what his father's opinion on the mating season was. Finn would have to talk to him.

King Nereus was in his chamber which, while one of the larger caverns, was still a hovel compared to the luxuriousness of the palace.

"*Father, do you have a moment?*" Finn asked as he hovered in the doorway.

"*For my favorite son, of course.*" King Nereus waved him in and directed him to the newly installed sponges.

Finn smiled and took a seat. "*I bet you say that to all your sons,*" he teased, in a way he would never have dared a few years ago.

"*You've caught me,*" his father replied. "*Now, what can I do for you?*"

"*I wanted to talk to you about the mating season,*" Finn said. "*It'll be here in a couple of weeks.*"

"*Yes, I know. Our scouts have been swimming in the area to check for land that is safe for the mer to go to.*"

"*Have they found any?*"

"*There aren't as many islands in the area as there were around Atlantis, but there are a few possibilities. There is one island a few miles away that appears to have been discovered by men but is uninhabited at the moment. There are also a few more that are completely deserted, but almost twice as far away.*"

"*Do we want to risk the one that men have been to?*" Finn asked.

"I think if we keep a close eye on it, the island may serve our purpose, at least for this first season. If it appears humans are returning there, we'll have to look to the other islands."

Finn chewed on his lip as he worked up the courage to ask the question he really wanted an answer to.

"There's something else, isn't there?" his father asked.

Finn nodded. *"I was wondering what your thoughts are about me going to land with Kyle during the mating season."*

King Nereus chuckled. *"I try not to think about what my sons get up to with their lovers."*

"That's not what I meant. It's just, well, you know, before..." Finn struggled to find the right words, ones that wouldn't offend the man sitting across from him. *"I wasn't allowed on land, and I wasn't sure whether I would be now."*

Finn's father reached over and took his hand. *"I'm so sorry for what your mother and I put you through. We should never have held you prisoner in the city. Of course, you may go to land with Kyle. I can't tell you how sorry I am that you even have to ask."*

At his father's words, Finn realized he didn't know *why* his mother had been so insistent Finn remain in the water. Having discovered his father could read his mind whenever he wanted to, Finn had assumed he knew the truth about that, too. Apparently, he was wrong.

"You really don't read your subjects' minds, do you?" Finn asked. *"You didn't read Mama's mind?"*

"No. Like I told you before, I try to avoid prying. Your mother's mind was probably the most tempting for me to look into, but I resisted, probably out of fear of what I might discover. Had I done so, I'd have discovered the truth about your paternity long before I did."

Finn nodded. *"You'd have found out something else, too."*

"What do you mean?"

"You'll remember I have a twin brother, Alex?"

"Yes. What of him?"

"He was born with legs and couldn't take mer form until his twenty-first birthday. That's why he lived on land."

"Ah. I did wonder why your mother left one of her children when she must have known bringing me two sons would have been a cause for a double celebration."

"He couldn't survive in the water," Finn said. "And I couldn't have lived on land, because I was his opposite."

"What do you mean?"

"Mama took me to land right before Kyle was banished. I had no human form."

King Nereus moved to sit beside Finn and pulled him into a warm hug. "Oh, Finn, I had no idea."

"Me, neither," Finn replied. "But I found my legs at the same time Alex found his fins. Mama didn't mean to be cruel by keeping me in the water. She did it because she thought it for the best."

"I'm glad you told me," King Nereus said. "And I'm pleased you have your human form now. You have my blessing to go to land with Kyle. I hope that one day you, Kyle and Jake might make things official."

"Thank you, Father."

With his mind eased, Finn left the cavern and went to track down Kyle. It didn't need to be the mating season for Finn to want his lover in his arms.

Despite his joy at being treated like any other merman, there was one thing that did bother Finn, and that was his mating trigger. He had found it hard enough to admit to his lovers what it was he needed to break his mating fever. Over time he had become more comfortable with expressing his needs, and had even confided in Justin's partner, Lucas, that his trigger was being spanked on the arse by one of his lovers.

In the privacy of the bedroom, Finn had no hesitation in bending over the knee of one of his lovers, usually Jake's, as he eagerly anticipated the sharp sting of the slap of a paddle or a hand on his flesh.

The problem now was that there weren't going to be any bedrooms on whatever island they swam to. Anyone in the vicinity would be able to see and hear what they did, just as Finn and Kyle would be able to see the others. The thought made him cringe.

Finn spotted Lucas helping Justin learn his way around the new caverns. As a sightless merman, Justin had to be finding things difficult as they settled into their new home.

"Lucas, do you have a minute?" Finn called as he swam up to them.

"Of course, Finn, what's the matter?" Lucas, while he wasn't a prince himself, was, by virtue of his marriage to Justin, a member of the family and one of the few merpeople in the community who didn't call Finn by his title.

"Um, I wanted to talk to you about something we spoke of when you visited England."

"Yes?"

"Privately," Finn clarified, with a nod toward Justin. Finn wanted to make sure that Lucas would keep their conversation private, as Finn himself was doing. When communicating telepathically, as the mer did when underwater, it was far too easy to forget to direct thoughts to one person instead of anyone in the vicinity. Justin, who had lived most of his life on land, still sometimes struggled with this, much to his embarrassment, particularly when he sent some of his more intimate thoughts to Lucas during a family meal, only to have everyone in the cave hear him.

"*Of course,*" Lucas replied.

"*Do you remember when we talked about triggers?*" Finn asked.

Lucas nodded. "*Yes. What about it?*"

"*Have you told anyone what mine is?*"

"*No.*"

"*Not even Justin?*"

Lucas smiled. "*I swear on my life that I've not spoken to anyone about what you told me.*"

Finn breathed a sigh of relief.

"*What's the problem?*" Lucas asked. "*You were pretty open about what you need when we were in England. I didn't form the impression you were embarrassed, not like I was.*"

"*I wasn't, but it's different here.*"

"*What do you mean?*"

Finn gestured around him. "*Here I'm Prince Finn. Back in England I was a regular guy, no one special.*"

"*I think Jake and Kyle might disagree with that.*"

"*You know what I mean. I never liked being a member of the royal family, but I see now that it's part of who I am, whether I want it or not. The mer come to me for guidance, just as they do Justin.*"

"*Even more than Justin,*" Lucas pointed out. "*You were raised in Atlantis, and you've been missed a great deal while you've been living in England. The people love and respect you.*"

"*And that's the problem,*" Finn said. "*How can they respect me if they find out what my trigger is? If I were a regular merman I wouldn't care. I mean, I'd be a little embarrassed at first, but not enough for it to bother me.*"

"*You think the rest of the mer might treat you differently if they see you getting a spanking from one of your lovers?*" Lucas guessed.

Finn nodded. "*Maybe not everyone, but we all know there are those who would make a big deal about it.*"

Lucas rubbed Finn's arm in a gesture of comfort. *"I know, but you have to ask yourself... Do you care what mermen like Otus think about you?"*

"I know I shouldn't, but I can't help it."

Lucas smiled. *"I think you're worrying over nothing, but if it bothers you that much, I promise not to say anything to anyone about your trigger, not that I would have anyway."*

"Thank you."

Finn left Lucas feeling a little better, but all it took was one sneer from Otus as they swam past each other for him to start worrying all over again.

Chapter Eighteen

Jake woke to the sound of a deliberate and pointed cough from the end of his bed. When he opened his eyes to see who had disturbed him, he nearly fell out of bed in surprise.

"Caspian? What the hell?"

Caspian threw him a robe and Jake quickly covered himself as he struggled to disentangle himself from the sheets. He wasn't sleeping well these days. The bed was too large for one person alone and he missed the presence of his two lovers.

"The new colony has been established," Caspian said without preamble. "We're going to start the transportation of your guests immediately."

Jake took a moment to check the date on the calendar. It had taken nearly five months for them to reach their new home. The mating season was imminent, as Jake was well aware, thanks to his still uncontrollable powers.

"Did everyone make it there safely?" Jake asked.

"Yes," Caspian replied. "They took longer routes when there was danger ahead, to ensure everyones' safety."

"And Kyle and Finn?"

"They are also with the colony."

Jake nodded. Time had run out for him to make his choice. It was still not safe for Kyle to return to England. Not only was Natalie still asking questions, there had also been several journalists snooping around. They couldn't approach the house, thanks to Medina's magic, but they were lingering around town with the persistence of dogs with bones. Jake didn't know when they would finally give up and find someone else to pester, but with Atlantis still in the news on a regular basis, it wasn't likely to be any time soon.

The US government had taken control of the island and various science and archaeology teams were making new discoveries all the time. Although it was no longer headline news, there were frequent reports from the city.

There was no chance that Kyle could simply come home and not be hauled in for questioning. If he had made it back quickly enough, they could perhaps have claimed the naked man to be a lookalike, but the longer he remained away, the less plausible that sounded. Unfortunately, the risk of having Kyle taken in for questioning and his secret discovered was too great.

"I'll go round everyone up," Jake said. "Delwyn will want to stay here with Fabian, of course, but everyone else is eager to return to the ocean."

With life in the ocean no longer an option for Fabian, Jake knew he and Delwyn were also eager to leave and start a new life together. They would probably have moved out before now but had stayed in the crowded mansion to help with the evacuees. Jake was very grateful for their kindness. He wasn't sure he would have been able to cope on his own. Delwyn especially had been invaluable, with many of the mer happy to approach him, whereas Fabian and Jake were human, and worse, Atlantean.

Jake roused Fabian and Delwyn first, setting them both to the task of gathering everyone together in the hall.

"What about Marin?" Delwyn asked. "You know he wants to return to the ocean, but if Caspian is doing the transporting, he won't take him."

"I don't know. Maybe Medina can take him there? I'll go wake him and see what he wants to do."

Delwyn snorted. "We already know what he wants to do."

"He's not ready to take on Urion," Fabian said. "He'll end up getting himself killed."

Jake suspected Fabian was right, but there was no telling Marin that. He was a grown man and free to make his own decisions.

"Marin, are you awake?" Jake called through the door.

The door opened to reveal Marin. From the shadows under his eyes, Jake suspected Marin hadn't slept at all.

"Are you okay?" Jake asked.

"I'm fine. What is it?"

Jake pointed to the stairs leading down to the hall. "The mer have arrived at the new colony. We're gathering everyone together, so the gods can transport them there."

Marin nodded. "The new colony has no interest for me unless the sea dragons are there."

"They aren't," Jake said. "From what Caspian has said, they stayed close to Atlantis after the island was raised."

"Then Atlantis is where I need to go."

Jake shook his head. "The place is swarming with humans and all the mer have left the area."

Marin glared at him with a stubborn set to his jaw. Jake could tell he was gearing himself up for an argument and stepped into the room, closing the door behind him.

"Marin, I know you want to track down Urion and make him pay for what he did, and I don't blame you in the slightest."

"But...?"

"But if you're spotted in the waters around the city, you could put all the mer in danger of discovery."

Marin snorted. "And — let me guess — Calder wouldn't want that, right?"

"I wasn't going to say that."

"Then what were you going to say?"

Jake steeled himself. "I love Kyle and Finn more than anything, and I won't let you do anything that would put them, or their families, in danger."

"You think you can stop me from seeking revenge for Calder's murder?"

"If your revenge for the one you loved puts the men I love in danger, then yes, I'll do whatever I can to stop you."

"Love," Marin corrected without meeting Jake's eyes. "I still love him."

Jake put an arm around Marin's shoulders as the young merman began to shake. "I know you do."

"I can't let his murderer go unpunished," Marin said.

"Cari says that if you go after Urion, he'll kill you, too. She's seen your future."

"Possible future," Marin argued.

"Likely future," Jake insisted.

Marin pulled away and walked over to the window. "I don't care. At least then the pain would stop."

"You'd be with Calder again, I guess," Jake added.

Marin glanced back over his shoulder. "No, I'd return to the sea, as all mer do."

"You don't have any merpeople heaven?" Jake asked.

"No. We don't know that concept. We have one life before we become one with the ocean again."

Jake had never asked either of his lovers about the beliefs of the mer, though he knew they had no religion of their own. "No reincarnation, either?"

"What's that?" Marin asked, for the first time showing a spark of interest in something that wasn't training with his weapons.

"Um, in some human cultures, they believe that a person's soul leaves the body after death and is reborn again to a new life, but with no knowledge of the ones they have previously lived."

Marin smiled. "So, in that case, Calder would be alive again?"

"I guess."

"I suppose that would be better than imagining him gone forever, but the mer don't do that, either. When we're dead, we're dead, and that's it."

Caspian chose that moment to appear in the doorway, an impatient expression on his face. "What's taking so long?"

"Sorry," Jake said. "We were just talking."

"So I heard," Caspian replied. "I'm going to start transporting the mer to the new colony."

"I want to go, too," Marin announced.

"Absolutely not," Caspian snapped.

"You have no right to hold me prisoner on land."

"We both know that if I were to take you to the new colony, you'd simply swim right back to Atlantis and your death."

"It's *my* choice to make."

"I took a vow to protect all mer who set foot on land," Caspian said.

"I don't care about your stupid vow. I'm going to go back to the water with or without your help."

Caspian gave him a hard stare. "If you truly wanted to go back to the ocean, all you have to do is get Jake to drive you to the beach and swim from there. The fact that you haven't tells me that you're not so eager for death as you would appear."

"I've been training," Marin said. "I want to be prepared so I don't die."

"You can train for years and you'll still fail. No merman can fight a sea dragon singlehandedly, and certainly not you. Having an accurate aim against broken furniture won't help against a sea dragon. They fight back."

Marin bristled and grabbed his trident from where it rested again the wall. "Maybe I should try a moving target then." He pointed the trident at Caspian. "What do you say? It's not like it can kill you."

Caspian gave him a measuring look and nodded. "Very well."

"What?" Marin gaped at the god.

"If it keeps you from the suicide mission you seem to be desperate to undertake, then yes... Agreed."

"Oh."

Caspian smiled briefly. "Never bluff a god. We'll always know when you're lying. Pack your things and once I've finished escorting the mer to the new colony, I'll take you somewhere where you can practice as destructively as you like, and on me, if you wish."

Marin stood silently and made no move to do as Caspian had said.

Caspian turned to Jake. "Come on. Let's get everyone to the colony."

Jake hurried after the god, leaving Marin to pack. He wondered if the young merman had any idea what he was getting himself into. He suspected not.

* * * *

When the last of the merpeople had been transported to the new colony, Jake stepped forward with Maurissa in his arms. She was the last of the mer, save for those who were staying and Marin.

Cari reached out her arms to take Maurissa, but Jake didn't relinquish her. "I'll deliver her to her mother personally."

"Will you, indeed?" Caspian asked as he joined his sister. "Care to explain?"

"I've decided to go with the mer, to join Kyle and Finn," Jake explained. "You said I should be able to survive under the water."

Caspian frowned. "You're prepared to give up everything—your entire life—for them?"

"Yes."

Jake thought Caspian might have been about to crack a smile but put it down to his imagination. The bad-tempered God of Justice wasn't the most cheerful of people.

Medina's perfume filled the room and the Goddess of Love appeared a moment later. "Jake, darling."

Jake stepped back as the goddess practically flew at him, wrapping her arms around his neck and squealing madly. Maurissa cried at the noise and Jake struggled to quiet her until Cari took her from his arms.

"Can't…breathe…" Jake gasped as he tried to disentangle himself from Medina's embrace.

"I *knew* you'd make the right decision," Medina said. She stepped back a little and wiped tears of joy from her eyes. "You *do* know the meaning of love. Giving up everything for love proves it. I'm so happy for you. I don't mind saying that I was a little worried that you might choose to give them up, and if that had happened, you'd never be able to love again."

"Not anyone?" Jake asked.

Medina shook her head. "You were my gift to Finn, a lonely young merman who prayed to me for love. To turn away from Finn would be to turn away from me, and in doing so, you'd lose the ability to love at all. But we need not talk of such things. You've passed your initiation and no goddess could ask for a better offering from her priest."

Caspian coughed deliberately. "Touching as this is, Jake doesn't actually need to give up *everything* to keep his mermen in his life."

"I don't?"

"No," Caspian replied. "While I'm sure that dog of yours would be well-cared for by the Mitchells, I suspect you'd be much happier to take him with you."

"I don't think he'd survive at the bottom of the ocean," Jake pointed out. "He doesn't even like the pool that much."

Caspian rolled his eyes. "I wasn't suggesting you and the animal go live in the caverns."

"What were you suggesting, then?" Jake asked. He had been reluctant to give up Treacle. He and the mongrel had been through a lot together over the years. If there was a chance he could keep him and still be with Kyle and Finn, he would definitely take it.

Caspian turned to Cari. "Can you take Maurissa to her mother?"

"Of course." The goddess vanished from the room in an instant.

"You could at least have let me say goodbye," Jake said.

"You'll see her again soon, I'm sure. Go pack your things — and the dog's — and meet me back here in ten minutes."

"What?"

Caspian pointed at the staircase. "Pack, now."

Jake looked questioningly at Medina, but she merely shrugged in response. "Are my powers going to be under control?" he asked. With the departure of most of the merpeople, he was no longer being bombarded with the intimate thoughts of those around him, but he couldn't tell if that was because they had left or for some other reason.

"Your powers will continue to grow for as long as the Atlantean pantheon strengthens. They will peak eventually, and I suspect that after a couple of years, you'll have your abilities under control."

"Will there be any more surprises?" Jake asked. "No new powers like the permanent erection or anything like that?"

Medina laughed. "I see you've been talking to Fabian. No, if that one was going to manifest, it would have happened long before now."

Jake breathed a sigh of relief.

Medina nudged him and laughed again. "Like you aren't desperate for sex whenever you're in the presence of Kyle and Finn, anyway."

"Good point," Jake mumbled as his face flushed.

"Are you packing or not?" Caspian complained. "I don't have all day."

Jake raced up the stairs and hurried to the bedroom where he grabbed a suitcase. *How the hell am I going to fit everything in? Do I need to take Kyle and Finn's clothing, too?* Admittedly, they walked around naked a lot of the time, but since he had no idea where Caspian planned on taking him, he didn't know whether his lovers would need to be fully clothed or not.

"What's the hold-up?" Caspian asked from the doorway.

Jake nearly jumped out of his skin. "I'm trying to decide what to bring. It might help if I knew where we were going."

Caspian walked over to the case and pulled out the two jumpers Jake had already packed. "You probably won't need those any time soon."

"What about Finn and Kyle?"

"What about them?"

"Do I need to pack their clothes?"

Caspian snorted. "Leave them here. You can always buy them new stuff if they suddenly decide they enjoy wearing clothing, which I'm sure you know is highly unlikely."

"Then there are clothes shops where we're going?"

Caspian frowned. "No."

"Er, what about a supermarket?"

"No."

Jake stopped packing and stared at the god. "What are we going to do for food?"

Caspian sighed and grabbed a pile of t-shirts from the open drawer. "You'll be flying out for anything you need."

"Flying?"

"Yes."

"So there's an airport there?"

"No."

"I don't understand. Where are you taking me?"

Caspian moved onto the next drawer. "If you don't hurry up, I'm not taking you anywhere at all."

Jake could tell he wasn't going to get any sort of helpful response from Caspian, so he went to fetch Treacle's things. He piled his favorite toys, bowls, blanket, collar and lead into the dog bed. He also put all the food and treats into a carrier bag and left the entire lot in the hallway.

Treacle himself wasn't too hard to locate. He hadn't liked the crowds, probably because most of the merpeople were unfamiliar with dogs and reluctant to give him attention. The lovable mutt had instead sought shelter in Jake's bedroom, most often hiding under the bed. Jake didn't blame him and had often felt like joining him down there.

Jake found Treacle curled up under the bed, fast asleep. "Come on. We're going on a trip." He ruffled the dog's fur and Treacle licked his hand before crawling out and running to the door. Jake hoped he wouldn't be too disappointed that they weren't going for a walk.

Caspian waited in the hallway, two heaving suitcases at his side as well as the trunk from the end of the bed, which contained a wide range of sex toys. Jake hoped the god hadn't opened the box, but since he suspected he probably had, he kept his mouth shut rather than ask.

"Are you ready now?" Caspian asked.

"Will I need my passport?" Jake asked.

"For the love of... Yes, you'll need your bloody passport. You know the new mer colony is in the South Pacific."

Jake scowled. "Yes, I knew that, but I'm pretty sure you travel all over the world without one, right?"

"I'm a god. I don't need to use planes. *You*, on the other hand, will need your passport if you ever want to go anywhere once you arrive at our destination."

"What about Treacle?" Jake asked after he had located his passport, driving license and other documentation, along with those Caspian had conjured up for Kyle and Finn. "Does he need a passport? What about quarantine?"

Caspian ignored his questions and a moment later the world around them changed.

Instead of the mansion Jake had been living in, thanks to Caspian, they were now in an entirely different building. The old-fashioned rooms had been replaced with modern, airy ones. Tall and wide glass windows stretched along the entire wall opposite him. Treacle ran to the windows and barked excitedly.

"Where are we?" Jake asked.

Caspian held out some papers. "This is a private island in the South Pacific, about three miles north of the location of the new mer colony."

Jake took the papers. "Please tell me these aren't what I think they are?"

"Ownership papers," Caspian confirmed. "This island is in the names of yourself, Kyle and Finn."

Jake frowned. "I thought our future was in England," he said. "Cari showed me a life where the three of us were in our house there, with Summer and Alex and their children."

"Cari shows *possible* futures," Caspian reminded him. "Every decision you have made since she showed you that vision may have altered your course."

Jake wasn't sure he liked the sound of that. He had liked the vision Cari had shared with him.

"It may still happen," Caspian added. "You may decide to return there, when things have died down and it's safe to do so. You may live there permanently or simply visit. It is entirely up to you. For the moment, however, this is your new home."

"Is there anyone else on the island?" Jake asked as he approached the windows and savored the beautiful landscape. A small garden outside ended at a stone wall. At the other side of the wall were trees, and at the far side of those was the ocean.

"No."

"What happened to the previous owner?" Jake had visions of someone arriving on the doorstep demanding his or her home back.

"There is no previous owner," Caspian explained. "Until today, this island didn't exist."

"What?" Jake gaped at the god. "You don't think perhaps someone might notice a *second* island appearing out of nowhere?"

"No, this one cannot be seen from the air, the sea or by your satellites. Ships in the area will steer clear, though the captains won't know why they alter their courses to avoid the place. Planes will see nothing but sea. Only the mer will be able to find this island."

"How is that possible?"

"For a small island such as this one, it's quite simple," Caspian replied. "It's how the gods shielded the islands the mer used during the mating seasons."

"It's a pity you didn't do that with Atlantis itself."

"With the sea dragons hiding it, we didn't have to."

"And after the dragons left?"

Caspian sighed. "Atlantis is much bigger that this place, and to hide the entire thing would take more power than I and the rest of the allies of the merpeople have."

"You could have tried."

"We *did*," Caspian snapped. "Or we tried to hide the palace and surrounding buildings, at least. But with other immortals working against us, it was impossible to do so. Mariana wanted the mer discovered and driven from the city. We soon discovered that whatever we did to try to hide any part of the city was completely ineffective."

"I didn't realize."

"Of course you didn't. Why would you?" Caspian said. "The immortals don't have to tell you our every move."

"Sorry."

"It doesn't matter. And before you suggest that we should have tried to hide the city after it was raised, by then we had most of the pantheon working against us, and hiding the city then would defeat the purpose of raising it."

"I see."

"Anyway," Caspian continued, "the mer will be able to find this place without any difficulty. You'll no doubt get a lot of visitors to your beaches during the mating season."

Jake sat on a comfortable sofa and stared at the god who had done all this for him. "Why would you go to this much trouble for me?"

Caspian shrugged and avoided his eyes. "No particular reason."

"But this is so much and I'm an Atlantean, not mer. Your vow to help the mer doesn't extend to me."

Caspian sat beside him and gave a sigh. "Forget being Atlantean and forget that your lovers are mermen. You're just a man who loves someone — two someones — so much you'd give up everything for them. Do you have any idea how rare that is?"

"Not really."

"Speaking as a god who has lived for thousands of years, I can tell you it is very rare indeed. There are few who would do what you intended to do. I couldn't. But I once knew one who could. He…"

Jake remained quiet rather than prompt Caspian, who seemed lost in the past. He rather suspected that Caspian might have forgotten he was there at all.

Caspian stared at his hands for several long seconds. "I didn't deserve him, not at all. But I loved him."

"He was mer, wasn't he?" Jake asked softly.

Caspian nodded then seemed to remember where he was and who he was talking to. He jumped up from his seat. "Now, you'll want to know how to get off this island when you want to get supplies or go on a shopping spree. This way."

Jake followed Caspian, who was all business again, through the house and out the door. They walked down a path that sloped gently downward. Jake didn't bring up what they had spoken about, but his mind slowly put together a few more pieces of the mystery that was Caspian. Things that Cari, Fabian and others had said about the bad-tempered god he now saw in a different context. He didn't need to be told that Caspian had lost the merman he loved, that much was obvious. Although he knew the god wouldn't welcome his sympathy, Jake found himself feeling quite sorry for Caspian anyway.

"The beach is that way," Caspian said, pointing at a path to the right.

They didn't go to the beach. Instead, they carried on straight ahead until they reached a dock where a seaplane had been parked.

"Your new transportation," Caspian announced.

"Um, I have no idea how to fly one of those," Jake said, "or anything else, for that matter."

"You'll find you have the knowledge when you need it. Just remember to take your passport with you for when you arrive on the mainland."

Jake could barely believe it. An island of their own and a seaplane, as well. He hoped Caspian's knowledge of flying the seaplane was better than his knowledge of using other human technology. Perhaps he should take some lessons from a professional, just to be on the safe side.

Treacle yapped as he raced past them, chasing some exotic bird he had no hope of catching.

"What about him?" Jake asked. "How would we go about taking him with us if we went back to England?"

Caspian sighed. "Call myself, Medina or Cari and we'll transport all of you, mutt included, to England. I'm sure one of us will be available for infrequent visits such as those. What we aren't available for is monthly shopping trips."

"Thank you." Caspian might not welcome Jake's sympathy, but he could at least offer him his heartfelt gratitude.

Caspian gave him a brief smile, taking Jake by surprise. "You're welcome, Jake Seabrook."

Jake stood on the dock as Caspian vanished.

Now all he had to do is settle into his new home and wait for Kyle and Finn to track him down. The mating season was upon them, and he had no doubt they would be coming to land, eager for sex, sometime in the next twenty-four hours. He couldn't wait to see them again.

Calling Treacle to follow him, Jake headed back to the house. He found the cupboards and fridge full and set about cooking a meal for his men. He suspected they might have been missing human food during their time traveling in the oceans. A romantic meal to celebrate their reunion would be ideal.

Chapter Nineteen

Finn and Kyle arrived on land with a couple of dozen other merpeople. No one seemed to be shy about getting started the moment they took human form, except Finn.

Kyle guided Finn a little way down the beach, but there were still plenty of mer around. The island was pretty small, and Finn suspected that wherever they went, someone would be able to see what they were doing.

Realistically, Finn knew that most of the mer had no interest in watching others of their kind having sex, yet he still couldn't help feeling embarrassed at the idea of anyone discovering what he needed to break his mating fever. He caught sight of Otus a hundred or so feet down the shore and cringed.

It wasn't as if they could keep quiet, either. On this deserted island, so quiet and peaceful, the sound of Kyle smacking Finn's arse would ring out like gunshots, not that the rest of the mer would know what a gun was.

"You realize this is the first mating season since the three of us started our relationship where Jake hasn't been here?" Kyle said.

"I know. It doesn't seem right, does it?"

Kyle shook his head. "Unfortunately, he's on the other side of the world."

Finn sat on the sand and Kyle dropped down beside him. "Next season we're tracking him down. Agreed?"

Kyle nodded. "We're a trio, and even though sometimes I think we've all felt we weren't, without him we're not complete."

Finn couldn't agree more. Next mating season they were going to find a way to be with Jake, too, and curses on any of the gods who tried to keep them apart.

Kyle stretched out on his back and planted his feet in the sand. Finn crawled closer and knelt between Kyle's legs. He ran his hands down Kyle's inner thighs, easing them wider apart with smooth strokes.

As he teased his lover, he watched Kyle's erection rise from the bed of dark curls at his groin. Leaning down, Finn swiped his tongue along Kyle's length, licking him from root to tip.

"Finn!" Kyle cried out as he bucked up, driving his cock into Finn's mouth.

With a moan of pleasure, Finn sucked his lover, closing his eyes as he savored the taste he had missed so much during their long journey to the new caverns.

"Fuck me," Kyle demanded. "Please, Finn. I need you in me or I'm going to burn up."

The mating fever could do that to a person. Finn often felt as though he might burst into flames at the peak of the season. He had no intention of waiting much longer before taking Kyle. With one final suck on Kyle's cockhead, Finn sat back and gazed at the glorious sight in front of him.

"I wish we had some lube," Finn said.

"Yeah, me, too," Kyle admitted. "We've been spoiled, haven't we?"

"Just a bit."

Unfortunately, without a pharmacy around the corner, they would have to make do with saliva, like the rest of the mer did.

Finn prepared Kyle as best he could, fingering him far longer than usual in his attempts to make things easier for his lover.

"Finn, for the love of the gods, fuck me!" Kyle shouted, when it seemed Finn had taken too long in his preparations.

They kissed briefly, their tongues touching for a fraction of a second before they parted. Finn lined his cock up with Kyle's arse and entered him with one swift thrust.

Kyle screamed out in pleasure, though Finn fancied there was a little pain there too.

From the moment Finn buried himself in Kyle's arse, he felt the feverishness to Kyle's skin recede. With a few hard strokes, Kyle came, spilling his cum across his abdomen and chest.

"It's a good job you don't need to feel my seed inside you," Finn whispered. "Then we'd have a real problem."

Kyle choked off a laugh. "Your cock is enough to break my fever, but I know what you mean. Now, how about we switch places? You get on your hands and knees and I'll get rid of that pesky fever of yours."

Finn froze mid thrust. There were mer just a little way down the shore. Any one of them might see and hear what Kyle did to him.

"Finn, what is it?" Kyle pulled back and sat up, Finn's erection slipping free from him.

"I can't," Finn whispered.

"Can't what?"

Finn nodded subtly to the mermen and mermaids coupling down the beach. "I'm supposed to be a prince, a leader."

"You *are*."

"My position, much as I hate it, requires the people to respect me. How can they do that when they see what I need — what I *desire* — to break my mating fever?"

Kyle sighed loudly and pulled Finn into his arms. "We can go somewhere more private, if you wish?"

"This is a small island. Wherever we go, someone will see us, and even if they didn't, they would hear." Finn sobbed softly and buried his face in Kyle's chest. "I hate the pain of the mating fever, but I see no other way to keep the respect of my people."

Kyle held him close, and Finn took what little comfort he could from being in the arms of his lover.

"Human!"

The cry came from the far end of the beach. By the time Finn had risen from the ground, half the mer in the locality were already back in the water.

"Jake!" Kyle shouted. "Finn, it's Jake!"

Finn couldn't believe his eyes. He sprinted down the beach and into his lover's embrace. He was aware of Kyle calling the rest of the mer back to land, assuring them it was safe to do so. Not everyone could hear him, for many had already dived below the waves, but some of them cautiously swam back, gazing at Jake, who, in his human clothes, must appear quite strange to most of them. As they drew close, some recognized their former host and greeted him with shy smiles and waves.

Kyle joined Jake and Finn a moment or two later.

Jake raised his hand to Kyle's brow. "I see I've missed some of the fun, haven't I?"

"We didn't know you were here," Kyle said.

Jake stroked Finn's skin. "You're still feverish, baby."

Finn's face heated.

Jake smiled and kissed him softly. "We have a house on the other side of the island. It's not far."

"We?"

"You, me, Kyle and Treacle."

"Treacle's here?" Finn asked, at the same time the dog in question bounded up to them, yapping and jumping in excitement. Finn bent down and gave Treacle an affectionate pat. "Aw, you've missed me, haven't you?"

"We both have," Jake said. "Now, how about we take this somewhere a little more private? You know I'm not a fan of public sex."

Finn grinned widely as relief swept through him.

Taking Jake's hand, Finn let him lead them along a path. Treacle ran ahead of them and Kyle planted himself firmly on Jake's other side.

Finn glanced over his shoulder at the other mer, who, now that the excitement was over, were returning to their previous activities.

The house Jake brought them to was modern and new, and Finn loved it immediately. The moment he walked through the door, he felt as if he had come home.

"The bedroom is up those stairs," Jake said, pointing to a spiral staircase at the side of the room. "It's the only room up there and has windows in all directions. I've been up there watching out for the mer all day, but I guess I was watching the wrong side of the island."

"The scout had told us about the building here," Kyle explained. "We deliberately came to land at the beach that was out of sight of the structure."

"Ah, that explains it," Jake said. "I'd not have found you at all if it weren't for Treacle constantly barking in the direction where you were. I think he knew you were here long before I did."

"Clever dog," Finn praised as Treacle ran to one of the cupboards and looked up at it longingly.

"I guess he deserves a treat for his work this evening," Jake said as he gave the dog a bone. "It'll also keep him busy while we're otherwise engaged."

"Sneaky," Kyle teased.

"Yes, but also effective." Jake pointed over to the dining room. "I've made us dinner. Do you want to eat now or later?"

"Later," Finn immediately replied. "Bed first, then food."

Jake winked and gestured to the stairs. "After you, my loves."

Kyle went up the stairs first and Finn followed right behind him. He was halfway up the stairs when he felt Jake pat him on the arse. It was a light tap, but enough for his already straining cock to take note. He was about to get what he needed after all, and well away from the rest of their people. No one need ever know of his shame. He said as much to Jake as they took their places on the bed.

Jake halted Finn when he moved to rest himself over Jake's lap. "Wait a moment, Finn. What do you mean about shame?"

"He was embarrassed at the idea of the other mer seeing him break his fever," Kyle explained before Finn could say a word.

"I don't care if they see me have sex," Finn muttered as he sat back up. "I just don't like the idea of them knowing what I desire most is being spanked."

Jake kissed Finn briefly. "I've told you before, but it bears repeating. What happens between us, here in our bedroom, stays between us. No one need ever know. But, Finn, you have nothing to be ashamed of."

"I like being spanked," Finn whispered. "I'm supposed to be a leader, someone my people look up to."

"And they do," Kyle said. "They love you as much as they love Justin."

"But they wouldn't if they knew the truth," Finn replied.

"You don't know that," Kyle argued.

"I'd rather not find out for sure," Finn countered.

Jake shook his head. "Now is not a time for arguments. We're finally back together again, and tonight we're going to christen this bed thoroughly. Finn, if you don't want your people to know what you desire, then they won't. We have a house here, and the privacy to do what we want in it. No one will see or hear what we get up to unless you want them to."

Finn nodded and this time when he bent over Jake's lap, Jake didn't try to stop him and held him securely in place.

"Kyle, the chest is over in the corner," Jake said.

Finn glanced over his shoulder and saw Kyle was already rummaging through their trunk of toys.

"This one?" Kyle asked as he raised a paddle for Finn to see.

"Yes," Finn replied, and Jake held out his hand to Kyle.

"Are you ready?" Jake asked. "Comfortable?"

"Hmm…"

Kyle hurried to kneel on the floor beside them, perfectly positioning himself to kiss Finn.

Finn grinned and leaned as far as he could to bring his lips to Kyle's. Their lips connected right at the moment Jake brought the paddle down on his arse for the first time. Finn's cock, already hard, ached with renewed need. He grabbed the back of Kyle's head to hold him in place and deepened their kiss. He moaned into Kyle's mouth as the paddle connected for the second time. His buttocks burned and his cock throbbed.

The third stroke on his tender arse nearly tipped him over the edge. He broke away from Kyle as he cried out in pleasure.

"Harder, fuck, Jake, harder, please."

Jake increased the intensity of his strikes and Finn howled in delight.

"So beautiful," Kyle praised. "I love seeing you like this."

"Me, too," Jake said. He halted his smacks and ran his fingers lightly over Finn's arse. "I never thought I'd enjoy the sight of my lover's bum, all red and tender, over my lap."

Finn squirmed as Jake stroked him, easing his buttocks apart and slipping a finger between his cheeks, teasing his rim.

"How close are you?" Jake asked.

"Very," Finn replied between gasps of delight.

"Good," Jake murmured in his ear. "Because I'm close enough to come in my pants, but I'd much rather be in you instead."

Finn moaned long and low and his buttocks clenched around Jake's probing finger.

"Soon," Jake promised as he took away his hand and picked up the paddle again.

Finn raised his arse as high as he could, meeting the paddle mid stroke. "Yes!"

In front of him, Kyle stroked himself as he leaned in to kiss Finn again.

They tangled their tongues as Jake continued to deliver strong, hard, smacks to Finn's arse, each one driving Finn a little closer to his orgasm.

Finally, when Finn thought he couldn't take any more without bursting, Jake put aside the paddle and instead used his hand.

Finn whimpered in delight as Jake spanked him several times in quick succession, each smack sending sparks of desire to his dick.

The moment he started to come, Jake gathered him into his arms and Kyle climbed onto the bed beside him to join in their embrace.

Held safely in the arms of his two lovers, Finn climaxed, his seed spilling over all three of them.

He was still seeing stars when Jake touched his forehead, checking that his fever had broken, just as he always did, as though the cum staining his shirt wasn't evidence enough.

Finn rested his head on Jake's shoulder and closed his eyes. "Thank you," he murmured.

Jake chuckled. "You know there's no need to thank me for that. I love watching you come."

Finn let Jake place him in the middle of the bed and tend his buttocks with a cooling lotion, before he opened his eyes again. "What about you?" he asked.

Jake glanced down at his jeans and gave a rueful grimace. "I'll have to fuck you later," he said. "I'm afraid it's been too long since I've been with the pair of you. I've not as much control tonight as I usually have."

Kyle knelt beside Jake and reached down to unfasten his zipper. "May I?"

Jake nodded and Finn licked his lips.

Kyle pulled Jake's jeans down, swiftly divesting him of both those and his cum-stained underwear.

Jake closed his eyes as Kyle licked at his cock and balls, lapping up his seed and cleaning him thoroughly.

"Kiss me," Finn said, eager to enjoy the almost-forgotten taste of both of his lovers at the same time.

Kyle finished cleaning up Jake and turned his attention to Finn, kissing him messily.

Finn moaned as he thrust his tongue into Kyle's mouth, searching and finding Jake's taste.

From the corner of his eye, Finn could see Jake watching them with a small smile playing on his lips. Finn held out his hand and beckoned Jake to sit up and join them.

Their lover understood him immediately. The three of them fidgeted and shifted positions until they were able to comfortably exchange the three-way kisses they enjoyed so much.

Kyle was hard again. Finn and Jake both seemed to realize it at the same time and they reached to take him in hand. Together, they leisurely brought him to the brink, and by the time he came for the second time that night, both Finn and Jake were half hard again.

Finn was about to get on his hands and knees, ready for Jake to carry out his earlier promise to fuck him, but Jake surprised him by climbing off the bed instead.

"Dinner?" he suggested with a grin.

"Now?" Finn replied as he gaped at his lover.

"Yes, why not?" Jake asked, his grin growing wider. "I think I'll need my strength tonight."

Finn stuck out his lower lip. "Tease. I think you want to torment me."

"That, too," Jake said. "Come on. If we leave it much longer, it won't taste as nice. Besides, Treacle has been barking like crazy. I'd better see what his problem is."

Finn and Kyle followed Jake down the stairs. "It's all right for you," Finn told Kyle. "You've just come."

Kyle laughed. "It wasn't that long ago you did."

Finn supposed he was right, even if he ached so much it didn't exactly feel like it.

By the time they arrived in the dining room, Jake was already dishing up the food. He still wore his shirt, half unbuttoned, and begging to be ripped from his body. He hadn't bothered putting his jeans back on and his erection was on display as he strode back and forth from the adjoining kitchen.

"Now there's a sight for sore eyes," Kyle said to Finn as Jake turned around, flashing his arse in the process.

Jake blew them a kiss. "Take a seat, boys. I'll get the wine."

"Wine?" Finn and Kyle, like the rest of the mer, had no tolerance for alcohol at all. They usually gave the stuff a wide berth and stuck to fruit juices.

"Non-alcoholic," Jake called back. "Caspian has provided us with a fully stocked kitchen and all the alcohol appears to be made with you lightweight mermen in mind."

"What was Treacle barking at?" Kyle asked.

"I don't know. He's quiet now. Probably he's not used to being in a strange place."

Finn took his seat, a little gingerly, since his arse was still sore, and Kyle sat beside him. Jake returned a moment later with a bottle and glasses. He poured them drinks and raised his own glass for a toast.

"What shall we drink to?" Jake asked.

"To our new home?" Kyle suggested.

"How about to a fresh start, not only for us, but for the rest of the merpeople, too?" Finn replied.

"To all of us," Jake agreed as they clinked their glasses together.

As Finn sipped his wine, he thought perhaps he might get to enjoy the best of both worlds. He had Jake and Kyle, men he loved more than he ever thought possible, a new home on land and the sea right on his doorstep whenever he wanted it. He would miss his brother and his parents, but they had their own lives to lead.

"I've brought all your human papers with me," Jake said. "So if we ever want to travel the world the human way, you can do so. Caspian says he or the other gods will be happy to commute us all to England for the occasional visit. And until then, we actually have a phone here, if you want to call your parents."

"How do you do that?" Finn asked. "It's like you read my mind or something."

Jake smiled. "I'm finally getting a handle on my powers and yes, I did read your mind, though not intentionally. You were thinking of the love you have for your family."

Finn nodded. "I'm going to miss them, but I feel my life is in the ocean. It's different for Alex. He grew up on land and has a human girlfriend. Mama probably finds it most difficult, but she won't leave my dad and she'd never be welcome in the new colony. The bitterness between her and my father is too recent."

"You can call your mum whenever you want, though you might want to remember the time difference. I doubt she'd appreciate being woken in the middle of the night."

"Thank you."

Finn turned to Kyle, who was uncharacteristically quiet. "What's the matter?"

Kyle startled. "I was thinking about my own mother, wondering where she is. I think I need to find her. I would much rather her be here in the new colony than out there in danger."

Finn squeezed Kyle's hand. "We'll find her together. I promise."

"That's a lot of ocean to search," Kyle said. "It would take years to swim it all, and even then, we might not find her if she's traveling around."

"We'll find her," Finn promised, "as well as the others in your clan who chose not to stay in the sunken city."

Kyle nodded, a sheen of moisture on his eyes. Finn vowed to find a way to bring Kyle's family back together. His lover and friend had given him so much, he, more than anyone else Finn knew, deserved to be happy.

Chapter Twenty

The next morning, Kyle woke to the familiar feeling of having been thoroughly fucked by the men he loved. He opened his eyes to see Finn watching him with a smile.

"How long have you been awake?" Kyle asked.

"A while."

"And how long have you been staring at me?"

"The same." Finn leaned over to kiss him. "We should probably head back to the colony in a little while. My father will be sending out a search party for me, if we don't return soon."

Kyle stretched and yawned. "You go back. I think I'll stay here in this nice soft bed for a few more hours."

Finn stuck out his lower lip. "You're supposed to be my bodyguard."

Kyle laughed as he pulled Finn down on top of him. He wrapped his legs around Finn, holding him in place. "Maybe you should fire me?"

Jake groaned beside them. "What time is it?"

"Just before five," Finn replied.

"For fuck's sake," Jake grumbled. "Go back to sleep, the pair of you, or I'll throw you both back into the ocean."

"You're not tired, are you?" Finn teased.

Jake opened one eye and glared at them. "We only went to sleep a couple of hours ago. How can you possibly be this bloody chirpy?"

Kyle laughed as Finn pounced on their lover, causing Jake to curse and swear, while burrowing under his pillow.

"Kyle, help," each of his lovers cried at the exact same time.

Deciding to take pity on Jake, Kyle pulled Finn off him, giving Jake time to recover.

"Traitor," Finn muttered as he half-heartedly attempted to escape Kyle's embrace.

"Now, now, Finn," Kyle teased. "You've got to remember that Jake isn't as young as we are. As he gets older, he's going to struggle to keep up with us."

"Hey!" Jake exclaimed. "Who are you calling old? You're less than three months younger than me."

Finn raised a brow at Kyle. "He's got a point. You're both a lot nearer to thirty than I am."

Kyle and Jake exchanged a look before tackling Finn.

Early in the morning or not, they were all wide awake now, though he suspected it would be quite a while before they headed back to the ocean.

* * * *

When Finn and Kyle finally returned to the colony, after another round of sex, a full English breakfast and nearly an hour on the phone to their friends and family in England, they were immediately summoned before King Nereus.

"*I told you he'd be sending out a search party,*" Finn said as they swam into the largest cavern, which had been declared the king's new audience chamber. Several mermen and mermaids congregated in the chamber, though few Finn recognized.

King Nereus swam to meet him. "*Finn, my son, I expected you back here hours ago.*"

"*We've been on the island,*" Finn replied. "*Jake is living there.*"

"*Jake? You mean your human lover? Isn't he back in England?*"

"*He was, but not any longer. Caspian took him to the island, along with our dog. We spent the night with him, and I guess we lost track of time.*"

King Nereus didn't seem appeased. "*I've received a disturbing report about this human.*"

"*He startled some of the mer when he arrived,*" Finn admitted. "*But they swam off before we could explain he was a friend.*"

"*That's not what I'm referring to.*" King Nereus flushed and wouldn't meet Finn's eyes.

"*Father, what is it?*" Finn had a sinking feeling in his stomach.

"*I've been advised that this human has used violence toward you,*" King Nereus finally said.

"*Who has told you this?*" Kyle asked.

King Nereus glared at Kyle. "*You will remain silent. As Finn's personal bodyguard, it's your job to protect him.*"

"*Kyle protects me perfectly well,*" Finn argued. "*Now, how about you answer his question?*"

King Nereus turned his fury on Finn, and for a moment Finn saw a fleeting glimpse of the man who had sent them from Atlantis. Then he seemed to visibly rein himself in. *"Otus returned from the island an hour ago and felt the need to report to me what he had seen immediately, due to concerns for your safety."*

"Otus? What are you talking about?"

"The leader of the guards was concerned when you were a long time returning to the ocean," King Nereus explained. *"He ventured to the human structure to check that you were unharmed."*

"What?" Finn searched the room for Otus, finding him hovering nearby, a gloating smile on his face.

"When he saw the human beating you, he swam back here at once."

Finn shot a venomous glare at Otus. *"Did he really?"* he asked sarcastically. Even if Otus had crept into their home and watched them, there was no way he'd swum right back here to the king. If he had, he'd have been back hours ago and King Nereus would have sent someone to bring him back as soon as Otus had raised the alarm. More likely the odious merman had waited until there were plenty of merpeople around before he decided to express his so-called concerns.

"Is it true?" King Nereus asked. *"Did this human raise his hand to you? Did he use some human instrument to beat you?"*

Finn felt Kyle take hold of his hand and squeeze his fingers in support.

"You have nothing to be ashamed of," Kyle whispered into his mind, for Finn alone to hear.

"Stop calling him 'the human'. He has a name," Finn snapped.

"Answer the question, Finn!"

"Jake helped me break my fever."

"That's not what I asked you," King Nereus replied. *"Did he strike you?"*

"He gave me what I needed last night." Finn knew he was avoiding saying the words out loud, but there were so many spectators in the room, and even if he sent his words to his father alone, he could tell the king was projecting his voice for everyone in the cavern to hear.

"Answer the question!" King Nereus roared.

"Yes!" Finn shouted back. *"And I loved it."*

The king reeled back at Finn's response. *"What are you saying?"*

Finn glared at Otus, hating that he had been forced into this position by a merman who simply wanted to stir up trouble. Finn wished he had sent his words privately to his father, but it was too late now, even if he didn't know that Otus would be telling anyone who would listen about what he had seen.

He turned back to his father. *"My trigger is being spanked,"* he said quietly. *"I enjoy it, as I'm sure Otus could tell when he invaded our privacy last night."*

King Nereus sat on the luxurious sponge that he had been installed as his throne. *"Come here, Finn. Everyone else, please leave the room."*

Finn kept hold of Kyle's hand, not wanting to be left alone when he was feeling so vulnerable.

"You too, Otus," King Nereus said. *"I'll speak with you later."*

When the cavern had cleared, Finn approached his father, drawing Kyle with him.

"Tell me the truth, Finn. Is that really your trigger?"

"Yes."

King Nereus frowned. *"And this human – Jake – he treats you well outside of the mating seasons?"*

"He always treats me well," Finn replied. *"You know our triggers are what bring us the most sexual pleasure. I know*

it isn't befitting a prince, but it's what I enjoy, and on the solstice, it's what I need."

"I want to speak to him personally," King Nereus said.

"Not if you're going to shout at him. He's given up his entire life to be near me and Kyle, and I don't want you saying anything to him to make him regret his decision."

"You don't trust me?"

"Not when you're in a temper," Finn muttered.

His father took his hand and pulled him onto the sponge beside him. *"Finn, I just want to make sure you're being treated as you deserve — not because you're a prince, but because you're my son, whether we're blood related or not."*

"I am. I swear it."

Finn let his father hold him and finally released Kyle's hand so he could hug his father back.

When they parted, Finn retreated to Kyle's side.

"We'll have to make sure we lock the door next time," Kyle said. *"I don't know about you, but the thought of Otus watching us last night makes my skin crawl."*

"Mine, too," replied King Nereus, reminding them both that he could hear even their private communications. *"I think perhaps Otus needs to be reminded of his place."*

With a roar that startled both Finn and Kyle, King Nereus shouted for Otus to be brought before him.

The guard appeared a few moments later. No doubt he had been hovering right outside the cavern.

"Otus," King Nereus said, *"can you tell me why you chose to follow the prince and his lovers into the human's building?"*

"I was concerned for Prince Finn's safety," Otus explained.

"Why?"

"Humans are treacherous."

"Having met Prince Finn's human lover for yourself, it should have been obvious to you that was who he greeted. Again, I ask you, why did you follow them?"

Otus remained silent, and Finn had the impression he was trying to think of a reason that might sound plausible.

"I'll tell you why, shall I?" King Nereus said as he swam right up into Otus' face. *"You're jealous of what my son has with his two lovers. You thought to spy on them for your own pleasure. Then you decided to embarrass His Highness for your amusement."*

"No," Otus argued. *"I was concerned for the prince's safety. I swear on my life that I saw the human strike him, many times."*

"If that is the case, why did you not intervene?" King Nereus asked. *"If the prince was in danger, was it not your duty to protect him?"*

"It would have been three against one."

King Nereus raised a brow and smiled. *"Then you didn't believe Prince Finn was in danger, because if he had been, he'd have welcomed your intervention, and it would have been two against two, or three mermen against one human, depending on whether the prince's bodyguard chose to assist you or the human."*

Convicted by his own words, Otus hung his head.

King Nereus pointed his trident at Otus' throat. *"You are hereby stripped of your position as leader of the guards. If you wish, you can remain in the ranks, in a more junior position, but if you dare to lie to me again, I'll see you banished from this colony for life."*

Otus snorted and glared at Kyle and Finn. *"Banishment for life doesn't mean much around here."*

King Nereus' face went purple with rage. *"Get out, now, and never show your face here again."*

Otus seemed to realize he had made a mistake, but King Nereus prodded him with the trident and urged him out of the cavern. *"Guards!"*

Several mermen swam up at the king's call.

"See this merman is escorted from the colony," the king demanded. *"He is not to return for as long as I draw breath."*

"But he's the leader of the guards," one of the mermen said. *"Who will take that position now?"*

King Nereus faced Kyle. *"Do you want the position?"*

Kyle shook his head. *"No, Your Majesty. I will be leaving to search for my mother. I cannot take charge of the guards."*

The king appeared disappointed, but he nodded. *"All guards are to report to me in one hour. I'll make my decision as to Otus' replacement by then."*

Finn watched as the guards led a furious Otus away. He truly hoped he never saw him again.

All around him, curious mermen and mermaids gazed at him with wide-eyed stares. Finn fancied every one of them was imagining him bent over his lover's lap, having his arse spanked. He inched closer to Kyle, seeking his hand and support.

King Nereus swam over and patted his arm. *"Don't worry so much, my son. I promise none of those present are thinking of you in such a way. Most are wondering what Otus has done to be banished, and a few are glad to see the back of him. He isn't very popular, it seems."*

"I wonder why?" Kyle muttered.

Finn nudged his lover and turned back to his father. *"They might not be thinking of me now, but we know word will spread of what Otus saw."*

"And what if it does?" his father replied. *"You are a prince, and no one would dare to say anything to your face."*

"*I know, but I don't like to think of them saying anything behind my back, either.*"

King Nereus raised Finn's chin with his finger. "*Hold your head high, my son.*"

Kyle nodded. "*You have nothing to be ashamed of, my love.*"

Finn took their advice, and when he looked around again, he saw the crowd had dispersed, everyone returning to their chores, the banished guard and the prince apparently swiftly forgotten. *Perhaps it will be all right, after all.* Finn certainly hoped so.

Chapter Twenty-One

Once his lovers had returned to the water, Jake set about doing a little more exploring. The plants in the garden weren't yet ready to be harvested, but there appeared to be a variety of fruits and vegetables. Jake was pretty sure some of them shouldn't flourish in the current climate, but he guessed Caspian had something to do with that.

Treacle happily explored the house and the island, nosing into everything he could find. Jake made it a top priority to fence in the garden before the animal dug it all up.

Jake suspected Caspian had also had a hand in the decent mobile phone reception and the electricity in the house. At first Jake had thought the latter must be from a generator, but despite searching high and low, he couldn't find any trace of one.

The fresh water running from the taps was another mystery he had yet to solve.

Jake wondered whether they would be getting any bills for the supplies, and if so, who they would be from. *Hell, will we be getting any post at all?* Though he'd be happy to see the back of the junk mail.

Jake and Treacle walked the length and breadth of the island, exploring every nook and cranny.

Although the island was comparatively small, much of the terrain wasn't ideal for walking, and by the time Jake returned to the house, it was mid-afternoon, and his stomach was growling.

"Come on, Treacle. I bet you're hungry, too." Jake quickened his pace as they walked up the path from the beach to the house.

As they neared, Treacle ran ahead, barking madly. The dog charged around the side of the house, heading for the garden. Jake ran after him, hoping he caught up before the dog had dug up half the plot.

When Jake rounded the corner, he found Treacle, not destroying the garden, but growling at a vaguely familiar man sitting on the doorstep. Jake thought he might be one of the guards who had helped with the evacuation of the mer, but he couldn't recall his name. The guards had all gone to the cave network outside the city before the immortals had raised the city.

"It's about time," the man said.

Jake studied the man who was naked and apparently not bothered by the fact. *Definitely a merman, then.* "Can I help you?" he asked.

"You're the prince's human lover."

Jake shrugged. "What of it?"

The merman rose, revealing he was an inch or two taller than Jake. "What makes you think you have the right to touch a member of the royal family?"

"I don't see Finn complaining," Jake said as he brushed past the merman, refusing to be intimidated.

"The prince is easily led, usually by his cock."

Jake spun around and pushed the merman up against the wall. "Watch your mouth when you speak about Finn."

The merman shoved Jake away. "You think you can fight me?" He laughed loudly. "I'm leader of the Atlantean guards. There's not a merman in the world who can take me on and beat me."

Jake laughed. "I don't care who you are. What you should be asking yourself is who I am."

"I *know* who you are, some random human who thinks he is good enough for our prince."

"I'm also a direct descendant of the Atlantean Goddess of Love, and I don't take kindly to *random mermen* turning up at my home and telling me who I can and can't be with."

"You should leave this island," the guard said. "It can be dangerous living alone in a place like this."

"I can take care of myself," Jake replied. He had a feeling the merman was threatening him, but he refused to rise to the bait. He turned his back on the merman and opened the door.

A moment later, everything went black.

* * * *

Kyle and Finn swam to the island with King Nereus close behind. The ruler of the colony had insisted on accompanying them back there, so he could speak to Jake for himself as well as see where Kyle and Finn would be spending a lot of their time.

They arrived on the beach just as the sun was setting, and once they had got their legs, they walked along the path to the house.

"You'll like Jake once you get to know him properly," Finn said. "He's a wonderful man, kind and generous. And he loves me and Kyle so much."

Finn's father nodded but didn't comment as they approached the house.

"Is that Treacle barking?" Kyle asked.

"It must be," Finn replied. "I doubt there are any more dogs on the island."

"A dog?" King Nereus asked.

Finn called out for Treacle to come to him as Kyle did his best to explain about the human affection for the animals that were known as man's best friend.

Treacle, who usually came to Finn more than even Jake, ignored his shouts. Finn quickened his pace as Kyle and King Nereus hurried to catch him up.

As they approached the house, Finn continued to call for the dog and finally Treacle came charging down the path toward them, barking loudly.

"What is it, boy?" Finn asked.

Treacle continued to yap as he ran ahead, then back to the men, seemingly trying to encourage them to go faster.

When they reached the house, Treacle ran around the side to the back door, where he continued to bark while jumping up at the handle. The dog barely even noticed the others arriving behind him.

Finn tried to open the door, but found it locked.

"Let's go back around the front," Kyle suggested.

Finn encouraged Treacle to come away from the door and they all went back to the other side of the house.

Kyle had an uneasy feeling as Finn slowly opened the front door. "Finn, wait! Where's Jake? He wouldn't leave Treacle running around on his own in a strange place. If he'd gone exploring the island, he'd take Treacle with him."

"I don't know," Finn said, "but I'm going to find out."

"What if there are wild animals on the island?" Kyle asked. "Maybe he's been hurt by one."

"I didn't see any dangerous creatures last night," Finn replied. "And none of the mer came back to the colony with injuries or anything like that."

"That doesn't mean there aren't any."

"If Jake had been injured, surely Treacle would be with him?"

Kyle guessed Finn was right, but he still didn't like this. "Be careful."

"Stop," King Nereus said. "I'll go first."

"But—" Finn argued.

"Step aside," King Nereus ordered.

Finn did as his father asked, picking up the struggling Treacle and moving out of the way.

Kyle also let the king pass into the house first.

"Otus is here," King Nereus said in a low tone.

"How can you tell?" Finn asked.

"He's close enough that I can hear his thoughts."

"Can you hear Jake's?" Kyle questioned.

The king shook his head. "No, just Otus. Jake has not sworn any vows of allegiance to me and his mind is therefore closed to me. Clearly the guards didn't escort Otus far enough away."

Kyle wondered how far King Nereus' power to hear thoughts stretched. *Can he hear everyone on the island or do they have to be nearby?*

"Nearby," King Nereus replied to the unspoken question.

"You do know it's extremely annoying when you do that?" Kyle said. "Between Jake and the various immortals who keep popping in, there are way too many people in my head already, without my father-in-law poking in there, too."

King Nereus chuckled. "Father-in-law? I think I like the sound of that. I promise I do stay out of people's heads most of the time. I picked up on your thoughts because I was trying to scan a little farther to establish whether Otus was alone. I believe he is."

Kyle hoped the king did refrain from reading minds generally. He didn't want the intimidating merman hearing his more intimate thoughts about his son.

King Nereus shot him an amused glance. "I don't want to hear those thoughts either, so try to focus on the problem at hand, *please.*"

Finn snickered from behind them.

"You should wait outside," Kyle said.

"Not a chance," Finn replied. "I don't need to be protected. I can take care of myself."

"Quiet!" King Nereus ordered.

Kyle and Finn immediately obeyed and Kyle heard what the king had already picked up. Kyle pointed to the door leading to the dining room and kitchen. "Through there," he mouthed.

King Nereus nodded and strode over to the door. Kyle and Finn were right on his heels.

"Jake!" Treacle escaped from Finn's arms as Finn ran to his lover, who was passed out just inside the back door.

Kyle took two steps toward Jake before he felt something prod him in the back.

"Stop right there," Otus said.

Kyle froze, recognizing the sharp point of a spear at his lower back. Sending a lone merman out into the ocean without a weapon was tantamount to a death sentence. Obviously, the guards who had escorted Otus away from the colony had decided he could keep the spear.

"He's still breathing," Finn said.

Kyle relaxed a little at Finn's words.

Jake groaned and opened his eyes. "What the fuck?" he mumbled.

Treacle licked his face and Jake moaned, this time in a 'yuck, don't do that' sort of way.

"Hey," Finn said. "Welcome back."

Jake sat up slowly and rubbed the back of his head.

Kyle stepped forward again, only to find Otus jabbing him in the back again.

"Not so fast," Otus warned.

"You!" Jake shot to his feet—way too fast, from the way he was swaying.

"Otus did this to you?" Finn guessed.

"Yeah. The bastard must have knocked me out when I turned my back on him."

Finn snorted. "Well, that was a bloody stupid thing to do, wasn't it?"

"Apparently so," Jake replied. "A mistake I won't make again."

King Nereus ignored Otus entirely and walked over to Jake. "It's good to see you again. I'm glad to have the opportunity of thanking you properly again for opening your home to the mer. I'm sorry your kindness has been repaid in this manner." The king pointed his trident at Otus, though Kyle hoped he wouldn't use it while he stood between the two of them.

"You *dare* to attack the mate of His Royal Highness Prince Finn, second in line to the throne of Atlantis and all the waters of the world?"

The use of Finn's full title told Kyle the king was furious with Otus, even more than he had been when he'd banished him a few hours ago.

Otus sneered at Jake. "He's a human. He shouldn't even know we exist."

"Kyle, step aside," King Nereus said.

Although he could still feel the spear at his back, Kyle didn't dare disobey an order from the king. He eased his way over to Finn and Jake, standing between them and taking their hands in his own.

With an accuracy Kyle envied, King Nereus shot sea-fire from his trident, hitting the spear directly.

Otus dropped his weapon and shook his hands as though they had been burned.

"You know the punishment for striking a member of the royal family?" King Nereus asked. "Oh, of course you do. You reminded me of it when you reported what you'd seen last night, didn't you?"

"Last night?" Jake whispered. "Did I miss something?"

Kyle glared at Otus. "Seems we had a visitor last night, one who watched us in the bedroom before going back to King Nereus to tell him what he'd seen."

Jake gasped and turned to Finn. "Are you okay, baby?"

Finn nodded. "Yes, I'm fine. A bit embarrassed, but I'm dealing with it."

Kyle gave Finn a quick kiss on the cheek. "*We're* dealing with it together, right?"

Finn smiled and hugged Kyle briefly.

Jake leaned around Kyle to pat Finn on the shoulder. "If I'd known about this creep, I'd have been a lot more cautious or I'd have decked him on sight."

King Nereus appeared to be waiting for them to finish their conversation. He gave them a mildly impatient stare.

"Sorry, Father," Finn said. "Carry on."

The king returned his attention to Otus. "The penalty for striking a member of the royal family is banishment from the oceans of the world, or in extreme cases, death."

"That human isn't a member of the royal family," Otus argued.

"As Prince Finn's mate, he is," King Nereus replied. "You are hereby charged with harming a member of the royal family and I banish you from all the oceans of the world."

Finn coughed. "Can he at least go back in the water long enough to get off this island? I don't know about the others, but I don't want him hanging around here."

King Nereus nodded. "Otus, you have one month to swim for the land of humans. If you're still in the water when that time is up, I'll know, and I'll view your prolonged presence as an act of defiance punishable by death."

"You can't do that!" Otus argued.

"I can and I will." King Nereus gestured to the door with his trident. "I would suggest you swim fast, Otus, because one month isn't as long as you might think."

Otus scrambled for the door, casting one last poisonous look at Kyle and his lovers.

"Good riddance," Finn called after him.

Treacle, who appeared to agree, chased after Otus, barking and growling as he saw him from the premises.

"Do you think he'll go to land?" Jake asked. "Can you tell if he doesn't?"

"Oh, I can tell, but it would take a lot of energy to do so. As long as whoever has been banished doesn't show their face again, I don't tend to check up on them." King Nereus shot Kyle and Finn a glance. "Unless they're family, of course. When I couldn't sense Finn in the ocean after he left, I thought I'd lost him forever."

Finn hurried to his father. "Not forever, Father."

"For which I am eternally grateful," King Nereus said. "When you swam back into my audience chamber that day, I thanked every god and goddess of Atlantis for bringing you back to me."

From the corner of his eye, Kyle could see Jake rubbing his head. "Are you sure you're okay?"

Jake moaned but nodded. "Yeah. I suspect I'm going to have a bit of a headache, but I'll be fine."

Kyle nudged him to one of the large comfy chairs in the living area. "Come and sit down so I can take a look at it."

Jake seemed as though he might argue, but one glare from Kyle had him scurrying to a seat and meekly letting Kyle examine his head.

"You have a nice home here," King Nereus said as he gazed around the room.

"Courtesy of Caspian, God of Justice," Jake replied. "He thought I might find this preferable to living in an underwater cave."

"You were going to live in the caves?"

Jake smiled over at his lovers. "I go where Kyle and Finn go."

Finn squeezed in beside him and smiled. "I don't think you'd like the caves much, but you will have to visit them."

"We'll get you swimming at depths before you know it," Kyle added.

"And what of you two?" King Nereus asked. "Where are you intending to make your homes? Here or in the caves?"

"Here!" Finn replied without hesitation.

"He's been very spoiled with human amenities during his time in England," Kyle teased.

"And you haven't?" Finn countered.

Jake laughed. "You've *both* been spoiled."

King Nereus gave them all an indulgent smile. "Well, since the three of you seem to have made up your minds already, I'll leave you to settle into your new home. I hope you won't mind my visiting occasionally."

"You'll always be welcome," Finn said. "We can introduce you to human foods."

King Nereus smiled. "That would be *interesting*, but not today. There is much to do in the caverns and I should return there."

"We'll come and help," Kyle said.

"No, you stay here. I know you three will have a lot to catch up on, and I suspect there was little talking taking place last night."

Kyle's face heated and he could see his lovers' faces were equally flushed. King Nereus didn't need to read their minds to know some things. King Nereus smiled knowingly and let himself out.

Jake patted his lap and Kyle needed no more invitation than that to slide onto it.

Finn snuggled up against Jake's other side.

This was how it was meant to be. Their ménage finally reunited once more. He vowed that nothing would separate them again.

Epilogue

Jake filled his days by working in his garden, a task he found to be fulfilling and enjoyable.

Kyle and Finn sometimes joined him, but more often than not, their work required them to be in the caverns with the rest of the merpeople.

Word had spread throughout the oceans of the new colony and more merpeople were arriving every day.

They had located ground suitable for growing sea fruits, but until the first harvest, times would be tough. Jake's crops would be essential in the coming months. As such, he was never short of helpers, with several of the gatherers working alongside him.

Today, however, the garden could wait.

The beach was crowded with merpeople and humans, many of them having been brought to the island for a temporary visit by Medina and the other immortals.

"This isn't actually a temple," Medina pointed out.

"It doesn't have to be," Caspian replied impatiently.

"But it would be nice," Medina said. "Maybe a little shrine over in the clearing."

"No," Caspian snapped. "Now, is everyone here?"

Jake nodded. Although he had no birth family present himself, his two lovers did.

King Nereus was there, along with Malcolm and Coral, the former queen of Atlantis. They were all doing their best to stay out of each other's way, rather than risk causing upset for Finn on his special day. Finn's brother Alex stood beside him, with Summer and their young twins just behind them.

Lynna and her family were also close by and Medina had even tracked down Kyle's mother and brought her to the colony for the occasion. Kyle had expressed his hope that she would stay permanently.

Jake, Finn and Kyle stood before Medina in a triangle, holding each other's hands.

The churches Jake had attended growing up might not accept their relationship, but the Atlantean gods had no such reservations. Medina had been delighted when they had approached her to ask whether she might consider officiating over the ceremony.

Jake spoke the words after Medina, recognizing the concept of marriage, even though the words were somewhat different to the more traditional ceremony. He didn't mind in the least. Theirs wasn't a traditional relationship, after all.

Kyle spoke his words second and punctuated each sentence with a squeeze of his hand.

Finn went third, his voice sure and steady as his gaze flitted between Kyle and Jake.

"I now declare you married," Medina said, her voice cracking a little as she dabbed her eyes daintily.

The three of them hugged and exchanged — for them — a very chaste three-way kiss, before their guests crowded around them to offer their congratulations.

Jake was aware their marriage might not be recognized around the world, but here, among their friends and family, it was, and for Jake and his two husbands, that was all that mattered.

Want to see more from this author?
Here's a taster for you to enjoy!

One Perfect Wish
L.M. Brown

Excerpt

Scott Baxter woke with a strange feeling something wasn't quite right. Half asleep and with his eyes still closed, he tried to figure out what could be different. The bed seemed too soft and far more luxurious than the cheap hotel mattress he vaguely recalled crashing on the night before. A thick duvet covered him and he could feel warmth similar to the heat that usually came from another body close up against him. He couldn't recall ever waking in a hotel with such contentment as he felt this morning.

After working nearly forty-eight hours straight, he had flown back to England on the red eye, practically sleepwalked to a taxi, then had finally fallen into bed exhausted. Long overdue for a break, he told himself he'd take one after his latest consulting project had been completed. He told himself the same thing every time, even though he knew his boss would have another job lined up for him before the final work had been finished on this one.

"Morning," a sleepy voice murmured into his ear.

Scott froze. His unexpected bedmate moved and Scott noticed he had some serious morning wood pressed against his arse.

He opened his eyes. Only his companion's arm wrapped around Scott's chest stopped him falling out of bed from the shock. Had the relentless pressure of his job finally caused him to snap?

The hotel room had vanished and instead he appeared to be in someone's house. The drapes over the patio doors had been pulled back and a snow-covered garden stretched toward a frozen pond. Light snow fell from the cloudy sky. The landscape outside the doors seemed more like January than May.

"Scott, are you okay?"

Scott didn't know what to say. Had he been drugged and kidnapped? And if so, why? He wasn't anyone important and his family didn't have the money to pay any ransom.

"Ah good, you're awake," a second voice said. Like the first, this voice also belonged to a man, though he seemed to have a slight accent Scott couldn't place.

Scott wondered how many men he had climbed into bed with last night, before he saw the second speaker stood at the end of the bed with his arms folded across his bare chest. With baggy silk trousers and golden metal cuffs on his wrists, he could have stepped straight out of *Arabian Nights*.

"What the *hell* is going on?" Scott shouted as he tried to untangle himself from the arms of the man sharing his bed. His companion wasn't exactly helping him and instead seemed to be frozen in place like a statue. He poked the man with a finger. His skin felt normal, yet the other man didn't react at all.

"You're here to fulfill a wish," the man at end of the bed told him. "I'm a djinn and I'm here to explain your present situation."

Scott stopped contemplating the statue man beside him. "Excuse me?"

The djinn nodded. "I'm sure you've heard of my kind. We grant wishes to those who summon us. Well, I'm here because someone wished for you."

A headache started behind Scott's eyes. He didn't have time for this nonsense. "I don't believe in magic."

The djinn shrugged. "Your belief isn't necessary to my job. You have been wished for, and therefore here you are. It's only for today, so I suggest you enjoy yourself and make the most of the opportunity. This place is certainly an improvement on the dump I found you in."

"You're out of your mind." Scott finally managed to climb from the bed. He realized he was naked and searched for his clothes. "I'm calling a taxi and getting the hell out of here."

With snap of his fingers, the djinn produced Scott's mobile phone and tossed it to him. "Good luck with that. Do you even know where you are?"

Scott ignored the sarcasm. He opened the drawer of the bedside table, trying to find something with an address on as he called his usual taxi company. The irritating automated voice telling him the number was not available did nothing to improve his temper. He tried a second number with the same result. Then he worked his way through his friends, only to find every number he tried gave him the same annoying message. If it weren't for the crack on the bottom left of the casing, he'd have thought the phone wasn't his.

"Okay," the djinn declared after Scott had tossed the phone aside. "Here's how today is going to work. You and Cameron over there are married."

"What?" Scott gaped at the frozen man in the bed.

"Married," the djinn repeated.

"This guy wished for us to be married?" Scott had no intention of tying the knot and had spent the last ten years happily playing the life of a single man, albeit a single man who didn't have much time for dating.

"Not exactly," the djinn hedged. "But for today you will be enjoying wedded bliss. I can even produce a marriage certificate if you wish."

"The only thing I wish is for you to send me back to my hotel."

"You'll be returned at midnight, and before you start complaining about all the things you need to do today, rest assured, no time will have passed when I return you. It'll be as if today never happened, though you'll retain all your memories of your stay here."

"I think I'd rather forget my brief lapse of sanity," Scott muttered.

The djinn stepped up into his face and glared at him. "I suggest you lose the attitude and listen to me. From Cameron's point of view, you've been married for six months. You're madly in love with each other and today happens to be one of your rare days off together. Today you get to enjoy domestic wedded bliss with a man who adores you. Then at midnight I'll send you home."

"And if I don't want to play along with this ridiculous charade?"

The djinn's smile became truly evil. "Then you'll never go home."

"Midnight has to come eventually."

"Not while time stands still," the djinn explained. He pointed to the window and Scott saw Cameron wasn't the only thing frozen in time. Each falling snowflake hung suspended in mid-air. "Every time you attempt to say or do something to shatter Cameron's perfect day with you, time will freeze, just as it is now. Your return home will come a lot swifter if you do what I tell you."

"Maybe I should spend the day hunting for your magic lamp so I can wish myself home."

"That won't work."

"Why not?"

"Well, for one thing, I don't have a lamp. I'm bound to a ring and that particular item of jewelry isn't here for you to find, no matter how much time you waste searching. And, of course, any time you do spend trying to locate my ring will be frozen, and will therefore prolong your stay here."

Scott huffed and sat down on the end of the bed. "So what you're telling me is I'm stuck here for a day, playing husband to some guy I've never met, and I won't be able to go home until he's had his full day with me."

"That's right."

"What's to stop me from simply walking out of here?"

The djinn gestured to the interior door with a smug smile. From the expression on his face, Scott could tell that leaving the room wouldn't work, but he had to try anyway. Sure enough the moment he stepped through the door he found himself back in the bedroom, as though he had walked in from the patio. When he tried leaving via the patio entrance, he ended up on the other side of the room.

Scott glanced back at the man in the bed. "If I'm married to this guy, he'll be expecting sex, right?"

"Of course."

"I'm not some kind of man whore."

The djinn snorted with obvious contempt. "What was the name of the last man you slept with?"

"Huh?" Scott's mind went blank. He had vague recollections of a young junior executive in the New York office, but his name escaped him completely.

"You don't remember? How about the one before then? No? Your sexual relationships consist of nothing except one-night stands."

"They do *not*. I've dated people."

"Your longest relationship is six weeks, back when you were in college. Since then your love life has been a string of sordid encounters that last no longer than the time it takes for you to get your rocks off."

"You're missing my point."

"Which is?"

"I'm not going to jump into bed with this guy, just because you say so."

The djinn gestured toward Cameron. "If you really don't want to have sex with him, he won't force you. All you have to do is make up a believable excuse, ill health perhaps, and he'll spend the day pampering you instead of making love. It's up to you how you let the day pan out, though you *will* stay here for the full day regardless."

"Fine, I'll stay here and play happy families for the day, satisfied?"

"Quite." The djinn snapped his fingers and Scott found himself back in the bed, with Cameron, his husband, wrapped around him. "Have fun," he advised, right before he vanished into thin air.

"Are you awake?" Cameron asked.

"Yes," whispered Scott, conscious of Cameron's erection once more. If he planned on playing the ill health card, now was the time to do so. Yet he remained silent. Maybe the djinn was right and this wasn't so different from a one-night stand. Perhaps he could pretend they'd hooked up at some club and come back here to Cameron's place the night before. Yeah, if he kept telling himself that, he could make it through the day without losing his mind completely.

Cameron reached down and cupped his testicles, squeezing them slightly. Scott whimpered at the contact. Cameron touched him right where Scott liked it most, almost as though he knew. Any lingering thought of declaring himself sick vanished. It had been so long since he'd been with another man, even for a one-night stand.

Scott soon surmised that Cameron probably did know what Scott liked and how he liked it. In Cameron's mind they'd been married for six months and together for goodness knows how long. Scott, meanwhile, had no clue what Cameron liked. He didn't even know if he preferred to top or bottom, though from the way Cameron pressed up against him, he suspected he might be more amenable to topping his lovers.

Cameron sucked on his neck as he continued to fondle his balls, stroking his length and tugging his cock to life with an expertise Scott had never known with his previous hook ups.

"I'm glad we decided to stay here today," Cameron whispered. "If we'd gone away we'd be stuck on the motorway about now and I couldn't do this."

Scott chuckled at the idea of them getting frisky in a car. No, this was much better.

Maybe he *could* get into this fantasy. A day getting laid by a man who apparently adored him didn't seem so bad. It had been a long time since he'd taken a day off and he'd never been one to turn down an offer of sex with a good-looking man. This didn't have to mean anything.

Scott pushed from his mind the thought that he didn't even know what Cameron looked like, having caught barely a glimpse of him during his escape from the bed. Instead he forced himself to relax and let Cameron touch him as he wished.

He closed his eyes and moaned as Cameron quickened the pace of his strokes. He quivered in his arms. It had been a few years since he'd been fucked, yet he found himself open to the idea of letting Cameron inside him.

"Need to see you," Scott pleaded.

Cameron changed his position and eased Scott onto his back.

Scott blinked and studied his fake husband properly for the first time. Cameron gazed back at him from under a mess of rumpled blond hair. His husband had a bad case of bedhead.

Cameron's blue eyes sparkled with desire and Scott's chest tightened as he tried to draw breath.

The full pink lips begged to be kissed and Scott leaned up to capture them with his own.

"Fuck, you're gorgeous," he whispered after they had reluctantly separated.

Cameron laughed. "You're acting as though you've never seen me before."

Shit! Scott had a feeling he might be making a few gaffes during the day and if he wasn't careful this would be one of many. He scrambled for something to say to smooth over his goof. "Each time I look at you, it takes my breath away."

Cameron snorted and smacked him lightly on the chest. "Idiot."

"What?" Scott asked, hoping he wasn't digging the hole bigger.

Cameron climbed on top of him and rubbed their groins together. "You're such a corny bastard," he teased.

Scott had never thought of himself as corny, yet his line seemed to have steered him away from trouble, so he didn't intend to argue the point.

Cameron rocked against him, slowly and deliberately. Scott had been hard from the first touch of Cameron's hand and he ached for release.

"What do you want?" Cameron asked.

"You," Scott answered immediately.

Cameron laughed. "I know that. Would you like me to ride you or fuck you?"

Any capability of forming words disappeared as Cameron scooted back a little and slipped his hand between Scott's legs, inching his way to his hidden pucker. He rubbed his index finger against Scott's entrance.

Scott pushed against the thick digit, whimpering when Cameron moved his hand away without offering him any sort of relief.

Cameron grinned at him. "I think I know what you want this morning." He eased Scott's thighs apart and knelt between them.

Scott strained his neck to see Cameron's cock. Here he was, spreading his legs for another man without even bothering to consider what he would be letting himself in for. Thankfully for Scott's arse, Cameron wasn't hung like the proverbial horse or likely to split him in two when he fucked him. Not that he was small. In fact Scott suspected he might actually be perfect in girth and length. He could only see one problem.

"What about—?" Scott halted when he saw time—and Cameron—had frozen again.

The djinn hovered at the side of the bed, though he stood facing away from the couple. Scott could see his ears had turned bright red and he suspected the man might be a little embarrassed. "Sorry, I don't mean to interrupt, but you're about to mention condoms."

"What are you, a bloody mind reader?"

"I already told you, I'm a djinn. You and your husband have been going bareback for quite a while now. I would advise against spoiling the mood by bringing up latex and causing Cameron to wonder whether you've lost your mind."

"Um, okay." Scott wondered how he could tactfully suggest the djinn bugger off before he ruined the mood entirely.

Before he could say anything the djinn vanished without another word and Cameron moved again. "What about what?" he asked.

"Er…" Scott fumbled for some way to finish his sentence that wouldn't make him sound like an idiot. "Lube!" Saved, he thought as Cameron grabbed the bottle from the bedside table and poured a generous amount onto his palm.

"You're acting very strange this morning," Cameron commented as he coated his dick with the lubricant.

"Am I?"

"Yes."

"Just because I want you to use lube?" Scott couldn't imagine any reality where he would let a man fuck him without the stuff, but then again, he couldn't see himself as married either.

"It's like you've forgotten I usually prepare you with my tongue first." Cameron shook his head and frowned. "I don't know. There's something different about you today. I just can't put my finger on what."

Scott grinned and grabbed Cameron's hand, placing it on his erection. "How about you put your fingers right about here and don't worry about it?"

Cameron stroked him once before reaching down to his entrance again.

Scott had never been particularly enthusiastic about being fingered. He much preferred to rush ahead to the main event. Yet he found himself enjoying being expertly teased and thoroughly explored by Cameron. Each crook of a finger sent shivers rippling through his body.

Finally, Cameron seemed to tire of tormenting him. He lined his cock up with Scott's nicely stretched hole and slowly eased his way inside.

Scott savored the sensation of being entered without anything between them, knowing this wasn't likely to happen again once today was over and his life returned to normal.

Cameron filled him completely and held still while Scott took the time to adjust. Scott frowned as he realized he wasn't struggling to accommodate Cameron, as he would have expected after going for so long without being fucked. It was almost as though he regularly took someone up the arse. Then again, if he'd really been married to Cameron for six months, he supposed he probably did. He guessed the djinn must have worked some magic on him to ensure Cameron didn't suspect anything untoward.

Scott wrapped his legs around Cameron and urged him to move. He grabbed Cameron's arse and kneaded the flesh as he encouraged his lover to quicken his pace.

As they moved together, Cameron appeared to read his every thought. He changed angle just as Scott desired. His strokes quickened or slowed before Scott could even make the suggestion. Cameron touched him in the places Scott liked to be touched, the spots Scott had discovered long ago, but no lover had ever been around long enough to learn. Cameron appeared to know Scott's body as well as Scott did.

"Come for me," Cameron demanded as he continued to pound Scott's arse.

Scott reached for his dick, but Cameron nudged his hand aside.

"No hands," he ordered. "You know I love it when I make you come without a touch."

Scott had never managed to come untouched before. He always needed a hand with it—literally. Yet Cameron clearly seemed to think otherwise.

Cameron moved position again, this time nailing Scott's prostate with ease. The stimulation wasn't enough to send him over the edge. It had never been enough to make him come. Yet, his orgasm built with every stroke. Cameron was touching something at the very core of his being, in a place no other man had managed to discover.

"Look at me," Cameron ordered.

Scott faced his lover and the moment their eyes met he lost control. He was dimly aware of the heat of Cameron's release filling his arse and his husband collapsing across his chest.

"Oh fuck," he managed to gasp out between breaths.

Cameron blinked up at him with a sated smile of contentment. "I love you," he whispered before laying down his head on Scott's chest.

Scott opened his mouth to reply, but once again Cameron had frozen. "What the hell have I done now?" he asked the irritating djinn.

"Nothing, just don't say the words unless you mean them."

Scott sighed with frustration. "If we're married, like you say we are, won't he be expecting me to say them?"

"Cameron is already asleep and won't know whether you've said the words or not."

Scott supposed at least that got him off the hook for another lie on top of the rest he would no doubt be telling during the course of the day.

The djinn disappeared and time began to move again.

Sure enough, Cameron had fallen fast asleep. He snored contentedly, clearly not bothered about the fact they would be extremely sticky when they finally emerged from the bed.

Scott tried to be bothered about the mess, but found he didn't care. It wasn't as though he'd be around long enough to have to wash the sheets.

About the Author

L.M. Brown is an English writer of gay romances. She believes that there is nothing hotter or sweeter than two men in love with each other…unless it is three.

When L.M. Brown isn't bribing her fur babies for control of the laptop, she can usually be found with her nose in a book.

L.M. loves to hear from readers. You can find her contact information, website details and author profile page at http://www.pride-publishing.com.